⊘ **W9-AEO-719**

## Fear and Respect

For the first time in years, Cole found himself frozen in fear. The first reaction of a person to a grizzly, that being to run like hell, was often fatal. As clumsy as they seemed while lumbering about, grizzlies could outrun a man, even a man on a horse.

He pulled his Winchester from its scabbard and began backing his horse, figuring that his *best chance* was to get away slowly before the bear decided to drop back down to four legs and charge him.

The Winchester represented his *last chance*.

For a short while, it worked. The bear watched the mounted rider as though bewildered by the jerky backward motion.

At last, the grizzly decided that despite an apparent backward movement, this intruder represented an interloper at his supper table.

With an angry snarl, the beast charged.

The roan bucked, and Cole felt himself losing his balance.

In the process of trying not to lose his rifle, Cole lost his reins.

For a moment, he felt himself sliding sideways from a galloping horse.

In the next instant, he was colliding awkwardly with the ground.

The Winchester, on which he had lost his grip, dropped about six feet away.

The sound of the bear galloping toward him was like thunder.

He literally threw himself toward the gun.

Grabbing the rifle in mid-tumble, Cole fired without aiming.

# BLADEN COLE:
# BOUNTY HUNTER

## BILL YENNE

GCLS/GREENWICH BRANCH
411 SWEDESBORO ROAD
GIBBSTOWN, NJ 08027

**B**

BERKLEY BOOKS, NEW YORK

**THE BERKLEY PUBLISHING GROUP**
**Published by the Penguin Group**
**Penguin Group (USA) Inc.**
**375 Hudson Street, New York, New York 10014, USA**

Penguin Group (Canada), 90 Eglinton Avenue East, Suite 700, Toronto, Ontario M4P 2Y3, Canada
(a division of Pearson Penguin Canada Inc.) • Penguin Books Ltd., 80 Strand, London WC2R 0RL,
England • Penguin Group Ireland, 25 St. Stephen's Green, Dublin 2, Ireland (a division of Penguin
Books Ltd.) • Penguin Group (Australia), 250 Camberwell Road, Camberwell, Victoria 3124, Australia
(a division of Pearson Australia Group Pty. Ltd.) • Penguin Books India Pvt. Ltd., 11 Community
Centre, Panchsheel Park, New Delhi—110 017, India • Penguin Group (NZ), 67 Apollo Drive,
Rosedale, Auckland 0632, New Zealand (a division of Pearson New Zealand Ltd.) • Penguin Books
(South Africa) (Pty.) Ltd., 24 Sturdee Avenue, Rosebank, Johannesburg 2196, South Africa

Penguin Books Ltd., Registered Offices: 80 Strand, London WC2R 0RL, England

This is a work of fiction. Names, characters, places, and incidents either are the product of the author's imagination or are used fictitiously, and any resemblance to actual persons, living or dead, business establishments, events, or locales is entirely coincidental. The publisher does not have any control over and does not assume any responsibility for author or third-party websites or their content.

BLADEN COLE: BOUNTY HUNTER

A Berkley Book / published by arrangement with the author

PUBLISHING HISTORY
Berkley edition / November 2012

Copyright © 2012 by Bill Yenne.
Cover illustration by Cliff Nielsen.
Cover design by Diana Kolsky.
Interior text design by Kristin del Rosario.

All rights reserved.
No part of this book may be reproduced, scanned, or distributed in any printed or
electronic form without permission. Please do not participate in or encourage piracy of
copyrighted materials in violation of the author's rights. Purchase only authorized editions.
For information, address: The Berkley Publishing Group,
a division of Penguin Group (USA) Inc.,
375 Hudson Street, New York, New York 10014.

ISBN: 978-0-425-25054-9

BERKLEY®
Berkley Books are published by The Berkley Publishing Group,
a division of Penguin Group (USA) Inc.,
375 Hudson Street, New York, New York 10014.
BERKLEY® is a registered trademark of Penguin Group (USA) Inc.
The "B" design is a trademark of Penguin Group (USA) Inc.

PRINTED IN THE UNITED STATES OF AMERICA

10  9  8  7  6  5  4  3  2  1

If you purchased this book without a cover, you should be aware that this book is
stolen property. It was reported as "unsold and destroyed" to the publisher, and neither the
author nor the publisher has received any payment for this "stripped book."

ALWAYS LEARNING                                                    **PEARSON**

# PROLOGUE

◆━━◆✦◆━━◆

"WHO CALLED ME THAT?"

The big man who had been leaning on the bar at the Palmer House Saloon for the past hour, gregariously telling tall tales, turned suddenly, jerking his head so hard that you'd have thought somebody had slugged the side of his chin.

"*Who* called me that?" Stewart Webb repeated.

All eyes were now on the man at the end of the bar. He had spoken to Webb, calling him by another name.

"That you?" Bladen Cole said, holding up a yellowish sheet of paper and tossing it on the bar. "Is that you . . . Alonzo Sims?"

Stewart Webb glanced at the stranger, at the gun on his hip, and finally at the paper. The only words that he could read at this distance were the one at the top—WANTED—and the ones beneath—ALONZO SIMS. Stewart Webb recognized the picture as one that had been taken of himself some years back, when he still *was* Alonzo Sims and when he led a different life.

Alonzo Sims had disappeared, and Stewart Webb had

been leading his new life in Green River, Wyoming, for eight years. It had been long enough for Stewart Webb to believe that Alonzo Sims had gotten away clean and disappeared forever.

Stewart Webb led his new life under a purloined name, borrowed audaciously from another.

Stewart Webb was no more Stewart Webb than the Palmer House was *the* Palmer House. Just as the saloon's founder had poached its name from the legendary Chicago hostelry to lend his place undeserved prominence, so too had the man taken the last and middle names of Alexander S. Webb, a Union general who earned a Medal of Honor at Gettysburg. It gave this man leading a new life an aura of importance. Alonzo Sims had been at Gettysburg as well, but as far down in the enlisted ranks as Webb was high in officer rank.

Stewart Webb had lulled himself into the belief that this day would never come.

Now it had.

"That you?" Bladen Cole repeated.

"Don't recognize that name," Webb lied, swallowing hard. He gritted his teeth, wishing that he could, by force of will, banish from his bloodstream all the alcohol he had consumed over the past hour.

"That's not me," Webb insisted. "My name's Stewart Webb. I'm a prominent member of this community. Ask anybody."

Even as he nodded toward the other patrons in the bar to vouch for his prominence, they were scuttling discreetly toward the door. Only the bartender remained, and he had moved as far as he could from where Stewart Webb was standing.

"Tell the man, John," Webb demanded of the bartender.

Nervous silence.

Barely out of his twenties, John did not want to die. He imagined that he had a life of some promise ahead of him and had no interest in seeing it cut short in the sort of cross fire that often followed the sort of fighting words that were being tossed about in his bar this afternoon.

"Tell him, *John*," Webb repeated.

The bartender nervously edged toward the wanted poster, stopping when the words were visible and Webb's portrait was clearly identifiable.

It surprised him not in the least that Stewart Webb was not *really* Stewart Webb. Lots of men who came west—and not a few women—changed their names to avoid a past and get a new start.

John had pegged Webb as a scoundrel the first time that he had seen him, and that pegging had been borne out over the months that he had watched Webb cheat people at cards, run his petty scams, and become modestly rich from it.

However, not every scoundrel and cardsharp with a sketchy past who haunted the taverns of transient railroad towns like Green River was wanted for *multiple* homicides in Cheyenne like the man on the poster who had Stewart Webb's face.

"Don't know anybody by that name," John said truthfully, not going so far as to say that it was not Webb's likeness in the picture.

"No?" Bladen Cole asked, even though he could read the opposite answer on John's face.

"Never heard of this man," John said in a confirmed tone.

"You sure?"

"Yep."

"Then I'd say that this is very good news," Cole said with a broad smile. "Then Mr. Webb has nary a worry in the world."

"Huh?" Webb said, now confused.

"I hate to see a man wrongfully accused," Cole said seriously. "It puts him in all manner of danger."

"Huh?" Webb repeated.

"We just have us a case of mistaken identity," Cole

grinned. "You and I'll just take the train back over to Cheyenne, and you can state your innocence. You can show the law over there that it's all a misunderstanding. We can get things all straightened out, and you can be back standing at this bar in two days' time."

"I don't think that's really necessary," Webb said, relaxing—just a little. "*You* could go . . . you could go'an tell 'em . . . explain to 'em."

"I think you and I both know that *you're* the one who's got to do the explaining," Cole said. "Till then, I think you had better relieve yourself of that gun you're carrying. If you would not mind, sir, I'd like to ask you to take it out of the holster and just lay it there on the bar."

Stewart Webb had always known that his life might come to this moment, but over time he had gradually deluded himself into believing that the odds were gradually growing less and less.

"I surely want no trouble," Webb said, reaching slowly for his gun.

His eyes locked on Bladen Cole as he lightly grasped the butt of the Colt with his thumb and forefinger.

Watching the stranger's eyes for any flicker of a blink, Webb rammed his hand into his holster, grabbed the gun full, and jerked it free.

He heard the shot at the very instant that he felt his wrist being shattered.

The wave of excruciating pain came over him a moment later in a blinding flash.

He now felt himself falling backward.

The gun was still in his hand, but in that hand, all feeling and all control had been severed by the impact of the bullet to his wrist.

Swimming out of the blinding flash, Webb could see the stranger coming toward him, his gun held at his side.

As his right hand dangled uselessly, there was still one card left to be played in Webb's metaphorical hand.

Being a gambling man, he had an ace up his sleeve, though it was not among those in his marked deck.

As Bladen Cole reached the fallen man, he suddenly found himself staring into the delicate double muzzle of a little twin-barreled, over-and-under Remington derringer.

GREEN RIVER, WYOMING, BEING A RAILROAD TOWN, WAS one of those places where you could get just about anything. For ten years, since they drove the Golden Spike at Promontory, linking the West to the East with steel rails, Green River's Palmer House had had reasonable access to the same finery and sophistication as the original Palmer House in Chicago.

In Green River, you could find a glass of whiskey on just about any corner. If you paid the right price, you could find a glass of whiskey that tasted more like *whiskey* than it did like the Green River.

In Green River, you could find a lady with lips the color of the juicy red apples on your grandmother's tree. If you paid the right price, you could find such a lady who would tell you that you were the wittiest and most handsome man in creation.

In Green River, you could also find a carpenter. If you paid the right price, you could find a carpenter who could craft you an heirloom-quality rocker that your grandmother, the one with the apple tree, would envy. For a more reasonable price, you could take your pick of many carpenters who were well practiced in the construction of six-foot boxes.

With the reward money having been wired to Bladen Cole, Stewart Webb left Green River for Cheyenne on his last train ride. Cole kept the derringer. It was still loaded when he'd slipped it into his vest pocket.

Cole was like a lot of young men who had come west after the War Between the States. They came west to seek their fortune or to answer the irresistible call of the horizon of the sunset. Many young men from his part of the country went west because there was literally nothing left for them at home.

Born in Caroline County, Virginia, Bladen Cole and his older brother, William, grew up on a prosperous horse farm and were educated in the best of schools. Bladen turned thirteen in the first year of the war and was seventeen when he rode with his brother against the Yankees in the war's final months. When he was growing up, Caroline County was known as the birthplace of the great explorer William Clark. When Bladen and his brother left in 1865, to follow William Clark's footsteps into the West, the county had become better known as the place where they had killed John Wilkes Booth.

With skills as horsemen that had been second nature throughout their young lives, Bladen and William Cole were able to find work herding cattle in Texas and later hunting buffalo for railroad work crews in Kansas. Gradually, they worked their way farther west, following the promising trail toward the gold and silver strikes out in New Mexico Territory.

Tragedy struck the brothers in Silver City one night when William was gunned down by two lowlife drifters. Bladen shot and killed one and spent the better part of the next year hunting the other—to no avail. He had deliberately honed his skills with a gun to an unprecedented degree simply because, if he *ever* met that rat-faced man again, it would not be a repeat of the man's escape on that night in Silver City.

More than a decade later, that night continued to haunt Bladen Cole.

About a year or so after Will's death, Bladen had found himself in a small mining town not far from the bustling metropolis of Cripple Creek, Colorado. Through a series of auspicious events, he played a role in foiling a bank robbery and was asked by the city fathers to consider becoming their sheriff. By this time, he was starting to think that he should be thinking about his future, so he accepted, and decided to settle down. He even met a young woman, named Sally Lovelace, with whom there was a mutual attraction, and a seriousness that had led *almost* to a wedding.

However, before that could happen, Sally took a fancy to a high roller who swept her off her feet. J. R. Hubbard was one of those men who attracted the attention of good women like a magnet attracts iron filings. Sally swooned to his charms and allowed herself to be seduced by the honey of his sweet talk and by starry promises that could never have been fulfilled by a man on a sheriff's salary.

At about the same time that Hubbard swept Sally away to San Francisco, Bladen uncovered a rodent's nest of corruption in city government but was thwarted politically in his attempts to bring the perpetrators in high places to justice.

Cole realized, as he had on that day when he and Will first followed the setting sun out of Caroline County, that he was not the sort of man destined to be too long in one place—and that he had been in *this one* too long. Having angrily tossed his badge on the mayor's desk, he climbed on his horse and rode away.

A week or so later, in a mining town up in Wyoming Territory, he began seeing wanted posters of a particular bank-robbing duo, and he decided that the reward money looked good. It also looked like his future.

Several wanted posters, and several successful pursuits, later, his remarkable skill with a Colt .45 had found Bladen Cole with a new career—and one which allowed him not to be too long in one place.

# CHAPTER 1

—◆◆◆◆◆—

"WHEN THE RAILROAD REACHES GALLATIN CITY, WE SHALL all be rich men," John Blaine said with effusive enthusiasm as Virgil Stocker unrolled the map with a dramatic flourish.

Dawson Phillips, their partner, lifted his considerable bulk from the chair and made his way to the head of a large oak dining table still set with the dinner dishes, rumpled napkins, and Mrs. Blaine's fine Bohemian crystal—imported into Montana Territory from Chicago at great expense.

The wives of the three men had excused themselves to the parlor when Blaine had brought out the cigars and offered the first round of brandy. The ladies were discussing matters more to their interest, gladly leaving the men to their heavily odoriferous tobacco and their "man talk."

These gentlemen, who now talked their man talk in the atmosphere scented by brandy and cigars, were entrepreneur merchants turned land speculators who had become Gallatin City's leading citizens. They had arrived in Montana Territory by various paths and had settled down to become the biggest fish in a small pond, and to do so by successfully betting that their small pond would become an increasingly larger pond. Blaine was a dry goods merchant, while Phillips was the proprietor of Gallatin City's best hotel and restaurant. Stocker was an attorney, and their fourth associate, not present this evening, was Isham Ransdell, who owned the city's only bank.

"Hmmm," Blaine said, studying the area that had been outlined in pencil. "Are you certain the Northern Pacific will lay its tracks through Gallatin City by this route?"

"I have it on good authority from a man in the very office of Fred Billings, the president of the road," Stocker assured his fellow businessman.

Having gone into bankruptcy in 1875 with its intended transcontinental line barely started, the railroad had been recently reorganized under the wily financier Frederick H. Billings, whose golden touch was about to revive the foundering project.

"Are you sure that there is going to *be* a Northern Pacific?" Phillips said skeptically. "I know that there's been a great deal of positive excitement that he'll bring the road out of its three years of bankruptcy, but . . ."

"Billings is the man," Stocker insisted. "He has raised a great deal of money and has resumed construction."

"Hmmm," Phillips said thoughtfully.

"He's laid rails a hundred miles east of Tacoma on one side, and on the other his crews have crossed Minnesota, most of Dakota Territory, and within a year and a half, Billings will build the tracks straight into Gallatin City . . . straight into this wedge of land that we *own*," Stocker exclaimed, pointing at the areas on the map north and east of Gallatin City.

The arrival of the Northern Pacific, upon which these entrepreneurs had set their hopes and dreams, would transform Gallatin City, as the arrival of railroads was transforming so many towns-turned-cities across the West. New settlers would arrive with more money and a need for the goods and services which these businessmen would provide.

More even than this was the fact that land values would increase, so with this in mind, the gentlemen had pooled their resources to acquire tracts of land that were of marginal value in a region not served by a rail link to the outside world, but which would be radically transformed when the rails at last reached Gallatin City.

"We have done very well for ourselves controlling the land between here and the diggings at Confederate Gulch," Blaine chortled.

Discovered more than a decade earlier by some expatriate Southern Civil War vets, the "Gulch" had been the richest gold find in Montana history. Though much of the easy pickings had been picked, a railroad would invite further investment.

"At the moment, most of the gold is going out on Missouri River steamers," Stocker continued, thumping his tobacco-stained finger on the map. "When the railroad reaches Gallatin City, *all* of the gold will go though *here* . . . through the land which we own. The railroad will *need* our land."

"If you are correct, sir," Phillips said, lowering his heft into a chair near the unrolled map. "We *shall indeed* be very rich men. I'd say that at the very least, this calls for another shot of your fine brandy, sir."

"Gladly," Blaine said, topping off the three glasses. "We shall drink to the four musketeers."

"To the four musketeers, then," Stocker said, touching his crystal goblet to those of his partners. "If California can have its 'Big Four,' its Huntington, Hopkins, Crocker, and Stanford, then Montana Territory shall have its own Big Four . . . Blaine, Phillips, Stocker, and Ransdell."

The men chuckled that their toasts were being made not just to the richest men in the city, but to the future richest men in Montana Territory.

"Pity that Ransdell couldn't join us at this table tonight," the portly Phillips said, patting his ample belly. "That was a fine roast that Mrs. Blaine placed before us."

"It's his loss," Blaine said with a smile. He was pleased that his wife's cooking had received a compliment from a man so evidently fond of eating.

As the toasts were echoing around the dinner table, the doorbell chimed.

"I wonder who that could be," Blaine said, setting down his glass without taking a sip.

His wife was already at the front door.

"May I help you?" Leticia Blaine asked as she opened the door.

"Looking for Blaine," a large man announced, stepping across the threshold without being invited to do so.

"*Gideon Porter*," she exclaimed, recognizing the man as he stomped into her parlor ahead of three companions. "What do you want?"

"Where's Blaine?" Porter demanded.

"You are a very rude young man," Mrs. Blaine said sternly, her hands on her hips. "You always were."

"I insist that you leave my home at once," John Blaine said angrily as he entered the parlor. "You are unwelcome in this house. Take your brother Enoch and these other hooligans and get out of here immediately."

By this time, Phillips and Stocker had entered the room as well.

"My husband has ordered you to go and . . ."

*Crack!*

The sound of the man's having backhanded Leticia Blaine across the face reverberated through the room.

For a moment, there was no sound but that of her crumpling to the floor. Everyone halted as though in shock. The sight of a man striking a woman so hard as to draw blood with a single blow startled everyone.

There was a pitiful, gurgling sob as Mrs. Blaine put her hand over her bleeding face, and a red-faced John Blaine slugged Gideon Porter with such force that his hat went flying.

All eyes were on Gideon as he staggered backward a step. Though Blaine was an older man, well past his prime, his punch still packed a wallop.

But Blaine's fists were no match for what came next.

*K'poom . . . K'poom . . . mmm.*

The thunder of two .44-caliber cartridges exploding in the confines of a moderate-sized parlor were as deafening as they were unexpected. Gideon Porter had drawn his gun.

The room filled with a bluish, choking cloud of gunsmoke as John Blaine dropped to his knees with a flabbergasted expression on his face and dark red stains spreading across his starched white shirt.

"Murderer!" Dawson Phillips screamed as he fumbled in his vest for the derringer he kept there.

As Enoch Porter leveled his Model 1860 revolver at Phillips, Mrs. Phillips leaped to her feet and let fly a stream of verbal vitriol unbecoming of a lady.

Enoch shifted his gaze and the direction of his gun to Mary Phillips and squeezed the trigger.

Her husband, who now had his derringer firmly in the grip of his fleshy hand, paused for a split second, watching aghast as his wife was struck down.

His split-second pause was all that it took for the revolver to be redirected at him.

A fourth shot was fired in the once-genteel parlor and then a fifth.

Dawson Phillips's body fell with a crash.

Virgil Stocker stepped forward to aid his fallen partner, but felt the impact of Gideon Porter's gun butt across his face, first once and then again and again.

As Gideon whipped the attorney with the pistol, Enoch turned his gun toward Sarah Stocker, who remained seated on the sofa, frozen in terror at the sight of her husband being beaten.

Seeing this, Gideon deserted Stocker and grabbed his brother's arm.

"Not the women, dammit!" Porter shouted. "We weren't supposed to hurt the *women*."

"You slugged *that one*, Gideon," Enoch whined, nodding toward Mrs. Blaine, who was now crouched over her husband's body, blood still streaming from her own wound.

"Let's get the hell out of here," Gideon ordered, picking up his hat.

# CHAPTER 2

❖━━◆◈◆━━❖

"THAT COULD HAVE BEEN *YOU*," HANNAH RANSDELL TOLD her father in a tone that was a mix of horror and relief.

"I know," Isham Ransdell said somberly as he and his daughter watched people urgently coming and going from the two-story, Victorian-style home where John Blaine and his wife lived—and the home where Isham Ransdell had been invited to dine this very night. Had it not been necessary for him to meet with a client on an urgent matter, he *would* have been there.

He stared at the house feeling the shock of knowing this. So too did his daughter.

Only twenty minutes or so had passed since Sarah Stocker had been found running down Elm Street screaming that people had been shot. By now, it seemed as though every one of Gallatin City's two thousand citizens knew of the shootings, and half of them had come out to gawk.

Sheriff John Hollin walked from the house shaking his head.

"What do you know?" Ransdell asked.

"Three dead," he replied. "Blaine and Phillips . . . Mrs. Phillips, too. Stocker and Mrs. Blaine are both hurt real bad. The doc's in there with them now."

"That's terrible . . ." Hannah said, putting her hand over her mouth.

"Do you have any idea who did this?" her father asked.

"Mrs. Blaine said the one who hit her was Gideon Porter."

"He's a cruel man, that Gideon Porter," Hannah interjected. "Him and his no-account brother, Enoch. Having Biblical names didn't prevent those boys from siding with the devil all their lives."

"It was them," the sheriff nodded. "Was Enoch who killed Dawson Phillips and his wife. The women said there were two more. Somebody saw four riders heading out of town in a hurry . . . heading north."

"So what are you waiting for?" Hannah demanded. "You should being going out after them!"

"Gotta wait for first light," Hollin explained patiently. "No good tryin' to track 'em in the dark."


IT WAS A FEW HOURS AFTER FIRST LIGHT AND A FEW HOURS after the sheriff's departure, when a lone rider appeared on Gallatin City's main street. He was riding a strawberry roan and had the look of a man who'd been on the trail for all of those hours and more.

He dismounted, looped his reins around a hitch rail near a watering trough, and loosened the cinch on his saddle so that the roan would be more comfortable. As his horse drank thirstily from the trough, the man strolled into the Big Horn Saloon and ordered a beer to satiate his own thirst.

"Seems like a lot of excitement in town today," Bladen Cole said, making conversation with the bartender.

"'Twas a shooting last night," the man behind the bar replied.

"Hmmm," Cole said, taking another welcome sip from his mug. His tone expressed the sentiment that shootings were not sufficiently uncommon to warrant the kind of excitement that was swirling around on the streets of Gallatin City.

"One of the town's leading citizens was gunned down in his parlor," the bartender added, sensing the need to elaborate. "In fact, there was *two* prominent men killed . . . a third one in bad shape."

"Hmmm," Bladen Cole replied. The tone this time said that he now understood why the fuss on Gallatin City's streets was at a heightened level.

"One of 'em's wife was killed too," the bartender added when Cole's latest "Hmmm" also needed to be underscored, to stress that something *really* serious was going on. It was almost a matter of civic pride to emphasize the seriousness of Gallatin City's excitement.

"That so?" Cole replied.

"Yep," the bartender replied, happy to have gotten some actual words out of the stranger.

"'Nother beer," Cole said.

His thirst satisfied by his first, Cole savored his second beer as the bartender went about his work, sorting glassware and topping off the whiskey bottles on the back bar from one of the big oak barrels that had been shipped out here all the way from Kentucky.

The big clock on the wall, flanked by a pair of angry-looking wolf heads, was striking four o'clock when someone rushed into the Big Horn.

"Deputy Johnson just rode back in," the man shouted to the handful of patrons who were in the saloon. "They done got shot up. Sheriff Hollin got himself *killed*."

The bartender stopped what he was doing and just stared at the swinging doors as the man ran down the street repeating the bad news.

"What's that all about?" Cole asked, eliciting the sort of elaboration that the bartender seemed to like to provide.

"Sheriff went out this morning," the bartender explained. "Tracking the Porter boys."

"Who's the Porter boys?"

"Ones they figure did the killings last night."

Tossing a couple of coins on the bar, Bladen Cole turned and stepped onto the street.

A crowd was gathered around a man on horseback who was slumped in his saddle, a pained expression on his face. People were shouting for someone to fetch the doctor.

As Cole watched, they carefully removed the man from his horse and carried him into the Big Horn, where they placed him on a table. Judging by his badge, it didn't take long for Cole to ascertain that he was the deputy who had survived the ambush. Judging by the placement of his bullet wounds, it didn't take long for Cole to figure that he would survive. He had applied a tourniquet himself, and although he was in shock, he was able to speak.

The doctor arrived, concurred with Cole's unspoken diagnosis, and prescribed a stiff drink from behind the bar.

Within fifteen minutes, the color had flooded back into Johnson's cheeks, and he was relating the tale of what had happened.

"We trailed 'em up and across the mountains toward Sixteen Mile Creek," he explained, his narrative punctuated by coughs. "Sheriff was the first hit. Head wound it was. Couldn't really see 'em. Hiding up in the rocks . . . up high. Ben Neff . . . he was riding with us. Got his gun out and got off a couple of shots. Both of us was returning fire. Couldn't really see 'em except for the smoke from the rifles, but the wind was blowing and it was hard to see. Ben got hit too. Then me. Didn't want to run, but I figured I'd have to get back . . . tell what happened."

"Did you hit any of *them*?" someone asked.

"The sheriff definitely hit one . . . in the arm," Johnson said with a nod. "Saw him get hit. His gun went flyin'."

"I've already got a wire off to the county sheriff in Boze-man," a self-important man announced. "He'll get out a posse and catch 'em."

That seemed to satisfy the crowd, who began drifting away from the deputy and toward the bar.

# CHAPTER 3

———◆❖◆———

BLADEN COLE AWOKE TO THE YAMMERING OF BIRDS OUT-
side the window and to the unfamiliarity of waking up on
a mattress and between sheets for the first time in weeks.
He had treated himself to a hotel room, spending part of his
reward money on unaccustomed luxury. If he continued with
his plan for an extended hunting trip up into the Beartooth
Mountains, he wouldn't be within a hundred miles of a
mattress for the next month.

Snapping open his pocket watch, the sturdy brass mecha-
nism which he still thought of as *his father's* pocket watch,
he was stunned to realize how badly he had overslept. It was
not that he was on any kind of schedule, but being asleep
when it was almost seven o'clock in the morning struck him
as an egregious waste of daylight hours.

Having allowed himself the luxury of a hotel mattress,
he allowed himself the luxury of a "store-bought" breakfast
in the hotel dining room. He was just marveling at the
extravagance of drinking coffee from a porcelain cup when
a well-dressed man came into the dining room and started

staring at him. Cole straightened his right leg a little, so that his .45 would be easy to reach, and returned the stare. At last, the well-dressed man approached.

"You Bladen Cole?"

"Who's asking?"

"My name's Olson . . . Edward J. Olson. I work for Mr. Ransdell."

The man's tone made it sound like everyone knew who "Mr. Ransdell" was, and those who did not *should*.

"Who's Mr. Ransdell?" Cole replied, in a tone intended to make it clear that he didn't know and really didn't care.

"He owns the Gallatin City Bank and Trust yonder," Olson said, nodding in the general direction of across the street.

"Hmmm."

"So, *are you* Bladen Cole?"

"I am."

"Bladen Cole . . . the *bounty hunter*?"

"I am."

"Mr. Ransdell would like a word with you."

"I won't ask why, because the way y'all said 'bounty hunter' makes it sound more like business than pleasure. If you'd excuse me while I finish this cup of coffee, I'd be pleased to make the acquaintance of Mr. Ransdell."

Ten minutes later, Olson was rapping on the front window of the bank with Bladen Cole in tow. It may have seemed to Cole like the day was half-gone, but by banker's hours, it was not even opening time.

Isham Ransdell heard the tapping and hurried to get the door himself.

Stepping inside, Cole scoured the room with his eyes. Ransdell was a wiry man with a narrow string tie and white sideburns that looked like they hadn't decided whether to get really bushy like Burnside's or allow themselves to be trimmed away entirely.

What caught Cole's eye, and would not let go, was the sight of a young woman in a gingham dress. It was conservatively high in the collar, but cut right in all the right places, and the places were very right, indeed. Her long, chestnut-colored hair was tied up, though loosely, in a blue ribbon which matched the color of her dress. Her eyes were big and gray, and she wore a confident, assured expression.

"Mr. Ransdell, this is Mr. Cole," Olson said. "Mr. Cole, Mr. Ransdell."

"Pleased to make your acquaintance," Cole said, gripping the man's hand and forcing his eyes away from the young woman.

"The pleasure is mine, Mr. Cole," Ransdell said, in the smooth voice of a banker. "May I introduce my daughter, Hannah."

"Ma'am," Cole said respectfully, touching the brim of his hat.

"Mr. Cole," she replied with an almost smile.

Ransdell invited the two men to sit down at a table in the lobby which Cole guessed was normally used for signing financial paperwork. He guessed that financial talk would be taking place there now.

Hannah, who apparently worked at the bank, sat down at a desk apart from the men, though clearly within earshot of the "men's business" that was about to be discussed.

"Mr. Cole, I'm sure that you are aware of the shooting that took place here in Gallatin City two nights past?" Ransdell began.

"I am."

"You may not be aware that the three men who were present at the shooting . . . including two who died in cold blood . . . were business associates of mine . . . partners in some important business ventures."

"I'm sorry for your loss, sir," Cole nodded politely.

"I know that you are also aware that Sheriff John Hollin and another man were murdered by the same men who did this . . . and that Deputy Marcus Johnson was injured."

"I watched him taken from his horse yesterday," Cole

said, nodding toward the place where the sheriff's last ride into town had come so dramatically to its end.

"I know," Olson interjected. "I saw you there. Thought I recognized you from the papers. We heard about what you did down in Green River."

"Your reputation precedes you, Mr. Cole," Ransdell said, smiling.

"Well . . . that's a good thing or a bad thing, depending," Cole said thoughtfully. He knew that they were getting around to the place where the business talk was about to start. "What can I do for you?"

"There are four men at large who must be brought to justice," Ransdell said.

"I know," Cole agreed, "but from what I heard yesterday, the Gallatin County sheriff from down in Bozeman was being sent for. It would seem to be his job."

"Well, there's a little bit of a problem in that," Olson responded.

"Is?"

"Yeah. The Porter boys are headed up north. They'd be clear into Meagher County by now. That would put them out of Gallatin County jurisdiction."

"Why doncha send a wire to the Meagher County sheriff?" Cole said, asking a question that seemed to him an obvious one.

"Well, that would be up in Diamond City," Olson said, referring to the boomtown which had grown up in the heart of the Confederate Gulch diggings.

"So?"

"Let me put it this way," Ransdell interjected. "The law hasn't really taken root in Diamond City. Meagher County isn't quite as lawless, literally, as Choteau County, but it's not exactly as refined in its ways as places like Bozeman or Denver."

"I understand," Cole nodded. Nineteenth-century civilization had reached the West, but it had done so in narrow swaths.

"You sure it was the Porter boys?" Cole asked.

"Three witnesses recognized them."

"There were four . . . Did the witnesses know the other two?"

"Milton Waller and Jimmy Goode. They are known to ride with the Porters . . . do whatever Gideon Porter tells 'em to do. He has a way of mesmerizing others less long on mental acuity . . . of manipulating them."

"Hmmm," Cole said thoughtfully, in his typical manner, intentionally evoking a sense of thoughtfulness.

"Soon as the state judge down in Bozeman wires through a warrant, I'd like to employ you to go get the Porter boys and bring them in to face the music," Ransdell said emphatically, getting down to business.

"What sort of money are we talking?" Cole asked, also getting down to business.

"We are prepared to offer you a sum of three thousand dollars," the banker said.

To Cole, this was a great deal of money. It was more than most laboring men could expect to earn in a year. However, the sum said a lot about Ransdell, and one of the things that it whispered in Cole's ear was how important this affair was to the man. The other thing it whispered was that there was more money on the banker's table.

"Well," Cole said reticently. "I had a number a little north of four in mind."

"I suppose we could split the difference at thirty-five hundred," the banker said after a long pause to scratch some numbers on a piece of paper.

Cole smiled to himself. The man was used to dickering and anxious to cut a deal.

"Well . . ." Cole drawled thoughtfully. "I did say that I was thinking of a number *north* of four. There *is* four of them and one of me."

"Okay, I'll make it *four*," Ransdell said. "And I'll pick up your tab at the hotel, and for your horse last night at the livery stable . . . and stake you to whatever provisions you'll need for this manhunt."

This time, the voice in Cole's head told him that they had reached the end of the dickering phase and it was time to extend his hand.

As Ransdell was writing out an agreement for them to sign, the boy arrived from the telegraph office with the warrant from the judge in Bozeman.

"Well, that makes it official," Olson observed.

Ransdell read the paper and handed it Cole.

"Longest telegram I've seen," he observed.

"Written by lawyers," Ransdell said wryly.

"Hmmm . . ." Cole said, half reading the document out loud. "Hmmm . . . 'armed and dangerous,' it says. Would have thought that this goes without saying."

"That's a way of saying they're wanted 'dead or alive.' It's a way of saying they're to be brought back by any means necessary, and in any condition necessary for them to be brought back."

"Most folks here in Gallatin City would rather see them *dead* than alive," Olson interjected.

Ransdell just nodded his head to confirm the assertion.

When they had finished signing an agreement and shaking hands a second time, Cole explained that he would be starting out first thing in the morning.

"Don't you want to get started right away?" Ransdell asked urgently. "You've got your warrant and they've already got almost a two-day head start."

"That's right, Mr. Ransdell," Cole agreed. "And at this point there's no way that hard riding will ever catch up to them. The only way that they're gonna get caught is if they can see that there's nobody coming after them. If they think they got away, they'll relax. They'll slow down. They'll get themselves caught. In the meantime, I'd like to spend what's left of this day taking a look at where the shooting happened and talking to them who was there."

"That sounds reasonable, I suppose," Ransdell admitted. "I guess you need to know who you're dealing with ... Hannah, could you take Mr. Cole over and see if Mrs. Blaine is up to receiving a caller?"

"Yes, Father," Hannah said with a nod of agreement.

Bladen Cole smiled, but Hannah scowled slightly. She found the tall stranger easy on the eye and a bit captivating in a dangerous sort of way, but she didn't want him to know that such was the case.


"WHAT DO YOU KNOW ABOUT THESE PORTER BOYS, MISS Ransdell?" Cole asked as they walked.

"They're no good," she said emphatically. "I knew them in school. A lot of the boys had a bit of the nick to them, but those two were just plain cruel ... cruel to animals ... cruel to people. Enoch was the worst. He had a taste for blood ... torturing and killing cats and dogs ... in ways I'd rather not describe ... or *recall*."

"They ever kill any *people* before?"

"Not that I know of ... Of course, I have never made it my place to know all of what the Porter boys were up to."

"Why do you suppose they did it this time?"

"I dunno ... some kind of grudge, I reckon." Hannah shrugged. "Gideon used to work for Mr. Blaine but got himself fired."

"What about the others?"

"Like my father said, they'll do anything Gideon Porter says to do. Milton Waller is dumb as a post ... quit school in the second grade ... Jimmy Goode is known all over Gallatin County as 'good for nothing.'"

"What do they do for work, these boys?"

"They cowboy around. There's a lot of need for extra hands on the ranches at branding time ... roundup time. Man who's good with a horse and rope, you don't care if he's dumb as a post or that he used to kick puppy dogs around."

As they turned the corner onto Elm Street, the wind shifted and Cole caught a whiff of her perfume. It was just a trace, just barely there, not like the dolls in Denver who liked to really slather it on. She was naturally, and almost perfectly, beautiful, but the little threesome of freckles on her nose added a humanizing touch, softening the classical perfection of that beauty. This and the easy way that she smiled—now that she had relaxed and stopped forcing her jaw into a perfunctory scowl—made her quite attractive.

The Blaine home was guarded by a man with a rifle whom Hannah knew. It was not so much that anyone expected the Porter gang to return to finish her off, rather he was there to give Mrs. Blaine the assurance of security. Hannah instructed Cole to wait outside while she went in to inquire as to whether Mrs. Blaine was up to a visit from the bounty hunter hired to avenge her husband's death.

While she went inside, Bladen made conversation with the man with the rifle. Asked about the four perpetrators, he echoed Hannah's opinion, though his description of Gideon Porter's evilness, and Enoch's atrocious way with small domestic animals, was a good deal more graphic.

Finally, Hannah called from the front door and Bladen climbed the steps. He made a point of removing his hat and wiping his feet, something that had become his second nature growing up in Virginia, where a man was measured by his politeness.

"I want you to *get* that Gideon Porter once and for all!" Leticia Blaine exclaimed without the formality of an introduction.

She was seated in a large, overstuffed chair in a small room opposite the parlor. He figured that she was avoiding the parlor, and understood that she had good reason. Another woman about her age, probably a friend, was hovering nearby. The side of Mrs. Blaine's face was deeply black-and-blue, and she had a long cut in her lower lip that had been stitched.

"Yes, ma'am," Cole said.

"I want that Gideon Porter six feet under."

"Yes, ma'am," Cole repeated. "He's the one who done this to you?"

"Darn tootin' he is," the spunky widow confirmed.

"And shot your husband?"

"Yes sir," she affirmed angrily. "He is a *madman*. John rose to my defense and lost his life for it!"

"Ma'am, if you don't mind me asking, do y'all have any idea *why* they did this? Why they came to your home to shoot people?"

"My husband fired that cur six months ago, and he had to have his revenge, of course."

"Why do you reckon that he waited so long?"

"How should I know?"

"He just came here asking after your husband?"

"That's right. I answered that door right there and . . . they barged through . . ."

"Into the parlor here?" Cole asked, stepping into the other room. The bloodstains on the rich oriental-style carpets, now turned dark and all the more deathly, painted a vivid picture of the place where each victim had stood. In the room beyond, the dinner dishes from that night still had not been cleared.

"That's right," she shouted, remaining in her chair as Cole left the room. "My husband was in the dining room with Virgil Stocker and Dawson Phillips. They all came into the parlor when they heard the commotion. Porter shot John, then his brother murdered Dawson and then Mary . . . it was *terrible!*"

On this note, Leticia Blaine dissolved into tearful sobbing, and her friend moved in to comfort her. Bladen Cole thanked her for her time and expressed his sympathies, as he and Hannah Ransdell retreated out the front door.

"Any chance I could go talk to this man, Virgil Stocker?" Cole asked as he put on his Stetson.

"I suppose we could do that," Hannah said. She was kind of interested in the bounty hunter's "investigating," and she certainly didn't mind being seen around town with a handsome stranger. Nor did she mind taking an occasional glance at the whiskers that studded his face. His were a bit on the shorter side for her tastes, but she did have a fondness for a younger man with a beard.

"You been long in the Territory, Mr. Cole?" she said as they walked.

"No, ma'am. I passed through a couple years back and was headed back up north to do a little hunting when your father's friend, Mr. Olson, approached me in the cafe."

"Hunting?" Hannah said with a knowing tone. "I'd speculate that in your line of work that has a little bit of a double meaning?"

"Yes, ma'am, it does," he nodded. "But in this case, it was mule deer I was after . . . some for trade . . . some to dry for winter."

"Heard the stories about you down on the Green River," she said.

"Justice required . . . justice done," he said, phrasing his few words in such a way that he hoped to close out the topic.

"How did you get into this . . . mmmmm . . . line of work, Mr. Cole?"

"I sorta fell into it, Miss Ransdell."

"How does one . . . ?" Hannah began.

"When one finds that he's good with a gun, he can find himself on one side of the law or the other."

"And you picked . . ."

"I don't mind sleeping with one eye open sometimes," he interrupted. "I just figured that I couldn't live with having to sleep with *both* of them open."

LETICIA BLAINE'S ANGER WAS A MERE TRIFLE BY COMPARISON to the rage expressed by Virgil Stocker, and the expletives he used were considerably stronger than "cur."

Likewise, Stocker's facial injuries were of an order of magnitude greater than those endured by Mrs. Blaine. She had suffered under the fist of her attacker, while he had been struck by the butt of a gun. Even the jagged cuts that remained unbandaged would leave a permanent reminder of that night in the mirror of Virgil Stocker.

As to the question of *why* this happened, Stocker's opinion coincided with the conventional wisdom. Angry at being fired, Gideon Porter had come for retribution, and things got horribly out of control.

"And the women . . . the poor *women*," Stocker's wife interjected. She had sat quietly through her husband's tirade but felt the need to insert her own perspective on that terrible night. "Gideon Porter said that the women were not *supposed* to be hurt, but . . . poor Mary . . . For a man to strike a woman . . . much less shoot her . . . poor Mary Phillips. To watch her . . . writhing . . . writhing on the carpet . . . that terrible expression . . ."

"What do you think he meant by saying the women were not *supposed* to be hurt?" Hannah asked.

By this time, Mrs. Stocker was sobbing uncontrollably, reliving the horror of the deaths of friends with the survivor's guilt of knowing that of the six, only she remained unscathed—physically.

"She's been through *hell*," Virgil Stocker said, rising to his feet and moving toward his guests in a gesture signifying the end of their visit, with Hannah's query unanswered. "She's been through *enough*."

"Mr. Cole," Stocker said from the doorway as Bladen and Hannah crossed the porch. "I understand that the warrant has language in it that says . . . or at least insinuates . . . 'dead or alive.'"

"It does," Cole nodded.

"I hope you make sure that *none* of that bunch ever again breathes the air of Gallatin County."

*   *   *

"THERE'S ANOTHER THING YOU SHOULD KNOW," HANNAH said as they walked back in the direction of Main Street.

"What's that?"

"You know how my father said those men were his associates?"

"Yeah."

"Well, they were all having dinner at the Blaine home . . . the associates and their wives. My father was supposed to have been there, but he had a meeting."

"So he nearly . . ."

"Yes, he nearly wound up in the line of fire. That's why this is sort of personal. The reward money is coming from him . . . personally."

"Guess he and your mother are counting their blessings," Cole said.

"Um . . . actually my mother passed away three years back. If he *had* gone to that dinner party . . . he would have taken *me*."

# CHAPTER 4

"IT'S HIM. IT'S JOHN HOLLIN," EDWARD J. OLSON SAID, THE color draining from his face as he was overcome by the stench. "I recognize his shirt."

The sun was just coming up as Bladen Cole and the three men from Gallatin City descended the trail toward the place where Sixteen Mile Creek emptied into the Missouri River. When he had told them that he planned to leave "first thing in the morning," he had meant it. To the three men who had asked to accompany him as far as the ambush site to recover the bodies, it had been the middle of the night.

Cole studied the bluffs above the place where the bodies lay as the men from the town began the grisly chore of wrapping the deceased in canvas. They would soon be loaded on mules for their last ride home.

"Reckon this is where we part company, gentlemen," Cole said, touching the brim of his hat.

"Good luck, Mr. Cole," Olson said, his tone of voice suggesting that he figured the bounty hunter would *need* it.

With that, Cole rode north.

The breeze was rustling in the changing leaves of the
cottonwoods as he paused to let his roan drink before they
forded the creek. The Porter boys had left no tracks, but they
were easy to follow.

After killing men whose deaths were guaranteed to raise
the ire—or at least the attention—of Montana's powers that
be, the next leg of their trail after the ambush was obvious.
To have crossed west of the Missouri River would have
taken them on a heading toward the territorial capital at
Helena, while staying to the east would have taken them
through Diamond City, which all agreed was an outpost of
lawlessness.

Cole reached Diamond City as the autumn sun was dip-
ping toward the mountains in the west and stepped into the
Diamond Bar Saloon on the main street of Meagher County's seat for a late afternoon beer.

"Hello, darlin,' buy a girl a drink?" the seductively attired
woman asked with an enticing smile.

After observing that the floozies were out early, and
appreciating the attractiveness of Hannah Ransdell by comparison to this girl, Cole smiled broadly and did, indeed,
buy the girl a drink.

He knew the end to which the proprietor who employed
her intended the interaction to lead, and he knew where *he*
intended it to lead.

She had a few years on Hannah, and she had led a much
different life. Her name was Aggie, or so she said. She had
come to the lawless West with her father, a preacher, or so
she said. Bladen told her that he had come west in the wake
of the war, because there was nothing for him in Virginia,
which was more or less true.

He let her sit on his lap, and she let him touch her leg. It
all felt good to Cole, and he was tempted to allow it to play
out as the proprietor had intended.

Knowing that her drink contained little but cherry extract

and soda water, he insisted that she chase it with a beer. He knew that she wanted to, and so she did, and it loosened her tongue.

When she was at last comfortable, and had shared her fictional life story with him, talk turned to his "old friend" Gideon, who Cole was hoping to catch up with on the trail.

"Yeah, I believe I reckon to recall a man by that name was in here," she reckoned to recall. "I remember the name because it's from the Bible . . . and my daddy was a preacher, y'know. But you missed him . . . not my daddy . . . your friend Gideon. Day before yesterday, I think."

"He buy you a drink?"

"No, not me . . . I think Crystal . . . no, Crystal, she was talkin' with the one with his hand all bandaged up. I was with their partner. Your friend was in here with a couple of partners."

"Three partners?"

"Yeah . . . I believe there was three . . . total of four with your friend, Gideon. I was with this squirrely little fellow who kept saying he was good."

"Goode?"

"Yeah, that's what I said . . . *good* . . . 'cept your friend Gideon kept callin' him 'good-for-nothin,' and that made him mad. As it turned out, he wasn't very good at all . . . if you know what I mean . . . and that made him *real* mad."

"Sure wish I'd not missed 'em," Cole said, trying not to laugh out loud at Aggie's previous remark. "They say where they were headed?"

"Up Smith's River way," she said thoughtfully. "They were talking about Fort Benton and Blackfeet country."

Having gotten the essential information he needed, Cole let the small talk spin off in another direction, allowing their discussion of the man named "good," who *wasn't* very good, to be buried in the blur of other topics touched upon.

When at last Aggie got around to telling him that it was

time to seal the deal of their implied contract, Bladen told her that it was time for him to get his horse taken care of for the night.

"I'll be right back, darlin,'" he promised as he touched the brim of his hat.

He had lied.

BLADEN COLE BEDDED DOWN IN THE HILLS EAST OF TOWN. Sleeping with your head on a saddle was not nearly as desirable as sleeping with your head on a pillow—and not *alone* on that pillow—but if that pillow was in Diamond City, these arrangements in the hills east of town went further toward guaranteeing that your saddle would still be around in the morning.

Aggie was beautiful in that striking way that comes in part from being skilled at the brushwork that transforms a woman's cheeks and eyelids—and she was shrewd in that resourceful way that comes in part from being skilled at identifying what you want and knowing how to get it.

Naturally, he had also found himself comparing Hannah Ransdell to Sally—or more to the point, Sally as he had first known her. When you spend five years with a woman, she becomes a benchmark of comparison when a man finds himself crossing the paths of other women, even though in his present frame of mind with regard to Sally, it was more a contrast than a comparison.

Hannah did remind him a little of the younger Sally, the Sally with whom he had fallen in love—if it really was *love*. After all, he was not sure he knew what "love" meant.

Hannah was easy on the eye in a way that was different from the beauty of a woman such as Aggie. The color in Hannah's cheeks was as natural as the blush of a Georgia peach. Her girlish grin and those freckles on her nose were enough to make a man smile back just by watching her.

Hannah reminded him a little of Sally, when he had first

crossed her path. Each woman was as sharp as a tack, and like Sally had been, back then, Hannah had that streak of stubborn idealism that comes from being long on brains yet still short on the experiences that come with years. For Hannah, these would come over time. With Sally, the time and experiences *had* come, and would continue coming. Naturally, Cole chose not to allow his mind to wander down the road of speculation as to the *nature* of the experiences Sally had been sharing with J. R. Hubbard out in San Francisco.

Cole fell asleep dreaming that the three stars in the heavens directly above his head were the freckles on Hannah Ransdell's nose.

COLE WAS BOILING HIS COFFEE WHEN THE NEW DAY WAS just a narrow, pinkish-purple sliver on the distant horizon.

It was growing noticeably colder as the man and his horse made their way through the Little Belt Range, heading ever northward. Cole had ridden this roan for more than a year without naming him. The closest he got was "*whoa, boy,*" "*hya, boy.*" He figured the roan didn't mind going nameless. The naming of horses had always been a matter of pride to the planters back in Virginia. Maybe that was why Cole now shied away from the practice.

They camped a second night where the Little Belts give way to the Plains and where Cole could look out and see the lights of the scattered, distant settlements and farmsteads along the Missouri.

If the Porter boys had kept to the plan that Aggie had overheard, they would certainly have come this way. They were running from the law, so wintering in Blackfeet country was a logical thing to do.

They could have crossed the Missouri to head north at any number of places between the Great Falls and Fort Benton, but provisioning at Fort Benton made sense. As a river steamer port, it was both big enough and transient enough for them to get what they needed and not attract too much attention.

With this, Cole naturally wondered, aloud, whether boys who were as witless as the Porter boys were supposed to be would think so logically.

Riding alone for the past couple of days, Cole had been doing a great deal of wondering. He had been going over the Gallatin City shooting in his mind and had been wondering about a lot of unanswered questions.

The Porter boys were impulsive punks who he could easily picture drawing their guns in a barroom brawl, but he had a hard time getting his head around Gideon Porter harboring a grudge for half a year before drawing his gun.

Cole also wondered why Gideon Porter had barged into John Blaine's house, with his gang, in order to shoot his former employer in front of a room full of witnesses. From the universal impression of Gideon Porter, he seemed to be the type of lowlife who would be more at home shooting a man in the back in the dark of night.

Another question that nagged Cole was one Hannah Ransdell had asked of Mrs. Stocker. What indeed had Gideon Porter meant when he told the impetuous Enoch that the women were not *supposed* to be hurt?

He hadn't said "don't hurt the women," he had said the women were *not supposed to be* hurt.

To Cole, this implied that the men *were* supposed to be hurt, and by "supposing" anything, the statement implied that they had gone to Blaine's house with a *plan*. This explained why it took four men. It was not an angry madman settling a score, it was a deliberately conceived *plan*.

The conundrum that Bladen Cole pondered most particularly as his campfire turned to embers that night was *whose plan* it had been.

As much as he was taken with the memory of gazing upon the loveliness of Hannah Ransdell, Cole wondered about her father. Why had Isham Ransdell *not* been at the dinner party? Of course, he had a reasonable explanation that was certainly believable, but why had he not been there, *really*?

Why had he been so anxious to hire a bounty hunter—at great expense and with his own money? Of course, his stated reasons were both reasonable and understandable, but why had he been in such a hurry to hire Cole, *really*?

Whose plan, indeed?

# CHAPTER 5

———◆◆◆———

THE TOWN DOWNSTREAM FROM THE GREAT FALLS, WHERE Bladen Cole reached the Missouri, was hardly a town at all. It was merely a little no-name collection of shacks that had grown up around a place on the river where cattle could be loaded aboard steamers or barges for shipment to buyers downstream. This time of year, when the river was low, it was barely that.

Naturally, as in any cow town in Montana, or in the West as a whole for that matter, civic life was centered on the watering hole. Cole limped into this place, a combination saloon and general store, noticeably favoring his left leg, and ordered a whiskey.

"None of my business, but it's a little early in the day for whiskey, ain't it," the proprietor said as he poured a generous shot and scooped up the coin that Cole tossed on the bar. As was often the case in very small towns where the saloon doubled as a general store, the owner was more used to selling salt pork or horseshoe nails when the sun was this high in the sky.

There was another man in the place, noticeable by his especially large hat, which was tall in the crown. He was examining the wares in the general store part of the place and seemed to pay Cole no mind.

"Medicinal," Cole said sheepishly, nodding to his leg. "Part of the problem with camping for the night where others have camped."

"How's that?"

"Cut my foot on a piece of broken glass when I was answering the call of nature."

"*Ow-ee*," the man said, commiserating.

"Yep, two nights ago. Ain't feeling much better. I fear it'll be infected."

"If you been stepping where your horse been answering the call of nature, it shore 'nuff *will be*."

"Do you know where a man might find some doctoring around here?"

"Which way you headed?"

"North."

"Nearest place would be Fort Benton."

"Thank you greatly," Cole said, holding out his shot glass for a refill.

"Must be something goin' on," the man said as he took Cole's coin. "There was another fella by here yesterday who was stove up with an infection. Nasty goddamn thing on his wrist. Also headed up to Benton. Around here that counts as an epidemic."

"Not Benton," interjected the man with the large hat. "They was headed *east*."

"Well, then I guess the doctor will have time for me when I get there," Cole said, finishing his drink and turning to leave. "Much obliged, good day to y'all."

When he had limped back out to his horse, and the second man had thought him sufficiently removed from earshot, he began berating the shopkeeper.

"Damn you, man. They told us not to tell nobody which way they went."

"That fellow was no lawman," the shopkeeper said, referring to Cole. "I could figure that out, and so could you. Besides, he wasn't askin', I was tellin'."

"They told us not to tell *nobody*."

Hoping that the disagreement would not go beyond verbal, Cole mounted up and rode out of town.

His feigned limp had allowed him to open the door into talk of a man who was injured, and now he knew that he was gaining on the Porter boys. He had started out more than two days behind them and had halved their lead.

As the faint sound of the argument died away, the only sounds were the songs of the meadowlarks in the tall grass. Except for the trail Cole was riding, the vast landscape surrounding the Missouri River in the valley below was as devoid of the hand of humanity as it had been when Lewis and Clark had been the first white men to pass through these parts more than seven decades before.

Their journals of their westward trek on the river recorded no sign of another person for the weeks they took to cross most of the vast expanse of what became Montana Territory. The Piegan, Gros Ventre, and Blackfeet hunters, who no doubt noticed them from the high bluffs above the river, discreetly chose not to make their presence known. When the white men returned, traveling eastward, it had been a different story, but even after the passage of more than seven decades, this stretch of the Missouri, flanked by cottonwoods and aspen in their yellow autumn raiment, had not changed.

Downstream at Fort Benton, it was a different story. William Clark had been dead for less than a decade when this town was born as a bustling riverboat port serving the fur trade. Through the years since, it had grown in importance as gold was discovered and as cattle ranching proliferated.

The most navigable inland port on the Missouri, it was served routinely by steamboats heading downstream to the Mississippi at St. Louis, the Gulf of Mexico at New Orleans, and thence to the whole outside world.

With hyperbole based lightly upon fact, its boosters called their port city "the Chicago of the West." With hyperbole more closely rooted in reality, Fort Benton's detractors, complaining of gunslingers and river pirates, called its main street "the bloodiest block in the West."

Fort Benton was a place where four men on the run could lose themselves, and where a man with a wrist infected by a bullet wound could seek medical attention without the embarrassment of intrusive queries. So too could a man with a limp, who feared an infection of his own.

As had been the case in Diamond City, and as in the recent no-name cow town, the window into the soul of Fort Benton was the pair of swinging doors that led to the saloon. The only question when there were so many was *which* saloon?

Cole bypassed the places on the main street—especially the one from which a fistfight had spilled across the boardwalk and into the street—and picked a smallish tavern on a side street that seemed more likely to cater to locals.

Once again, he affected a limp, and once again he explained his need for whiskey as "medicinal."

"You oughta get that looked at," the bartender offered in the way of advice.

"Reckon I oughta," Cole said in a tone that lacked conviction. There was no sense in his betraying *too* much eagerness to find a doctor who catered to strangers with suspicious injuries—especially not when he was tasting good whiskey. And the whiskey *was* good. The closer a man was to the port to which the whiskey had been shipped, the lower the percentage of native water that was likely to have been added to "extend" it.

"Looks like winter's comin' on," Cole said, changing the subject.

"Saw some snow in the air the other night," agreed the bartender, who drifted away to deal with some other patrons.

When he returned to Cole, the bounty hunter grimaced a little and asked for another shot.

"If I was to want to have this looked at," he said as his shot was poured, "where would I find a doc to do the lookin'?"

"Hear of Doc Ashby?"

"I'm not from around here."

"Second street over. He takes a lot of folks just passing through."

"Much obliged," Cole said, laying a couple of coins on the bar.

Doc Ashby's shingle hung above the door that led to the second floor of a red brick commercial building. The bartender hadn't actually said how many doctors practiced in Fort Benton, but Bladen Cole figured himself to be on the right track when the first one to come to the man's mind took patients who were "just passing through."

There was no sign saying *closed*, and the door was unlocked. Cole took this to be a good indication. A little bell tingled happily as the door opened, and he began climbing the steep and creaky staircase. At the top of the stairs, standing behind a desk, was an older man in wire-frame glasses wearing a vest over a white shirt that was a little dirty in the cuffs.

"I'm Dr. Ashby," he said, extending his hand. "Can I help you?"

"Well, Doc, I'm actually trying to catch up with some friends of mine."

"How . . . ?"

"Well, one of 'em had an injury on his hand, and I figure he'd be looking for a doctor such as yourself to patch him up."

"That so?" Ashby said, his friendly demeanor enveloped by a tone of suspicion. "I believe that your friend is my patient . . . but he's not really your friend . . . is he?"

"Nope."

"You a lawman?"

"No."

"Bounty hunter?"

"I am."

"A man who collects rewards for collecting people," Ashby commented, sniping at Cole.

"A man who enforces legally executed warrants," Cole said with more impatience than defensiveness. "Two men were gunned down in cold blood in the parlor of one of their homes . . . and then the wife of one of the men . . . and then the sheriff of Gallatin City, and finally a fourth man. I'm on the trail of men who've left a string of at least five bodies across this territory . . . I'm out to bring killers back to answer for those crimes."

"I'm afraid you will not be taking this man anywhere," the doctor said.

"Why's that?"

"Because within the next hour or so, he'll be going home to the Lord."

"That bad?"

"That bad. If they'd gotten him to me a day or so earlier, I might have taken off an arm and saved a life, but it's too late. The infection's spread . . . all the way to his heart."

"Can I see him?" Cole asked.

"Nothing wrong with that . . . I suppose." The doctor shrugged, nodding to a door on the wall opposite the head of the stairs. "Go ahead."

Inside, a man lay on a bed, his head on a pillow soaked in sweat. His boots and shirt had been removed. There was a fresh bandage on his wrist, but his arm and shoulder were deeply inflamed.

His eyes flickered open and rolled to look in Cole's direction, but otherwise he remained motionless.

"Which one of the Porter boys are you?" Cole asked.

"Ain't no Porter," he whispered at last. "Name's Waller . . . Milton Waller. If you're here to arrest me, you're too late. Sheriff done killed me already. He's a good shot. Thought he just nicked me . . . but he done killed me."

"Why'd you kill those people?" Cole asked. "Why'd you go after Blaine?"

"Got paid . . . paid good."

An attempt at an ironic chuckle was interrupted by a cough, followed by a choking sound.

"The railroad . . . land deal," the man explained between sputters. "They have to die . . . four partners . . . only one can survive."

"Who paid you?" Cole asked.

"Got paid to kill 'em . . . half up front," Waller continued, skating to the edge of deathbed delirium. "Had to get out of town without the rest . . . damn that Enoch Porter . . . he shot that woman . . . then it all fell apart . . . running out of time . . . had to get out of town quick."

"Who paid you?" Cole repeated.

"All fell apart . . ." Waller said. "He shot the woman . . . we're all scared . . . have to run . . ."

With that, Milton Waller ran out of time. His eyes went blank, his body flinched and relaxed.

Cole looked at Ashby, who nodded. Waller had gone home.

# CHAPTER 6

———◆◆◆———

BLADEN COLE HAD A STRANGE APPREHENSION THAT HE was congratulating a killer when he scrawled out a message to Isham Ransdell at the Fort Benton post office. He enclosed a copy of the death certificate and confirmed the death in his accompanying note. He wrote nothing, however, about Waller's last words, nothing about "only one can survive," because it had been Ransdell, conveniently absent from the shooting, who was the *one* who had walked away *completely unscathed*.

Cole had long been pondering the words of Gideon Porter as related by Mrs. Stocker that the women were not *supposed* to be hurt. From this, he had concluded that the killings were not a matter of an angry madman settling a score, but part of a deliberately conceived *plan*, leaving only the question of *whose plan* it had been. In his deathbed declaration, Waller's words had filled in this missing piece.

For Bladen Cole, justice, when applied to the Porter boys, was no longer a matter of "dead or alive." Justice could only be served by bringing the remaining outlaws back *alive* to point their fingers at Isham Ransdell.

The bounty hunter had hoped to continue his pursuit the morning after the demise of Milton Waller, but the time expended in getting two copies of the death certificate—one for himself and one to mail to Isham Ransdell—had cost most of the day. It had taken all morning and several trips back and forth to the county clerk's office to get copies of Waller's death certificate and to get them signed by both Doc Ashby and the coroner. He then had to chase down a notary whose office hours began only when he had slept off his night before.

Cole decided to sleep one more night between sheets in the fleabag hotel and bought his dinner at a little shack of a cafe near the levee. He decided to buy his whiskey at the saloon nearest his hotel, a typical Fort Benton dive, where trappers from the distant corners of the Plains and boatmen from the Missouri were being united with their first whiskey in months. The piano player was banging out some familiar Virginia marches, and it made Cole a little nostalgic.

He met a woman who craved companionship in a commercial, rather than nostalgic, sort of way, and he talked with her until he discovered that she had no information about the Porter boys. She too lost interest and drifted on to another prospect when she discovered that the only thing he was buying that night was drinks.

She had told him her name, but he forgot it right away. She too reminded him of Sally Lovelace in that way that most painted ladies now reminded him of Sally Lovelace. This one also had Sally's habit of making intense eye contact and telling him that she knew what he was thinking.

This night in this saloon reminded him of another night long ago in that other bar down in Silver City, where prospectors came down out of the Mogollon Mountains with too much gold dust and not enough sense.

The Cole brothers, William and Bladen, had been drink-

ing far too long for their own good that night—he would
grant that as a fact—but young men barely into their twenties cannot be told such a thing at the time.

So too had been another pair of young men barely into
their twenties. As often happens in circumstances such as
prevailed that night, neither pair of young men walked away,
as they should have, from a quarrel that had ensued.

Perhaps if Bladen had tugged at Will's sleeve and insisted
that they let the two men go, it never would have happened,
but he had not, and it did.

It happened so fast, and in such a fog, that Bladen never
really knew which man drew his gun first, but Bladen knew
he was the *last*. When the dust had settled, two men lay
dead, and one was Will. The fourth man, the cowardly one
with the narrow face of a rodent, had vanished into the night.

Through all the ensuing years, in saloons like this one
in Fort Benton, Cole had found himself scanning the patrons
who swirled in the kerosene glow, searching the room for
the rat-faced man who took his brother's life.

Through all the ensuing years, he had yet to see that ugly
face again.


DOC ASHBY HAD CONFIRMED WHAT AGGIE IN DIAMOND
City had said that she had overheard. The Porter boys were
headed across the Marias River into Blackfeet country. In
Montana around this time, you could more or less dance all
around the law with impunity, but *only* more or less. The
only place you could *really* outrun the law was where there
was *no* law. It was commonly stated that there was "no law
north of the Marias."

The cold wind blowing from the Arctic across the Cana-
dian prairies stung his face as Cole rode the undulating
landscape of apparently endless flatness alternated with
broad gullies cut by streams and filled with golden aspen.

It was, in the eyes of an outsider, a trackless wilderness

unpunctuated with landmarks, like the open ocean. To those who had been here for generations, each of the monotonous series of hills and gullies was as unique as a city street marked by a unique street sign.

The Blackfeet, called Siksikáwa in their own tongue, had inhabited this distant corner of the Plains for centuries. For the most part, the white man had yet to build up the momentum to exploit this place. Aside from a few distantly separated trading posts, there were no people living north of the Marias—in a vast region larger than Cole's native Virginia—whose grandparents had not been born here.

Late in the afternoon, Cole noticed a cluster of scavenging birds circling and squawking, and he detoured slightly to investigate. They were not the remains of three men ambushed by Blackfeet, but the bloody and scattered bits of something else that had recently been living. The pieces were so far dispersed that it took Cole a few minutes to ascertain that these remains were, or had been, a bull elk.

The big animal appeared to have been blown apart by a stick of dynamite, though in fact it had been attacked, killed, and partially consumed by a grizzly. A lump rose in Cole's throat as he realized that this slaughter had occurred within the past hour. The meat was fresh, the blood still runny.

The roan began acting nervously, jerking and snorting like a person who had come under the spell of an evil sorcerer. Cole had had barely a moment to understand why his horse was spooked, when he saw the reason in the corner of his eye.

The bear arose with a crash and a snort from a thicket of willows. From a crouching position, it unlimbered itself to a standing posture and bellowed ominously. The grizzly is an enormous creature, taller than a man standing in his stirrups while on his horse.

Cole felt the blood drain from his face as the roan reared.

The signature terror of the remote corners of the West, the grizzly was a creature so fierce that all others avoided it—when they could. The Indians approached it with a mixture of reverence and trepidation. White men avoided it because it could not be killed. As many a man had learned the hard way, its skull was so thick and the muscle mass of its body so dense that only a lucky shot, a one-in-a-hundred shot, could bring one down.

For the first time in years, Cole found himself frozen in fear. The first reaction of a person to a grizzly, that being to run like hell, was often fatal. As clumsy as they seemed while lumbering about, grizzlies could outrun a man, even a man on a horse.

He pulled his Winchester from its scabbard and began backing his horse, figuring that his *best chance* was to get away slowly before the bear decided to drop back down to four legs and charge him.

The Winchester represented his *last chance*.

For a short while, it worked. The bear watched the mounted rider as though bewildered by the jerky backward motion.

At last, the grizzly decided that despite an apparent backward movement, this intruder represented an interloper at his supper table.

With an angry snarl, the beast charged.

The roan bucked, and Cole felt himself losing his balance.

In the process of trying not to lose his rifle, Cole lost his reins.

For a moment, he felt himself sliding sideways from a galloping horse.

In the next instant, he was colliding awkwardly with the ground.

The Winchester, on which he had lost his grip, dropped about six feet away.

The sound of the bear galloping toward him was like thunder.

He literally threw himself toward the gun.

Grabbing the rifle in mid-tumble, Cole fired without aiming.

The bullet struck the bear with little more annoyance than a horse fly caused attacking a person. Cole might as well have poked him in the shoulder with a stick.

However, the sound of the shot, something this bear had never heard, and the smell of the gunsmoke, something this bear had never smelled, provided a momentary pause.

It is curious to contemplate the sorts of things that go through a man's mind when he is about to die. They say that your whole life flashes before you, but what do "they" know?

Bladen Cole thought about that Sunday in the Congregational Church in Bowling Green when he was about twelve, when he had thought about the effectiveness of prayer for the first time. The preacher's remarks had lost him in the bobbing sea of his own daydreams, and he had wondered whether prayers went answered. He guessed that most did not, but he wanted to believe that some *did*.

In that split second before the moment in which he expected his own violent and painful death, Bladen Cole prayed.

He also squeezed the trigger again, and saw the lead tear into the cheek of an angry bear whose rapid progress toward him was not slackened.

He could smell the disgusting stench of the grizzly's breath as he fired the *last shot possible* before ten angry, raging claws reached him and ripped him apart as they had the elk.

The slug impacted the bear's left eye, cleaving straight into his brain.

The inside surface of the back of the bear's skull, being too thick to be penetrated by the bullet, caused it to ricochet, then ricochet again. Each time that the bullet zigged or zagged in the soft tissue of the brain, it tore a separate path and ripped away another swath of the bear's consciousness.

Cole rolled to the side as the bear reached him.

He felt the pain of the bear's leg falling on his, but he barely avoided having the full weight of the animal's thousand pounds crush him.

He imagined that he was being mauled, and he struggled

to get away, but the frightening gyrations were merely the bear's death throes. By the time that he had at last gotten out from beneath the enormous mass, the grizzly had twitched its last.

Cole gasped to catch breath, inhaling the rankness of the sweaty monster, but was overjoyed just to be breathing at all.

# CHAPTER 7

—◆◆◆—

COLE CAMPED THAT NIGHT AMONG THE ASPEN, WASHING himself off and watering his roan in the trickle of a stream that ran there.

He awoke suddenly to the hot breath of an animal on his face, immediately imagining it to be another grizzly, but it was merely his horse. He now realized how his subconscious mind had shifted into wilderness mode. Would he have mistaken his horse for a grizzly two nights earlier when he went to sleep with the lights of Diamond City twinkling in the distance? He had not and probably would not have before the experience of the day just passed.

Waiting for his coffee to boil, he watched the stars wink out in the lightening sky of dawn. He thought of what he had read of seafaring people using the stars as navigational tools, and of how he had always used the North Star as a reference point in unfamiliar territory.

As he rode north with the gathering dawn and turned westward in the direction of the Rocky Mountains, he saw a small group of pronghorns at a great distance, but aside from that, the only sign of life was the usual companionship of the meadowlarks and a hawk circling in the distance.

Shortly after his lunch, which consisted of a scrap of hardtack eaten in the saddle as he rode, he saw them. Two riders had materialized out of nowhere, or so it seemed. One minute, the hill about a quarter mile ahead and to the right had been deserted, and now there were two men there. He could make out the golden hue of their buckskin shirts and the long black hair that framed their heads. The fact that he had seen them at all signified that they wanted to be seen.

Cole raised his hand to signify that he saw them and meant no hostility. The men returned the gesture and waited for him to reach them.

"Good morning, fellows," he said in English, more to establish that his intention was to greet them than in the belief that they could understand his words. "My name's Bladen Cole."

They responded with a gesture to the tongue, which signified their not being conversant in his language.

Cole knew a few Lakota words—as did most white men on the northern Plains, because the two groups had had much contact over the past three decades—but almost nothing of the totally unrelated Blackfeet language. What he did know pretty well, and what did unite the tribes on the Plains who could not communicate verbally, was the universal sign language.

Using this, Cole was able to explain that he was looking for three men, three *white* men, who had come into Blackfeet country in the previous couple of days.

Without saying whether or not they had seen the Porter boys, the two men replied that they had problems of their own. There was some sort of intertribal squabble going on, and they were on one side of it.

One of them pointed to the Winchester Model 1873 rifle that Cole had in the scabbard attached to his saddle. At first, he thought that they were proposing to trade. One of them carried an older model, U.S. Army–issue "Trapdoor" Spring-field, and he could see the distinctive bronze-colored breech of the Winchester '66 carried by the other. Neither gun was desirable in a trade for a '73 Winchester, so he declined.

At this, the man who was doing all the talking said that Cole was mistaken. They didn't want his Winchester, they wanted *him*. They indicated that their head man had sent them to "volunteer" his services as a rifleman.

Cole found it hard to stifle the laugh, which, when he suddenly guffawed, noticeably startled his new Siksikáwa friends. Bladen Cole, the hired gun, was being hired for a second job in parallel to that which had brought him north of the Marias.

The two men were looking at each other with bewildered expressions, when Cole let it be known that he *would* help them.

On one hand, allowing himself to become embroiled in a Blackfeet civil war was an unnecessary distraction from his purpose, but if he had any hope of completing a success-ful manhunt in this enormous land, he needed friends. And he was about to make some.

They had ridden together for about an hour when Cole started to see the blue haze of many campfires in the dis-tance. At last, as the sweet smell of smoldering cottonwood reached his nostrils, they came over a rise and saw a village below. There were more than a dozen tipis clustered along a quarter-mile stretch of a stream. People were going about their daily chores, and horses grazed on the hillsides.

As they rode through the camp, Cole smiled broadly at the children who eyed him curiously. One group of preteen girls giggled and turned away as he caught their eyes.

They stopped before a large tipi which was decorated with a variety of pictograms painted in both red and black. By its location in the center of the camp, Cole concluded that this was the chief's house.

The three riders dismounted, and one of the Siksikáwa

men approached the open flap of the lodge. He spoke to
someone inside and gestured for Cole to come in. The bounty
hunter grabbed a knot of smoking tobacco from a parcel that
he carried in his saddlebag and approached the opening. He
wasn't fully conversant in native customs, but he did know
that among the people of the Plains, it was always good
manners to present your host with a token gift of tobacco.

"*Assa, nápikoan, oki*," the man said cordially as Cole
appeared in his doorway.

Though he claimed less than the barest understanding of
the language, Cole did recognize the greeting "*oki*" and term
for "white man," "*nápikoan*." He had always appreciated
that it was a more literal translation than the Lakota word
for his race, which was the derogatory "*wasichu*," meaning
"the one who steals the bacon fat."

Cole handed the chief the tobacco, a gesture which the
chief seemed to appreciate. With this, the old man shot a
glance toward one of the younger men which needed no
translation. It said pointedly that "this white man isn't as
discourteous as you thought."

"*Ke-a-e-es-tsa-kos-ach-kit-satope*," the old man said to
the young man, who immediately spread a buffalo robe for
Cole to sit on.

The chief had a leathery, lined face that was deeply tanned
in contrast to his long, snow white hair. His eyes were bright
and sharp, and it was hard to judge his age. By those eyes, he
could have been thirty. By the texture of his skin and the color
of his hair, he could have been a hundred.

"*Nitsinihka'sim O-mis-tai-po-kah*," he said. introducing
himself. "*Kiistawa, tsa kitanikkoowa*?" he continued, pointing at his guest.

The words made no more sense to Bladen than water
gurgling over rocks in a stream bed, but by the gestures, he
understood that the man had introduced himself and wanted
to know his name.

"Bladen Cole," he replied, pointing to himself.

"Ahhh, Bladencool," the man said, leaning back on his buffalo robe.

With this, evidently believing now that "Bladencool" understood some of the rudiments of the *lingua franca*, the man began relating some sort of story. Though it was accompanied by gestures, Cole became completely lost. He recognized the sign for "horse," but beyond that, he couldn't follow the man's narrative at all.

Finally, this confusion became apparent, and the chief impatiently turned to one of the younger men, who got up and left, as though he had been sent to fetch something.

The chief continued, but with simpler and easier to understand sign language. The fellow was making what amounted to small talk. He asked how far Cole had come and nodded his understanding when Cole explained that he had been following the three men for four sleeps.

They were deep into their conversation when a shadow appeared in the doorway.

Cole looked up to see a young woman with dark, riveting eyes, who looked to be in her early twenties. Her features were as smooth and delicate as the old man's were hard-edged and textured. Her long hair, which she wore in braids, was as black as his was white. She was wearing a double-row necklace made of elk teeth and a buckskin dress, lightly decorated with porcupine quills.

She listened intently as the old man spoke to her, nodding periodically and glancing occasionally at the white man. Cole could not take his eyes off her and savored the grace of her movements as she was invited to sit on a buffalo robe near him.

"Mr. Bladencool," she said looking at him, appearing to work hard to choose her words. "My name is Natoya-I-nis'kim. My uncle . . . his name is O-mis-tai-po-kah . . . has requested me to translate his words to you."

She smiled bashfully and asked, "Do you understand my words? I have not spoken in English for many months."

"Yes, I understand you just fine," Cole replied, trying to enunciate clearly. "Actually my name is Bladen Cole . . . two words."

"I'm sorry . . . Mr. Cool. I understand. Two names . . . yes, I understand."

"You speak English very good," he said to compliment her. "Where did you learn . . . way out here?"

"I was taught at the mission school. I attended as a girl. I am happy I remember the words."

"Your uncle seems proud of you," Cole said.

"My uncle, who is named O-mis-tai-po-kah for the white medicine buffalo calf who was born at the same time as he, is *iikaatowa'pii*, very powerful with spirit power . . . great medicine."

"What is it that your uncle wants with me? I understood something about horses . . . but that was about it."

"There were Pikuni Siksikáwa renegades who stole many *ponokáómitaa* . . . many horses . . . from us," she said, gesturing elegantly. "They have become into one band with the Káínawa Siksikáwa who live in the red coats' country."

"So that I understand," Cole recapped, "some people from your own tribe stole some of your horses and they're running with some people from the Káínawa Blackfeet up in Canada?"

"Yes."

"And your uncle wants *my* help in getting the horses back?"

"Yes . . . and also to punish the Pikuni for riding with our enemy."

As with many tribes, including the pale-skinned ones from Cole's world, people who seemed indistinguishable to outsiders were often rivals—or worse. The Pikuni Siksikáwa of Montana and the Káínawa in Canada shared a language and a culture, yet they had been openly hostile with one another forever. Of course, in Cole's own generation, the Civil War had consumed nearly a million lives of men, men just like him, men who were on two sides but who nevertheless spoke the same language.

"Where are they now, the renegades and the Káínawa?" Cole asked. "Did they go back into Canada?"

"No . . . they went to the *Mistákists Ikánatsiaw*, the mountains which go to the sun," she said, ". . . one or two sleeps toward the place of the setting sun . . . to the west from here."

"Why does he need an outsider for this?" Cole asked.

"Because most of our young men have gone away to hunt the *iiníí* . . . the buffalo . . . far to the east . . . many sleeps. They stole the horses because we were in a moment of weakness. We need help."

"How did you decide to pick me?"

"Ikutsikakatósi and Ómahkaatsistawa," she said, nodding to the two young men. "They spotted you this morning as the sun rose. They told my uncle about the white man riding where white men usually do not come. He said to get the white man to help."

"You don't see too many white men out here, then?"

"No, not this side of the trading posts, not in many moons."

"I was told there were three others who came this way a day or two ago."

"I haven't heard of them, they must have gone some other way," she said. Her expression agreed with her words.

"Must have," Cole said.

The old man said something, but Cole didn't hear it; his rapt attention had been on watching Natoya's graceful gesture as she pointed to the west.

She heard it though and quickly translated.

"You will go now . . . you will go *aami'toohski* . . . westward at once."

The chief said something to the men that caused them to grimace and Natoya to giggle slightly.

"I have one more question," Cole said, turning to Natoya. "Why me? Why did I get singled out for this escapade?"

"Because Ikutsikakatósi and Ómahkaatsistawa could see by your guns that you were a man who could fight . . . O-mis-tai-po-kah could see by your eyes that you are a fighter who does not like to lose."

"If I would *not* have come with them . . . if I wouldn't have agreed to this . . . ?"

"They would kill you and take your guns," she replied, her expression very matter of fact.

THE THREE MEN RODE OUT OF THE CAMP TOGETHER, BUT when they crested the hill at the far side of the river valley, the Blackfeet reined their horses ahead of Cole's, deliberately shunning him. It was obviously a matter of hurt pride that a *nápikoan* had to be hired to help them do their job. Being thusly ostracized did not bother Cole in the least. If it was him, he would have felt the same way.

Nor did it bother him to be riding alone. He had long preferred it that way, he thought to himself. But, thinking of Will, he recalled that he had not *always* felt that way.

As they rode westward toward the descending sun of mid-afternoon, he thought about the Porter boys and about their biblical names. From what he recalled about his own Bible learning, which was not that much, Gideon's biblical namesake was called "the Destroyer," but he did his destroying on orders from God. There were a couple of Enochs in the Bible, but Cole could remember only the one who was the son of Cain, who had committed the world's first homicide. He wondered whether the missionaries had taught the Blackfeet children about these men.

The Porter boys were his reason for being out here in the first place, and his thoughts turned to their whereabouts, and how long it would take to find them in this country. They were at least a day ahead of him, but having crossed north of the Marias, they had crossed north of their past, and they would no longer be running. Their pace would have slackened, and they would have relaxed and made their presence known to the locals.

If not Natoya's band, then some other Siksikáwa band or other out here would have seen them, and word would spread. That word would not spread to ears accustomed to English, but it would spread, and sooner or later, Cole would know.

As he had done since crossing the Marias, Cole was keeping his eyes on the horizon. Yesterday, he'd had *potential* enemies in anyone who might choose to distrust a stranger. Now that he had taken a side in a civil war, he had *real* enemies. He could count on the wary eyes of his two companions to see danger first, but still, he kept his eyes on the horizon.

The last place that he had expected to see that horizon populated was in the direction straight behind him—yet there it was, a rider coming up from behind at a gallop.

The two Siksikáwa men reined up their horses and exchanged words which Cole did not understand, except that they were more of aversion than alarm.

Cole could see why. The rider was Natoya-I-nis'kim, loping toward them on a paint, her braids swirling about her head as she came.

"*Iiksoka'pii kitsinohsi!*" she said to the two men, laughing as she brought her horse to a stop. Even back home in Virginia, where women took to riding with great pride of accomplishment, Cole had never seen a woman who could handle a horse with such skill.

They spoke with her angrily, pointing their fingers back in the direction of their village. Cole chuckled as she told them off. At last, the argument reached an impasse. They turned their backs on her and resumed the westward trek, ignoring her as they had been ignoring the white man.

"What was that all about?" Cole asked.

"I told Ikutsikakatósi and Ómahkaatsistawa I am happy to see them," she said, smiling mischievously.

"They aren't happy to see *you*."

"I don't care," she said playfully.

"Why are you here?"

"Uncle told me to come," she explained. "There will be a need to translate. Ikutsikakatósi and Ómahkaatsistawa would not speak to you if they *could*, but they *cannot*."

"They don't want to speak to *you* either . . . at least not to say a civil word."

"This is not a place for a woman, they said," Natoya explained with a smirk.

"It isn't," Cole agreed. "This will be dangerous."

"*I* will be dangerous," she said with a slight grin, pulling back the edge of her buffalo robe to show him that she had a holster strapped around her waist that contained an older model Colt Navy revolver.

"Where did you get that?"

"Trader."

"Have you used it?"

"Yes."

Bladen Cole held his tongue. It really *wasn't* a place for a woman, even if she could handle a horse and use a gun. Where there was the probability of a gunfight, it was a bad place for a woman, but it was, he decided, not his place to tell an Indian girl, especially one displaying such confidence, that she was in the wrong place.

On the other hand, the old man was right, an interpreter *could* prove useful—not only in accomplishing the old man's purpose, but in accomplishing Cole's as well. It was just a pity, he felt, that there were so few men in the camp that the chief had to send his young niece.

"When will the other men be back from their buffalo hunt?"

"Before the snow," she said, looking to the north and speaking without her previous assurance.

"Your uncle is named after the white buffalo?" Cole said, making conversation after a mile or so of riding in silence.

"Yes, a calf was born when he was born."

"You didn't tell be the meaning of *your* name," he said.

"*Inis'kim* is the 'Medicine Stone,' " she said. " 'Medicine *Buffalo* Stone.' "

"That sounds important."

"My mother found one when I was in her belly," she explained. "It is the stone which sings. It is the stone bringing good luck. Long ago, in the winter that the *iiníí* . . . the buffalo went away, a woman found the first stone in a cottonwood tree when she went to a stream to get water for cooking. The *Inis'kim* sang to her and told her to take it home to her lodge. It said that buffalo will return and hearts will be glad."

"Did it work?"

"She taught the *Inis'kim* song to her husband and the elders. They knew that it was powerful. They sang. They prayed. The buffalo *came*."

"Does your mother still have it?"

"My mother has gone . . . Absaroka raiders. My father too."

"I'm sorry to hear that," Cole said meekly, knowing that he had touched a nerve.

"That's when I went to the mission school," she said, wiping a tear from her cheek.

Cole made another innocuous comment about the weather and the approach of winter, and afterward, they rode on without talking.

# Chapter 8

———◆❖◆———

THE WISTFUL GIRL WITH THE TEAR ON HER CHEEK REAS-serted herself at the camp that night. When the Siksikáwa men, each a head taller than she, insisted that water be fetched for cooking, an argument ensued. It ended with Ikutsikakatósi taking the basket to the stream.

Bladen Cole found this greatly amusing.

"We'd better build this fire good so we don't get a visit from a grizzly tonight," Cole said, shoving some cottonwood sticks into the fire.

"Yes . . . you are right," Natoya agreed. "It is a dangerous animal . . . and a powerful animal in many ways."

"That's for sure," Cole agreed.

"And he is a very powerful animal with *nátosini* . . . um . . . how to you say . . . medicine?"

"Supernatural power?"

"Yes . . . supernatural power, *nátosini*."

"So the grizzly is sacred to the Siksikáwa?" Cole asked.

"In the way that everything in the world is sacred,"

Natoya explained. "In the way that the black robes thought
we 'worshipped' trees and badgers."

Poking a stick to turn a piece of cottonwood in the fire,
she continued her recollections of the missionaries.

"There was *one* black robe who understood . . . but
mostly they did not, and we laughed at them behind their
backs. That is not very polite, I know . . . but we were
children . . ."

"I think it's funny," Cole chuckled, imagining a bevy of
Blackfeet girls giggling about the inability of the missionaries to understand the people they were teaching.

"Of all the *kiááyo*, all the bears, the *apóhkiááyo* . . . you
call him 'grizzly,' is feared and respected above all," Natoya
continued.

"So that makes him *sacred*?"

"I do not have the *Naapi'powahsin* . . . the English words
to explain. It is not 'sacred' in the missionary way of being
sacred, just as we do not 'worship' trees in the missionary
way of worshipping. *Apóhkiááyo* is *important* to the
Siksikáwa . . . not the same way as the buffalo . . . but . . . I
don't have the words . . . *apóhkiááyo* is greatly feared *and*
greatly respected. I'm sorry that is the best I can explain."

Cole disagreed. "You have very good English words," he
said. "I know a lot of white people who do less of a job
explaining things."

"Don't let me be selfish," she said.

"How do you mean?"

"I am so happy to have someone . . . so I can speak my
*Naapi'powahsin* . . . my English words."

"You're not selfish at all . . . I'm happy to have someone
to speak English words with myself."

She smiled and turned away.

"But about the grizzly . . . and it being sacred in the way
that it is . . . and I know that's the wrong English word . . .
There's something that I gotta tell you . . . gotta admit to."

"What's that?"

"I killed one yesterday. I killed a grizzly."

Natoya-I-nis'kim looked at him with a mixture of shock and bewilderment.

"Yeah, I was coming across the plains and I came across a fresh elk kill," he said. "The thing reared up and charged before I knew what was happening. I got off three shots . . . the last one was a lucky shot. So I killed a sacred bear. I'm sorry to say that, knowing that they're important to your people . . . to the Siksikáwa . . . but it was him or me."

"It is a very great thing to overcome *apóhkiááyo* in a fight," Natoya said.

She seemed impressed, rather than upset, a fact that caused Cole to breathe a sigh of relief.

"Because of their strength, and their great *nátosini* . . . It is hard to kill him in a fight. Most men cannot. Most men die. A man who kills him in a fight inherits his power."

"How does that work?" Cole asked.

"Power . . . medicine . . . comes to all animals from *Natosiwa*, the sun. When *apóhkiááyo* is beaten in a fight, his power is then granted to the man. The man receives the character and spirit of *apóhkiááyo*. Of course he was powerful in the start . . . the man. He has to be to overcome *apóhkiááyo*. You are a powerful man, Mr. Cool."

"I didn't feel any different," Cole admitted, "except kind of dirty from having this sweaty bear dead on top of me."

Natoya laughed.

"By the way," he said. "Since you seem to appreciate the grizzly, I'd like you to have this."

He reached into his pocket and took out a sharp and frightening six-inch grizzly claw.

"I took this from that one yesterday," he said, handing it to her. "I want you to have it."

She took the object as though it were a religious artifact, for to be given a grizzly claw by a man who had triumphed over *apóhkiááyo* in battle was an amazing gesture.

She looked at it with an expression of awe. It was, Cole

thought, like having handed a white woman a fistful of diamonds.

Natoya then looked at him with an expression of speechless gratitude.


IN THE MORNING, ONLY NATOYA-I-NIS'KIM AMONG THE three Siksikáwa accepted the coffee that Cole offered, though she found it not to her liking.

By the middle of the day, the jagged peaks of the Rockies could be clearly seen, rising abruptly from the Plains.

"*Mistákists Ikánatsiaw*," Natoya said with a nod as Cole pointed toward the snowcapped peaks. The trail of the horse thieves led toward the mountains, just as O-mis-tai-po-kah had predicted. They had not been hard to follow. It is hard to move a herd of a couple dozen *ponokáómitaa* without leaving ample evidence of their passing.

Cole could tell by the fragrance of the "ample evidence" that it was more recent than it had been during the previous day. Thanks to Natoya's having insisted that they break camp very early, they were now only a matter of hours behind their quarry. The fact that the thieves' pace had slowed meant that the renegades were confident of not being followed. Just like the Porter boys, Cole hoped.

Gradually, they passed out of the rolling hills dotted mainly with aspen and came to a ridge whose western, windward slope was covered with gnarled and windblown spruce. As they crossed the ridge, they were greeted with a breeze which blew colder than what they had experienced thus far.

Natoya reined up her horse and pointed through the trees.

In the distance, they could see a long, slender lake hugging the base of the mountains. The winter, which all expected, had already come to the high country. The jagged peaks were heavily cloaked in snow.

Natoya identified the lake as Natoákiomahksikimi, but she translated the names of the peaks they saw. There were

Red Eagle and Little Chief, and occupying a prominent place above the lake was Going-to-the-Sun. To the left, she pointed out one named for a man called Imazí-imita, whose name, Natoya explained, meant "Almost-a-Dog."

A short distance down into the valley of the lake, the horse thieves had steered their purloined herd onto a broad trail. Natoya identified it as being a main thoroughfare for the Siksikáwa which led down into the valley of the lakes.

The "ample evidence" was now exceedingly fresh, and the Siksikáwa men pulled their rifles from the scabbards. Cole instinctively drew his Colt and spun the cylinder to count the cartridges. He knew it was loaded—this was just a ritual. As he undid the leather thong that secured his Winchester in its scabbard, he noticed that Natoya's hand was resting on her holstered weapon as well.

They rounded a bend near the base of the ridge, and the landscape of the valley revealed itself. There, not far below and swirling about in a meadow near a stream, was the stolen herd. Cole counted eight men.

As he and his companions watched, their number increased by two with the approach of a pair of *nápikoan* riders.

Cole squinted hard, determining that these white men were not the Porter boys. One might have been, but the other was much too fat.

"Buyers," Natoya whispered.

Cole nodded. It was obvious that the two white men had been invited here to purchase the stolen herd.

"I think something better happen before this transaction is completed," he said under his breath.

Natoya nodded and repeated this to the Ikutsikakatósi and Ómahkaatsistawa, who nodded their agreement.

"Cover me," Cole said as he spurred the roan forward.

A few minutes later, the ten riders in the valley turned their heads at his approach. Hands tensed and touched guns.

Cole raised his hand in greeting and rode toward the two white men.

"Good morning, sir," the heavyset man said cautiously. "To what do we owe the pleasure of seeing you here?"

"Good morning, sir," Cole said, extending his hand. "My name is Bladen Cole. If I'm not mistaken, you're here to buy some Indian ponies."

"Name's McGaugh," the man said, taking Cole's offered hand. "Benjamin McGaugh. You'd be correct in your supposition. We were informed at the Indian Agency that a herd would be available here this morning. I'm here to pick out four or five of the finest of these ponies."

"Would it make any difference to your plans if I was to tell you that these animals are a herd stolen from my friend White Buffalo Calf, whose lodge stands about two days' ride east of here?"

"If that were to be a fact, it would certainly make a difference. I am not in the business of accepting stolen property . . . certainly not Blackfeet property on Blackfeet land."

"I hoped that would be your position," Cole said.

"Mason," the big man said, turning to his companion. "Ask these boys about that. *Is* this a stolen herd?"

The other man, who looked to be part Blackfeet himself, queried the apparent leader of the horse thieves, who vehemently denied the assertion. However, the opposite message was conveyed by the nervous apprehension of the others when they heard the question asked.

"There we have it," the man said. "A denial from the man with whom I am about to consummate a transaction."

"And an admission from the expression of the others," Cole added.

"Were I to accept the discrepancy that you have pointed out," said the man, who was certainly not one to use one word when three would do. "Then I would say that we are at a bit of an impasse. For argument's sake, if I were to accept this discrepancy and agree with your opinion, then I would be faced with refusing the deal being offered and riding away without my friends getting the gold which they desire."

"That would probably be the case," Cole agreed.

"This would make my friends angry," McGaugh continued. "I would not want them angry, nor would *you*. May I remind you, sir, that we are several days' ride inside Blackfeet country and outnumbered. I suggest that our conversation never happened, and you may convey my heartfelt condolences to your friend, Mr. White Calf."

"If I had ridden all this way from Mr. White Buffalo Calf's camp alone," Cole began, "and if we really *were* outnumbered, I would be strongly inclined to agree with you . . . but that is not the case."

Turning toward the hillside, he raised his fist.

As the eyes of everyone in the valley turned to follow his gesture, Ómahkaatsistawa rode out onto a bluff, raised his rifle over his head and shouted the Siksikáwa greeting *"Oki!"*

Moments later, Ikutsikakatósi, in a far removed place, repeated the greeting. Cole was pleased that they had moved apart. This suggested that a much larger contingent was present.

Realizing that the deal was off and their position compromised, the horse thieves immediately moved to secure their assets and get out of their present predicament. The only way to do this was to stampede the herd and make a run for it.

There was a crackle of rifle fire to spook the horses, and the mass began to move.

Cole knew that the first volley was meant to stampede the horses, but any second volley would be designed to remove the inconvenient *nápikoan*, so he drew his Colt.

Almost immediately, he watched the leader of the thieves draw a bead on a startled Benjamin McGaugh.

Hoping that he had the range to make a difference, Cole aimed and fired.

He watched the man jerk sideways and tumble off his horse as his rifle flew through the air.

Mason had pulled a rifle from his scabbard and gotten off a couple of shots, but McGaugh was having too much trouble controlling his spooked horse to draw his gun.

Another of the renegades rode at Cole firing his rifle.

Keeping low, Cole ran at him rather than retreating, which seemed to surprise him a little.

In the split second that the man's hand was on the lever of his Winchester, Cole aimed and fired. The bullet caught him on the jaw and the lower part of his face exploded upward in a pink cloud.

It was not so much a running gun battle as a swirling gun battle. The horse herd had been grazing when it all started, with individual horses facing in every direction of the compass. Therefore, when the stampede began, it was a stampede that went nowhere but to turn like a cyclone, folding in upon itself and creating confusion and panic among the undisciplined herd.

Some of the renegades were in the midst of this, first trying to straighten the herd, then just trying not to be knocked off and trampled.

Other renegades were on the outside the cyclone. One fired at Cole. The miss was so close that Cole heard the lead hiss past his head like an angry hornet. When Cole's return shot struck the man's chest, he knew that it was a fatal hit.

Out of the corner of his eye, he saw three riders coming at full gallop from the woods, firing as they came. In the center was Natoya-I-nis'kim. The Colt looked like a cannon in her small hand, yet she held it as steady as if it were bolted to her horse.

She had shed her buffalo robe, and it was obvious—at least to Cole—that her slender, bare arms were not those of a man. What would the renegades do when they saw that they were being attacked by a woman?

The answer was a split second of disbelief on the part of

the nearest horse thief as she entered the fray, a split second that cost the man his life. Cole saw the big pistol buck in her hand and the man topple awkwardly from his horse.

Suddenly, Cole watched in unanticipated disbelief as she pointed the Colt directly at *him*! For a moment, he froze as he stared down the muzzle with her riding directly at him. She was scarcely fifteen feet away when he found himself staring down a muzzle flash.

Almost at the same moment, he heard a horrific shriek that seemed to come from his own shoulder.

He turned to see a man hovering in the air, almost on top of him. Blood was splattering everywhere, and the contorted expression on his face was that of the most frightening banshee imaginable.

As Natoya and her horse raced past him like a rocket, so close that Cole could feel the heat of her sweating mount, he realized what had happened. While he was distracted by the sight of her coming into the fight, one of the renegades had come within two feet of him for a certain kill.

Natoya-I-nis'kim had just saved his life.


THE THUNDER OF HOOVES—BOTH PANICKED AND PURPOSE-ful, clamoring within an immense and growing cloud of dust—was punctuated by screams of anger and screams of pain—and by gunshots.

Bladen Cole looked around. His eyes probed the choking yellow dust. He had emptied his revolver, dropping three men. He had now drawn his Winchester from its scabbard, and his eyes searched for more targets. Suddenly, he saw them, two riders who had bolted, leaving the scene and riding north at top speed.

He raised the rifle to his shoulder, sighted, and squeezed the trigger.

One man tumbled off his horse.

He hated to shoot a man in the back, but there was a job

to be done. Again he aimed, but this time, before he could fire, he heard the crack of another rifle.

The rider jumped slightly, but did not fall. The dust from his horse faded and disappeared into the distance.

Cole looked down. Ikutsikakatósi was just lowering his Trapdoor Springfield.

As the dust settled, he saw Natoya, riding hard to round up the stragglers from the stampeded herd. Realizing that she was the one working while her companions merely gawked at the battlefield, Cole went into action, chasing some stragglers and getting them back to the group.

Benjamin McGaugh, who had started the day with a simple horse-buying trip, sat on the ground staring at the lifeless body of his hired man and gripping a blood-soaked sleeve.

He was uncharacteristically speechless when Bladen Cole knelt beside him, ripped off his shirt, and constructed a tourniquet.

"You seem to know what you're doing," he said weakly.

"Learned it in the war," Cole said succinctly.

"Oh yeah," said McGaugh with a nod. "The war."

The two men could tell by their respective accents that they had been on opposite sides. It had been a long time, but nobody who was there would ever forget the war.

Cole stood him up and walked him to the nearby stream so that he could get a drink.

As McGaugh sat at the edge of the water, he began to shake, not from the cold, because the afternoon had proved to be fairly warm, but from the onset of shock.

Natoya, who had retrieved her buffalo robe, rode up, dismounted, and without a word, wrapped it around his shoulders.

With that, she lay down and submerged her face in the gurgling waters of the creek. After what seemed to Cole and McGaugh to have been about two minutes, she sat up abruptly, shook her wet braids vigorously and, obviously

refreshed, smiled a smile which, had Cole been a poet—
which he was not—he would have called angelic.

"Thank you," Cole said, looking at her, she who had been
*his* guardian angel. "Thanks for saving my life out there."

She looked down and then off to the horizon, still smiling, and began to blush.

The only sounds were the gurgling of the stream and the
background racket of Ikutsikakatósi and Ómahkaatsistawa
searching for trophies among their fallen enemies.

# CHAPTER 9

━━━◆◆◆◆◆━━━

THE SUN WAS DROPPING INTO THE STORM CLOUDS ENVELOP-
ing the peaks of the Rockies when four horses and three
riders lumbered into the isolated trading post on the river
which the Siksikáwa called "Two Medicine" because it
flowed out of the mountain valley where the sundance
lodges of rival Siksikáwa bands stood side by side in a celebration of tribal unity. It was ironic, Cole thought, after a
day marked by such deadly tribal *disunity*.

Across the saddle of the riderless horse was tied the body
of the half-breed named Mason, whose Yankee father had
wed a Siksikáwa woman in this land many years ago.

Bladen Cole and young Natoya-I-nis'kim had accompanied the wounded Benjamin McGaugh to this place, having
agreed to a proposal made by Ikutsikakatósi and Ómahkaatsistawa that they be allowed to return the herd of recovered *ponokáómitaa* to O-mis-tai-po-kah. They had wished
to do this because it would allow them to save face in light
of the fact that the bloody work of actually killing the

thieves and the mundane work of rounding up the heard had
been done mainly by a *nápikoan* and a *woman.*

Cole was happy to go along with this. He had done his
part and paid the dues that bought him the credentials and
credibility among the Siksikáwa that he would need to move
about in their land and continue his manhunt.

Natoya was happy to do this as well. She was tired of the
jealous taunting of the young men and relished the respect
that she had earned, and now enjoyed, from this stranger
from a distant world.

Benjamin McGaugh had begun to regain his composure
by the time that he was delivered into the capable hands of
the trader at the Two Medicine trading post. The trader and
his wife were decidedly more conversant than the Porter
boys in how to doctor a bullet wound, and therefore, the
would-be horse buyer was spared the anguished fate that
had been that of poor Milton Waller.

When the bullet had been removed, the wound cauter-
ized, and a whiskey-sated McGaugh was left snoring in
another room, Cole sat down with the trader to ask some
questions.

"Three white men?" the man asked rhetorically in reply
to the bounty hunter's query. "Yes, done heard tell . . . about
three days ago . . . over around Heart Butte."

"Three *nápikoan* gunslingers show up out here, and
people tend to notice," the man's wife interjected. "Talk is
going around that these characters are hoping to winter out
in these parts."

"Damn fool thing to contemplate," the trader added.

"Guess that makes you and me a coupla damned fools,"
his wife said with an ironic grin.

At this, the two of them laughed hysterically.

The bounty hunter merely smiled. The phrase "stir
crazy" entered his mind but went unverbalized.

Natoya stared without expression. Either she didn't quite
grasp the joke, or she felt it insulting that someone would

consider it foolish to winter where her people had wintered since the beginning of time.

"Where *exactly* would they be wintering, if they *did* winter out here?" Cole asked.

"Oh probably over at Heart Butte," the wife said.

"Yeah," said her husband. "That would be old Double Runner's band. He's been known to take in all manner of scalawags and fugitives from down south of the Marias. Law can't touch 'em up here, and he likes using them as hired guns."

"I've seen that happen in this country," Cole nodded, with a knowing look at Natoya.


COLE AND NATOYA-I-NIS'KIM ACCEPTED THE HOSPITALITY of the trader, ate his food, and camped near the three-room building that constituted the trading post.

As Cole stoked the fire so that it would be with them through the entire night, Natoya reclined on the opposite side of the fire wrapped in her buffalo robe. She continued to relish the opportunity to use her English words with a willing listener.

"Do you know the story of A-koch-kit-ope . . . the one who the *nápikoan* call the 'Medicine Grizzly'?" she asked as the conversation turned to the powerful and magic creature of which they had spoken the night before.

"Nope, but I'd sure be happy to hear *you* tell it . . . and I like stories told around campfires . . ."

He was going to add the phrase "by beautiful girls with the firelight flickering in their deep, dark eyes," but he did not.

"If it was a *nápikoan* story it would start with 'once upon a time,'" she laughed.

Cole laughed too. He liked her sense of humor and her ability to make word jokes in a language not her own.

"Go ahead and tell it that way," he said with a smile.

"Okay, once upon a time, Stock-stchi, whose name means 'Bear Cub,' was telling stories about a war party he had led across the mountains to attack the Kotoksspi, the people who live over there to the west. You know, the people who the *nápikoan* calls the 'Flathead.' It was a warm summer night . . . not like this one . . . and he sent his wife to get water. She saw a stranger in the light of the moon."

Cole enjoyed the smoothness of her gestures as she signed the expression for getting water, then pointed to the moon.

"The stranger was part of a raiding party from the Piik-siik-sii-naa people, who call themselves A'aninin."

"What does Piik-siik-sii-naa mean?" Cole asked.

"'Snakes,'" Natoya said.

"'Snakes'?" Cole repeated with mock indignation.

"You white people call them by the name Gros Ventre, which means 'big bellies,'" she laughed.

Cole couldn't help shaking his head with an ironic half grin. Outsiders from all sides seemed to have unflattering nicknames for the poor A'aninin people. Of course, people everywhere seem to have derogatory names for *other* tribes. He recalled the names that his fellow Virginians had for the freed slaves, and how the Lakota had named white people "bacon thieves."

"The Siksikáwa attacked the A'aninin before they could attack," she continued, making a point of using the tribe's name for its own people. "And they killed the whole raiding party except one man, who was a *natoápina*, a medicine man. They shot many arrows at him, but he could not be killed."

"Reminds me of what my people say about the grizzly," Cole interjected, "that it can't be killed."

"*Exactly,*" Natoya said. "You are understanding the story already. The man shouted that his name was A-koch-kit-ope, and he had powerful medicine . . . and the Siksikáwa believed he did. He said he would stay to guard his dead brothers so the Siksikáwa would not take trophies."

"Scalps?" Cole asked, more as a statement than a question.

Natoya nodded, then continued.

"The next day, they killed A-koch-kit-ope, but it took all of them to do it. They discovered that he had an *apóhkiááyo* claw . . . like the one you gave to me last night . . . tied into his hair. They realized that he had the spirit and power of the grizzly, and they were frightened. So they burned his body."

Natoya nodded toward their own fire and explained, gesturing as she did, how they captured all the embers that escaped so that they could destroy and contain his grizzly medicine.

"Did it work?" Cole asked, entranced by the motions of her hands as she told the story.

"No," she said with a graceful shrug that eloquently added, "They should have known better."

"A-koch-kit-ope reappeared as the Medicine Grizzly," she said, signing that it was a fait accompli. "This huge *apóhkiááyo* followed their trail and killed many of them the next time they made camp. When the Siksikáwa went back the next year to camp in the place where the story started, a large *apóhkiááyo* came into their camp the first night, scaring the horses and killing the dogs. The people were so scared when they saw it was A-koch-kit-ope. They did not dare to shoot at him. Even now, he is seen in the same place by a lake . . . deep inside the mountains. He is seen only by night, and he is never attacked because he is A-koch-kit-ope, the Medicine Grizzly."

Natoya-I-nis'kim smiled and reached to a narrow rawhide thong that she had around her neck. She pulled it from beneath the front of her buckskin dress and showed it to him. Woven to the end, in an elaborate and intricate pattern crafted by herself, was the grizzly claw that he had given her the night before. .

"*Apóhkiááyo* gave you the power of his spirit," she said, the reflection of the fire twinkling in her eyes like stars. "And you gave that to me, and that was how you were saved from the Káínawa bullet today."

And that was the story told by the fireside that night.

BLADEN COLE AWOKE TO THE FEEL OF WARM BREATH against his cheek. His first thought was naturally of the grizzly, but this was not a grizzly.

Had it been only two days since he had awakened to the hot breathing of the roan nuzzling him awake?

Then, it was a snorting, nudging, rude awakening. Today—or, more properly, tonight, as no sun warmed the world—the bounty hunter opened his eyes to the most divine of apparitions.

It was a phantom that drifted like sweet incense in the indistinct dimension between dream and dream-come-true.

Above him in the moonlight knelt Natoya-I-nis'kim. Her body, the most perfect of bodies, was clothed as it had been at the moment of her birth. Her long, jet-black hair, freed from the tightly wound braids, moved and flowed freely and most elegantly in the light breeze.

"Wake up," the Siksikáwa maiden whispered in a tone as rude to the dreamer as had been the prodding of the roan. "We must go . . . quickly."

It was, alas, a vision that quickly melded into reality, as she moved to clothe her most perfect of bodies as it had been clothed yesterday.

Their plan had been to start out at dawn, but Cole saw no dawn on any horizon, only the billion tiny campfires that dotted the heavens from edge to edge.

"It's the middle of the night," he pleaded weakly as he watched her put on her buckskin dress and gather up her robe. He did not bother to look at the watch in his pocket, but guessed it to be no later than four.

"We must go," she insisted. "We must be in Moisskitsi-pahpiistaki . . . Heart Butte . . . at dawn. I wakened with a thought in my mind. As the words of three men coming were being told across this country, words of *you* are spreading as well. You have heard of *them*. They will hear of *you*. We must go quickly."

As much as he would have rather spent the next hour—or the next lifetime—watching her in the moonlight, Cole knew that she was right.

They bade good-bye to the trader's wife, who was making her way to the outhouse as they mounted their horses, and rode away, guided by the stars.

"*KOKUMEKIS KOKATOSIX KUMMOKIT SPUMMOKIT!*" NATOYA said happily, looking up.

"Yeah, I agree . . . it's fun to look at the stars," Cole laughed, presuming that her words celebrated the heavenly spectacle of a clear night on the cusp of winter.

"That is a saying we have," she said, continuing to gaze skyward. "I guess it is sort of a prayer . . . asking the moon and stars to give me strength."

"I sort of guessed that," Cole said, putting the stress on the phrase "sort of."

"They *hated* this prayer at the mission school . . . they wouldn't let us say things like that. Finally an old padre came and asked about our prayers. At last, there was a black robe who understood . . . He thought it was splendid too."

"Me too," Cole agreed, looking at the stars.

"He was also one who understood about the *nátosini*, the power of Es-tonea-pesta," she laughed, pulling her buffalo robe tight about her.

"Who's *that*?"

"The maker of cold weather," she smiled.

"Yeah, he's sure working overtime tonight," Cole agreed.

In the predawn darkness, Es-tonea-pesta had the temperature near zero by the reckoning of the white man named Fahrenheit, but Bladen Cole felt sufficiently warmed merely by the presence of the girl named for the elusive Buffalo Stone.

"Tell me about Double Runner," he said after they had ridden for about another half hour.

"His name is Isokoyokinni in Siksikáwa," she said. "He is named for the footrace between the antelope and the deer. He lives *nápikoan*-style in a wooden house and takes in strangers. You can always find at least one *nápikoan* in his camp."

"The trader made him sound like as much of a scalawag as the scalawags he takes in," Cole said.

"I do not know this word."

"It means rascal . . . troublemaker."

"I do not think this of Isoko-yo-kinni," she said. "He is self-important, and he likes to have property and *nápikoan* things, but he is not *bad*. I think the trader sees him as a rival. Not every *nápikoan* who sleeps in Isoko-yo-kinni's camp . . . who rides in Siksikáwa land . . . comes to make trouble."

Cole nodded in agreement. *He* was a *nápikoan* who was riding in Siksikáwa land.

Just as it was stirring to life for the day, they arrived on a bluff near the heart-shaped butte from which the settlement took its name.

There were many tipis and a few clapboard buildings, making it a metropolis by comparison with the other places that Cole had visited in Blackfeet country. Around and among the tipis, a few women were stirring cooking fires to life while their men still slept. A couple of kids were running about, shouting and laughing.

"You should wait here," Natoya said. "I will ride down and see what I can discover."

She was right. A white man with a Colt on his hip would

attract a great deal of unwanted attention. A lone Indian woman appearing in an awakening settlement would blend in seamlessly—so long as her own Colt remained discreetly concealed beneath her robe.

Cole watched as she dismounted and led her horse through the fringes of the encampment. He could see her breath in the cold air as she spoke to the women who were cooking the morning meal. He could see her gestures and those of the women with whom she spoke.

Demonstrating no particular urgency, she worked her way through the camp toward the cluster of wooden buildings.

At last, he watched as her head turned directly, though very briefly, toward him. Her quick, though characteristically graceful hand gesture indicated that it was time for the *nápikoan* to ride into town.

Following her lead, he came slowly and casually, winding his way, rather than riding directly toward the building near which she stood. His heart skipped a beat, however, when he saw her go inside.


GIDEON AND ENOCH PORTER SAT AT A TABLE EATING A porridge of venison, while Jimmy Goode poured a cup of coffee—a distinct rarity in Blackfeet country—near a cookstove, which was another rarity in this country. Double Runner, wearing a white man's shirt and vest, sat at the table with the Porter boys.

Their conversation stopped when the door opened and a young woman stepped in.

"*Oki, i'taamikskanaotonni,*" Double Runner said, greeting her and bidding her good morning.

"*Tsa niita'piiwa, Isoko-yo-kinni?*" she said politely and appropriately for a young person speaking to an elder, asking after his health.

"*Tsiiksi'taami'tsihp nomohkootsiito'toohpa, Natoya-I-nis'kim,*" he said, recognizing her, and knowing that she was a relative of O-mis-tai-po-kah, whom he knew well, and saying that he was pleased to have her visit his home.

"*Tsiikaahsi'tsihp nito'toohs*," she said with a smile, replying that she was happy to be there.

The white men sat in stunned silence, reacting to Natoya's uncommon beauty as Bladen Cole had when he first met her.

"Who's this pretty little thing that's just walked in here?" Enoch Porter said, pushing the tin plate of porridge aside and rising to his feet.

"Sit down and finish your goddamn breakfast," Gideon snarled at his impulsively brazen younger brother.

"To hell with eatin' breakfast," Enoch said, taking a step toward Natoya. "I'd be wanting me a little taste of *squaw*."

"*Tahkaa kiisto?*" she said angrily, demanding to know who he thought he was.

"Got a tongue on ya, doncha?" Enoch laughed. "Betcha this squaw knows how to buck."

"Sit down and leave her be!" Double Runner demanded, standing up and reaching for his rifle.

"Don't do it," Gideon said, firmly gripping the gun and pulling it away from its owner.

Turning to Enoch, he repeated his demand that his little brother sit back down.

Again, his brother ignored him.

"Gimme little kiss, *squaw*," he said, grabbing her arm.

As his face neared hers, the disgusting odor of his breath nearly gagged her, but she managed to let fly and spit into his face with as much force as she could muster.

He staggered backward, momentarily stunned.

"Oh, you *are* a fighter, you little bitch," he said as he wiped his face with his sleeve. "If it's a fight you want, a fight you shall have!"

With a laugh, he seized and twisted her wrist, and her buffalo robe fell to the floor.

With her other hand, she drew her old Colt.

Without hesitation, as his eyes grew to the size of the

plate from which he had been eating porridge, she squeezed the trigger.

*Cli-ick.*

The sound of the misfire echoed through the room, which was suddenly devoid of all other sound.

Enoch angrily snatched the gun from her small hand and threw it hard across the room.

Pushing her onto the floor, he grabbed roughly at her clothing and drew his knife.

"When I'm finished with this pretty little doe . . ." he said, licking his lips and touching her cheek with the steel blade. "I'm gonna mess up this pretty little face so's I'm the last one who ever lays eyes on—"

His words were swallowed by the thunder of an explosion, followed immediately by another.

The porridge of bone and flesh that had once been the back of Enoch Porter's head distributed itself randomly on the far wall of the room.

Jimmy Goode's quivering hand lost its grip on his coffee cup.

Gideon Porter's hand went for his own gun.

Bladen Cole's reproachful advice, supported by a gun aimed directly at Gideon's head, was that he should *not* do that.

# CHAPTER 10

———◆◆◆———

RELIEVED OF HIS SIDEARM, A SULLEN GIDEON PORTER SAT upon his horse, his wrists restrained by old army-issue prison manacles. The chain was looped through the gullet beneath his saddle horn, inextricably fastening him to the saddle. He bit his lip in reaction to the biting cold and to the bitter realization that he had been caught.

He watched as his little brother, now a rapidly cooling corpse wrapped in a cast-off scrap of canvas, was tied across the saddle on which he had ridden into Heart Butte the day before.

"Damn you, Enoch," his brother hissed quietly. Had it not been for Enoch's uncontrolled sadism, Mary Phillips would still be alive, and the cycle of events that had been neither anticipated nor desired by anyone would never have led to this humiliating moment.

They had gone to a house to kill three men, but by Gideon's reasoning, Enoch's killing a woman with no good reason had ignited the fires of outrage that had put a bounty hunter on their trail—a bounty hunter who had apparently not feared following that trail into Blackfeet country.

Gideon had assumed they would be safe in this land of barbarians.

Gideon had been wrong.

"Damn you, Enoch," his brother hissed quietly. "Why the hell did you have to go after that damnable squaw?"

Had it not been for Enoch's impetuous, hotheaded lust, there would have been three guns to take on the bounty hunter. At least there would have been *two*—because, after all, Jimmy Goode was good for *nothing*.

Barely fifteen minutes ago, Jimmy had been enjoying a cup of coffee—poor coffee, but still coffee—but now both he and Gideon were manacled to their saddles in the icy arctic wind. Events had unfolded more quickly and with more complexity than the limited capabilities of Jimmy Goode's mind could process.

A squaw on the floor, and Enoch's brains on the wall.

A *very angry* squaw with Enoch's knife, and Enoch's manhood in Double Runner's potbellied heating stove.

Normally, Double Runner would have been displeased to have guests treated so harshly and blood spattered all around his parlor, but after what he had seen Enoch try to do to Natoya-I-nis'kim, he agreed entirely with the fate meted out to Enoch Porter by the bounty hunter.

After what Cole had told him about them, Double Runner was doubly pleased to be rid of the surviving strangers.

The Siksikáwa leader was also delighted that Cole had made the gesture of presenting him with Enoch's finely tooled leather boots, a pair which Cole had seen him admiring. Double Runner was pleased with this favor and called for his son and two other young men to ride with the bounty hunter and his prisoners as far as O-mis-tai-po-kah's camp.

As they rode out, all were silent.

There was nothing much to be said.

The two outlaws rode in the center, their horses roped

together, flanked by the Blackfeet men, who were as eager to see them going away to justice as the bounty hunter. Cole rode behind, where he could watch his prisoners. He was flanked by Natoya, who rode parallel to him at a distance of about a dozen yards.

As Cole watched, over the first few miles, the taut muscles in her face gradually relaxed. Rage had turned to anger. Anger had been slowly but surely consumed by the soothing mitigation of retribution having been exacted.

At last she shot him a glance, and he saw that for the first time, the frown had disappeared from her face. It was not exactly a smile, but it was an expression of thanks.

Cole nodded and touched the brim of his hat.

In the space of two days, they had each saved the other in dramatic fashion, thereby establishing a bond not unlike that of soldiers.

Cole had experienced this in those frenzied final days of the war, when the skirmishing seemed to run the length and breadth of Virginia's fields and farmsteads. He had saved a man's life, actually several lives on several occasions, and found his own preserved by the intervention of others more than once.

His mind wandered to those days, and to the lives preserved and the lives lost. Back then, momentous events involving tens of thousands of lives moved rapidly. In those days, there would have been no way to imagine long hours on these infinite, windswept plains where the mind could be allowed to sink into the monotonous reverie of contemplation.

"How many sleeps?" Natoya asked, pointing to the two prisoners and the distant horizon.

"Maybe four," Cole said.

His mind, having been allowed to sink into reverie, had just been contemplating the immense scale of the West in the abstract. Making conversation in an attempt to break the icy silence that had prevailed between them, Natoya had brought him back from the abstract to the real.

"Maybe more," Cole said with a lessened conviction that

begged and received the addition of the phrase "maybe a week . . . or so."

She nodded.

Like him, she understood that it would take him longer to return with prisoners than it had for him to get here alone. A lone rider in pursuit of a quarry moves much more quickly than a man slowed by a pair of charges who would just as soon cut his throat as cast him a cutting glance.

Indeed, it might take a week. He would just have to see.

Montana Territory was a big place.

Around noon, as the glow of the autumn sun stood as high in the overcast sky as it would that day, he pulled a scrap of pemmican from his pocket and shared it with her.

For the first time since Heart Butte, she smiled.

So did he.

How could he not smile at the bashful way that she grinned and looked away with her face, but not her eyes. It was like when he had thanked her for saving his life.

After that, they made small talk. He asked about the missionary school. She asked about the place from which he came and wrinkled her forehead in bewilderment as he tried to explain how far away it was.

The West was a big place, and the East was still many, many sleeps beyond. He wondered what she would make of a place like Denver, or Kansas City, or Richmond.


THE LIGHT WAS FADING WHEN THEY FIRST SAW THE MANY smokes of O-mis-tai-po-kah's camp on the horizon, and nearly gone when they crested the ridge and saw the campfires.

The size of the camp had nearly doubled since Cole had seen it last, and the level of activity spread out before him between the tipis told him that the men who had traveled to the east to hunt buffalo had come home. By the looks of things, they had not returned empty-handed.

Riding through the edges of the camp, Cole noticed that Natoya-I-nis'kim was looking around intently.

Suddenly, she nudged the withers of her horse and galloped ahead a short distance, to where a group of hunters were unloading the fruits of their labors.

With one, graceful, fluid motion, she slid off her horse, shed her buffalo robe, and jumped on one of the men. Had he not been a tall, powerfully built man, she would have knocked him over. Instead, it was he who pulled her off her feet, raising her face to meet his. As they embraced, Cole understood in a moment who he was, and what he meant to her.

At last, as the hunter let her feet once again touch the ground, she turned and pointed to Cole. Pulling the man's hand, she practically dragged him to where the bounty hunter was dismounting.

Natoya introduced the tall man as Sinopaa, the man she loved and planned to marry.

As Cole signed a greeting, the man's expression said that her description of this *nápikoan* stranger with whom his fiancée had spent the last several days had painted him as one of the good guys.

"*Oki . . . napi*," Sinopaa said, grabbing Cole's hand in a reasonable facsimile of a white man's handshake. The bounty hunter knew enough Blackfeet to know that the greeting was a formal one, meaning "hello, friend," and was reserved for use between men who truly respected each other. "*Tsiiksi'taami'tsihp nomohkootsiito'toohpa, Mr. Cool.*"

"He is happy to call you friend, and he is happy you are here," Natoya translated.

"Tell him that I am too," Cole replied.

O-MIS-TAI-PO-KAH ROLLED OUT A WARM WELCOME FOR "Mr. Cool," inviting him to spend the night and to join in the celebration being held to welcome home the hunting party.

Even Ikutsikakatósi and Ómahkaatsistawa greeted Cole

cordially. Though the two men had taken *most* of the credit
for recovering the horses, they *had* acknowledged that the
*nápikoan* gunman had participated bravely. Cole could tell
by O-mis-tai-po-kah's wry grin that he understood the
extent to which the two men had embellished the details.
He was just glad to have his horses back.

The hunt having been successful, there were copious quan-
tities of fresh meat, happily consumed by people who gathered around large fires near the center of the encampment.
Being a guest, Cole was offered a hump steak, considered to
be the prime cut, which he enjoyed. Porter and Goode, who
spent the night chained to a pair of cottonwoods near the
stream, were fed less desirable parts of the buffalo.

As the dinner party unfolded, Cole's eye was drawn,
naturally, to his young friend, Natoya-I-nis'kim. He watched
in the flickering firelight as she and Sinopaa sat beside each
other on the periphery of the crowd, talking—and even
giggling—like the young lovers they were.

He was happy for her, happy that she had a man who
cared for her as much as he obviously did. At the same time,
though, he could not help being jealous of Sinopaa. She was
a beautiful woman for whom he had, himself, developed a
great fondness.

Though Cole had imagined himself with her, he knew
that such imaginings were unrealistic in the extreme. There
was no place for her in the world of the *nápikoan*, or for him
in her world. Sinopaa was a lucky man, and Cole knew that
he knew it.

At one point, Cole glanced away to converse briefly with
a man seated near him, and when he glanced back, Natoya
and Sinopaa were no longer there. He smiled and reached
to slice off another piece from the meat that hung over the
fragrantly crackling cottonwood.

# CHAPTER 11

———◆✦◆———

THE FOUR WHITE MEN—A BOUNTY HUNTER, HIS TWO PRIS-
oners, and the remains of the late Enoch Porter—were on
the trail even as the sun was a cold sliver on the eastern
horizon.

Estoneapesta, whom the Blackfeet believed to be responsible for bringing the cold weather, had been plying his
trade. It had not snowed overnight, but the frost was thick
on the windblown prairie grass, and everyone's breath was
visible, except Enoch's of course. At least the freezing temperatures made transporting a corpse more tolerable than it
would have been in the heat of summer.

The two men from Double Runner's band who had ridden
with them from Heart Butte had headed home, but as a
friendly gesture, O-mis-tai-po-kah had assigned Ikutsikakatósi and Ómahkaatsistawa to ride with "Mr. Cool" as far
as the Marias River.

He welcomed the company.

Though they were manacled to their saddles, the two
felons still presented the potential for danger. So long as

Porter and Goode were outnumbered three to two, they were unlikely to try anything, but once he was across the Marias, Cole knew that the tables would be turned.

As he had the previous day, Cole brought up the rear, positioning himself where he could watch without being watched. His helpers, meanwhile, functioned as outriders, ranging right and left of the manacled men. Because the country was so open, it was easy for four widely separated riders to travel abreast.

He had tied the horses ridden by Porter and Goode together with a forty-foot rope and ordered them to remain that far separated. Being tied together, and with Enoch Porter's horse tied to his brother's, they were unlikely to try to make an escape. This arrangement would also reduce, if not prevent, their talking to one another without him overhearing what they said.

It was not that either man was doing a great deal of talking. As yesterday, they sat silently and sullenly as the miles ticked slowly by.

Jimmy Goode, the young oaf who had, like so many young oafs, gotten himself in over his head with bad company, displayed a jittery fear more than any other emotion. He feared being brought to justice and hanged, of course, but he also feared the wrath of Gideon Porter if they ever came within an arm's length of each other. Then too Gideon had told him that they were within a hair's breadth—as Gideon had sarcastically phrased it in an aside the day before—of having their hair lifted with a Blackfeet hunting knife.

Gideon Porter's expression betrayed anger, directed both at the world at large and, for their being caught, at the hapless Jimmy Goode, simply for being, as usual, good for nothing.

As Goode twitched and Porter stewed, Cole's mind wandered.

The only element absent from yesterday in his carefully arranged procession across the Plains was the company of

Natoya-I-nis'kim. Though it was his preference to ride alone, he missed the pleasure of her shy smile and the pleasure of her company during long hours in the saddle in monotonous terrain.

"*Aakattsinootsiiyo'p* . . . we'll meet again" were the last words that Natoya had spoken as she waved good-bye that morning.

He was left to ponder whether she meant the phrase merely as a perfunctory "see you later" or as a more purposeful "we *will* see one another again." She probably meant him to ponder it—in a half-flirting, half "I hope you don't forget me" way. And so he pondered, all morning and into the afternoon.

She was perceptive beyond her years and no doubt knew how he felt. Like him, she recognized that they had developed a friendship that was and would remain, despite the unique bond of mutual life-saving, just and only that.

Soon she would be out of his mind—or so he insisted to himself.

They camped for the night overlooking the Marias. Of the four, five, or more sleeps to come, this would be the last one when Cole would not be alone with his captives. He had decided to avoid Fort Benton and stick to the open country as he headed south. The potential for complications associated with riding into an essentially lawless town with two criminals, two Indians, and a dead body was just too great.

BLADEN COLE AWOKE WITH A START.

It was bitter cold, but quiet. Had the north wind not died down, he never would have heard it.

There it was again.

It was a crushing, snapping sound like a bear might make. He glanced quickly to where the horses were. They were standing calmly. Had there been a bear or a wolf in the vicinity, they would have been snorting and pawing the ground. They were not.

As he got his hand on his Colt and began to roll out of his bedroll, he saw something, or someone, moving. A moment later, he identified this something and squeezed his trigger.

In the cold, still air, the sound of a .45-caliber round being fired had the comparative effect of five pounds of dynamite going off.

In the muzzle flash, he caught a quick view of an angry face.

Gideon Porter, who had tried to sneak noiselessly to where the horses were tied, had been caught in the act and needed an alternate plan, immediately.

As Bladen Cole came toward him, he reached for the nearest weapon that he could see in the light of the quarter moon—Ikutsikakatósi's Trapdoor Springfield.

Meanwhile, Ikutsikakatósi had awakened suddenly at the sound of the pistol shot, and he reacted by grabbing his rifle back.

Cole's instinct told him to take an easy shot and send Gideon Porter to join his brother at the Devil's table, but instinct was outweighed by his commitment to justice. For that to be done back in Gallatin City, Gideon Porter would have to point his finger at the man who planned the crime that the Porter boys had carried out, and dead men can't point fingers.

He fired a second shot, aiming to miss the shadowy form of Gideon Porter, but to do so by as narrow a margin as possible.

Both Ikutsikakatósi and Porter paused, but only for the second that it took Cole to reach them.

In the split second that followed, Cole saw the flash of Ikutsikakatósi's knife coming out of its sheath like a bolt of lightning.

In the flash of a further second, split narrower than the sharp edge of Ikutsikakatósi's blade, Cole slugged Porter in the face with his gun hand.

The impact of a metal weapon striking his face with the tremendous force of Cole's blow, combined with poor footing on dark, uneven terrain, sent Porter sprawling backward.

Two men moved like pouncing cougars toward the fallen man.

One reached him by a margin of a split second, sliced as thinly as a split second can be sliced.

Bladen Cole stomped his boot on Porter's neck, both because he knew it would immobilize him and because he knew that this neck was the destination of Ikutsikakatósi's eight-inch blade.

Cole fired a third shot into the ground eight inches above Porter's head. The feel of the gravel kicked up by such an impact was frighteningly indistinguishable from being hit.

As Cole had hoped, Ikutsikakatósi paused.

Cole dragged Porter to his feet in the moonlight, noticing that his face was sheeted by the dark shadows of blood, flowing both from his face and from his scalp.

Feeling Ikutsikakatósi nudging closer, with the probable intention of relieving Porter of that bloody scalp, Cole slugged the outlaw once again.

This time, Porter fell with a thud and made no effort to get up.

A half minute of gunsmoke and spattering blood was followed by nearly ten minutes of diplomacy as Cole tried, using sign language in the dim moonlight, to convince Ikutsikakatósi and Ómahkaatsistawa not to finish what Cole had left unfinished.

Finally, the negotiations reached a compromise.

Ikutsikakatósi agreed to forgo the taking of Porter's scalp in exchange for his boots, finely tooled like those of his brother, which were now on Double Runner's feet.

Cole also agreed to Ómahkaatsistawa's insistence that they throw in Enoch Porter's saddle, though not without some demonstrative complaining. Cole really didn't care. He argued only in the spirit of keeping up the bargaining, to add perceived value to the saddle. Enoch would certainly not be needing it.

With light already starting to appear in the east, the two Siksikáwa decided that it was time to get an early start on their trip home.

They said their farewells to "Mr. Cool," claiming, as he did to them, that they would be friends forever.

Nevertheless, Cole waited for about an hour before he made his way down to the river to get water to clean Gideon Porter's wounds. He was not fully convinced that these impetuous young men would not double back in the hope of catching Porter unattended.

In the gathering light of the promise of daytime, Cole could see what had happened. He had manacled Porter to a small aspen—mainly because there were no *large* aspen out here where the punishing winds blew—and the resourceful miscreant had actually climbed the tree to get the chain over the top. In so doing, he had bent the small tree over. The sound that awoke Cole had been that of the tree snapping back when Porter climbed off.

Just as Porter realized that he had dodged three bullets from Cole's gun in a literal way, Cole knew that he too had dodged a bullet of the figurative kind, whose potential was no less deadly.

If he had, as Natoya-I-nis'kim believed, inherited the medicine of the grizzly, such power had failed him.

Or had it?

# CHAPTER 12

———◆◆◆———

"FATHER, YOU HAVE A LETTER HERE FROM YOUR BOUNTY hunter," Hannah Ransdell said. She had just returned to the bank from the post office and was sorting the mail, as she typically did each morning.

"I hope that he has some good news," Isham Ransdell said, approaching his daughter's desk. Hannah had started working at her father's bank when she was still in high school, but her duties had gradually increased and evolved and had long since warranted her maintaining a well-used desk not far from that of Mr. Duffy, the accountant who kept the ledgers. Duffy may have been the custodian of the numbers, but Hannah was the custodian of the customers. She knew them all by name and knew what sorts of accounts they all had at the bank.

"When was it mailed?" Isham Ransdell asked.

"A week ago from Fort Benton," she said, looking at the postmark.

"Never thought I'd see the day when you could get a letter all the way from Fort Benton to Gallatin City in just a week," Ransdell said, taking the letter.

"It'll be a lot faster than a steamer down the Missouri to Fort Union when the telegraph goes in," Hannah observed, handing her father a letter opener.

She watched curiously as he slit open the envelope and took out two pieces of paper, one a letter and the other an official-looking document. He handed the latter to Hannah out of force of habit. Through her experience at his bank, she had become so adept at grasping the legal wording of official documents that he often joked with her that he did not need the high-priced legal services of his associate, the attorney Virgil Stocker.

"Mr. Cole writes that Milton Waller is deceased," Isham said, scanning the handwritten note. "He goes on to say that he will be pursuing the Porter boys into Blackfeet country. What does that document have to tell us?"

"Much the same," Hannah said, handing it to her father. "It's a death certificate for Mr. Waller, signed by the Choteau County sheriff and the coroner. The cause of death is 'complications due to a gunshot.'"

"Well, it seems as though Mr. Cole has earned part of his fee," Ransdell observed. "I wish him luck among the savages in Blackfeet country. I can recall the day when you had to worry about the Indians even in these parts."

"Yes, Father," Hannah said with a smile, humoring him as she always did when he reminisced about the "old days." Even though the "Custer Massacre" had taken place but three years before in the same territory where they were, the days of the epic struggle between two irreconcilably distinct civilizations seemed distant in time and place.

"In Blackfeet country, it's different," her father insisted. "General Miles may have run the Sioux and the Nez Perce to ground out here, but north of the Marias, it is an untamed world, untouched by civilization."

"Yes, Father," Hannah said with a serious face.

Hannah went back to sorting the mail, delivering three more letters to her father, and handing off a couple that required the attention of Mr. Duffy. She then set to work responding to the remaining queries and missives herself, as she typically did.

Most of the communications were as dry as the dust on Gallatin City's main street in August, but as she systematically worked her way through the pile, she came across one that she found particularly touching.

It was from Mr. Dawson Phillips, Jr., the son of the couple who had been murdered at the Blaine residence. In his letter to the bank, he expressed the great sadness of losing both parents to a violent criminal, and wrote that he would be coming to Gallatin City from Denver to settle the affairs of his late parents. He requested a meeting with Isham Ransdell, who was, of course, his father's banker.

Hannah checked the calendar that she kept of her father's appointments and noted that he would have time available in the week of Mr. Phillips's estimated arrival. She wrote back that a meeting could be arranged.

When she had finished the paperwork that required her immediate attention, she stamped the letters and put them into her bag.

"Father, may I get you anything?" Hannah said, sticking her head into her father's office. "I'm going to the post office with the outgoing and to Mr. Blaine's store for some ink and banker's pins."

"I find a lump in my throat at each mention of 'Blaine's store,'" he said sadly, looking up from his desk and wistfully removing his glasses. "It's hard to truly grasp the idea that he is gone."

"Yes, I understand," she said. "I feel that way myself."

THE GALLATIN CITY GENERAL MERCANTILE AND DRY Goods, known locally as "Mr. Blaine's store," was still draped in black bunting. Leticia Blaine had insisted on it, and the store's general manager saw no reason to argue with his boss's widow.

The whole town was taking it hard. The hierarchy of society in any community will have its highs and its lows. It will have its center, and it will have its fringe. In the society of Gallatin City, the front and center had, until recently, been occupied by the Big Four of Blaine, Phillips, Ransdell, and Stocker. The loss of two men and Mrs. Phillips from among the most prominent figures in the community had left a tangible and powerful void.

For Hannah Ransdell, the black bunting prompted an eerie feeling. Since that night, she had been haunted by the notion that a bullet meant for her father had gone untriggered in that room. She had come within the minute thickness of a hair from losing her father and everything that mattered in her life.

Hannah loved her father, but she had *also* come to derive great satisfaction from her job. Her father knew, without having commented, that she had deliberately made herself indispensable to the running of the family business. Mr. Duffy knew it, and was happy with the situation. He was nervous around people, more comfortable beneath his green eyeshade working with his numbers, while Hannah's cheerful demeanor and intuitive personal skills had become the face of the Gallatin City Bank and Trust Company.

Edward J. Olson, on the other hand, was a man who believed that a woman's place was not in the affairs of a bank, or in business matters of any kind. Though he spent most of his time managing Isham Ransdell's other affairs and was rarely at the bank, Hannah's father often referred to him as his "right-hand man."

Despite the role that Hannah had carved out for herself, her father had never referred to her as his "right-hand woman." Hannah knew that if anything ever happened to her father, his right-hand man would ensure that there would be no woman of any hand at the Gallatin City Bank.

This would leave her having to start considering offers from eligible bachelors, which was something she had resisted, knowing that few men in Gallatin City and its environs would be pleased with a wife who spent her days at a job outside the home.

"Hello, Miss Ransdell, how *are* you today, dear?"

The voice greeted Hannah almost the moment that she entered the store. It was Sarah Stocker. She was much more composed than she had been that night when she was found running down the street screaming about having witnessed the murders.

"Good day, Mrs. Stocker," Hannah said formally, affecting a slight curtsey, as was expected of younger women greeting older women in polite company. "I'm well . . . and you?"

"Thank you for asking," she said with a flourish. "It has been hard. The terrible memories . . . the nightmares . . . and poor Virgil."

"How is *he* getting on?" Hannah inquired.

"As well as can be expected under the circumstances. The wounds are healing . . . the physical ones, of course . . . but the doctor says there will be scarring on his forehead. The one on his chin . . . well . . . you know men and their beards."

"Yes, ma'am." Hannah smiled. She liked the look of a man with a beard.

"He is still haunted by the deaths of his colleagues, of course," Mrs. Stocker continued. "Your father must feel that way as well."

"Yes, ma'am, but of course he did not have to *witness* the horror of the attacks as Mr. Stocker did . . . and *yourself* as well."

"It is the worst terror of my life, *and* I can recall the war coming dreadfully close to our home in Pennsylvania."

"They say it was about revenge?" Hannah said, expressing her statement as a question. The killings had been, and continued to be, the talk of the town, and everyone had taken as fact the assumption that the motive had been revenge directed at John Blaine. Nevertheless, the wheels that turned in the back of Hannah's mind had left her wondering if there was more to it than that.

"Of course," Mrs. Stocker said, reacting to a skeptical tone which the younger woman had unsuccessfully disguised. "They burst in and started killing people."

"Right away?"

"What?"

"The first thing when they broke in, they started killing people?"

"Well," Sarah Stocker said thoughtfully. Though the events of that evening gave her nightmares, they had also given her an element of celebrity in the town. She had come to take a certain perverse pleasure in the attention and the sympathy she received from her victimhood.

"Well, the *first* thing was that they asked for Mr. Blaine . . . next, my husband was struck. Then Gideon shot John Blaine and that wicked Enoch Porter shot poor Mary."

"You mentioned when we spoke before about Gideon Porter having said that the women were not *supposed* to be hurt," Hannah reminded her. "What do you think he meant by that?"

"I don't know . . . maybe even Gideon Porter realized that his heinous brother had crossed the line into the sort of unbridled savagery that we normally associate with the Indians."

"I still wonder why, if they were after Mr. Blaine, they killed the others?" Hannah said, again phrasing her statement as a question.

"*Because*," Sarah Stocker said, raising her voice, "the Porter boys are baleful monsters . . . and if you will pardon me for being unladylike . . . they should all be hanged from the highest yard arm in Gallatin City and left hanging there until their bones are picked clean by the buzzards."

"Yes, ma'am," Hannah nodded, imagining the sight of skeletons covered by buzzards dangling on Main Street.

Sarah Stocker quickly regained her composure, and the two women politely bade each other "good day."

As Hannah turned her attention to a display of writing ink, the whirring motion of the wheels that turned in the back of her mind had slowed not in the least.

# CHAPTER 13

◆━◆━◆━◆

THE BUREAUCRATS IN WASHINGTON, OR IN CHICAGO, OR somewhere across the eastern horizon had decided for the Marias River to be the boundary between the ancient civilization of the Blackfeet and the encroaching civilization of the *nápikoan*—but none of them had ever been here.

They had ordered their cartographers to delineate one side as being as different as night and day from the other, but to a person riding the hills and swales of this limitless country, the landscape on the south side seemed identical to that on the north.

The cartographers pictured the Marias as a great and imposing boundary, but today, the river, flowing forlornly low as autumn waited for winter, looked to the three riders who splashed across it this morning—you couldn't really say they forded it—no more distinguished than any other stream.

"How long you reckon . . . Mr. Cole?" Goode shouted, turning his head as they climbed the bank on the southern side.

"How long for what?"

"How long you reckon till we get there?"

"Get where?"

"Back to Gallatin City."

"Guess you'll know it when you get there," Cole promised. He didn't know himself, and he did not care to speculate for the satisfaction of Jimmy Goode.

Porter shot Goode an angry glance, and he said no more.

This was the first time that Goode had spoken in a conversational tone since they started on this enforced adventure. Cole took it as a sign, an indication, that Gideon Porter, the mastermind whom Goode had obviously once idolized, might be losing his charisma.

Goode perceived himself to have been captured in Heart Butte not as an individual, but as part of the entourage of Gideon Porter, an appendage to his power and presence, a mere addendum to the man himself. Goode had dared not engage in conversation because Porter did not, and he was merely an extension of the great man's identity. Now, as the great man had been taken down a peg, Goode was flirting with the notion that he was, himself, a person with an individual identity.

Jimmy Goode had, Cole intuited, probably spent a lifetime kowtowing to Gideon Porter, and living in a deeper, more shadowy corner of his shadow than even Gideon's little brother, Enoch. In the past two days, though, Goode had seen Gideon Porter captured, humiliated, and beaten bloody. No longer was he the kingpin of a gang; he was now a humbled man chained to his saddle in his stocking feet, being fed like a baby from his own canteen by the bounty hunter who refused to unchain him for lunch, or even to take a drink. Gradually, Goode was realizing that he and Gideon Porter were essentially the same—except that Goode still had his boots!

Nothing more was said, though. Porter's glare was still cruel and still frightening. An hour passed, then two. The hours melted into one another as the skies grew dark and the wind picked up.

It was one of those days when the wind demanded that you keep your head buried so low in your collar that you never notice the first snowflake. The first ones that landed on the roan's mane disappeared almost immediately. It was when they started to stick that Cole decided it was time to look for a place to camp.

One side of him yearned to press on, to try to get far enough so that they could reach the Missouri River early tomorrow. The other side knew that getting caught in a blinding blizzard in a deficient campsite was a potential disaster.

Two ridges farther on, they came into a broad gulch where the streambed was populated with a handful of tall cottonwoods. Unlike the small aspen of the previous night, there was no way that Gideon Porter could ever climb these.

"This is it," Cole declared. "Off your horses."

Porter and Goode each struggled off his mount as gracefully as he could while being chained to the saddle horn. Cole uncinched Goode's saddle and let it slide to the ground, where the snow was starting to stick. Leaving Goode for a moment, he went to deal with Porter. With Cole's back turned, Goode could start to run, but he wouldn't get very far in a blizzard while anchored to a saddle. Cole was sure that he would not even try—after all, he had been told all his life that he was good for nothing.

"This snow is damned cold on the feet," Porter complained as Cole uncinched his saddle. "And *damn you* for givin' my goddamn boots to that heathen brute."

"Damn *you*, Gideon," Cole said, as he worked. "I didn't *give* your goddamn boots to the savage."

"Whadya call it when he rides off with *my* boots, and I walk away barefoot?"

"Tradin'," Cole answered succinctly.

"*Tradin'*?" Porter spat angrily. "Didn't see nobody get no goddamn thing in trade from that redskin."

"I expect that even if you're too stupid to notice that the Indian traded your *life* for those damned boots . . . you aren't blind enough not to have seen that knife he wanted to drag across your neck from one ear to the other."

"I saw the knife all right," Porter admitted.

"What do you think he wanted to do with it?" Cole asked sarcastically. "Play mumblety-peg with it?"

"Lost my goddamn boots," Porter said, trying to redirect the trajectory of the conversation.

"You still got your scalp?" Cole asked rhetorically. "Looks like, by the fact that you can feel the cold on your feet, you're still alive . . . Now, pick up that saddle and head over to that cottonwood on the far right."

Once he had each man chained face-forward around a separate cottonwood trunk, Cole started a fire. Fortunately, there were plenty of broken cottonwood scraps in the gulch to use as firewood. Soon a big fire was blazing, the horses were secured, and Cole sat down to cook some of the buffalo meat that O-mis-tai-po-kah had given him as a parting gesture of hospitality.

"What's gonna happen to us in Gallatin City?" Goode asked cautiously, keeping his voice low so that Porter, who was forty feet away, couldn't hear what he was saying over the roar and crackle of the fire.

"Reckon there's gonna be a trial," Cole said.

"I didn't shoot nobody," Goode insisted. "'Twas Gideon and Enoch who shot all those people in that house. Enoch shot a *woman* . . . an *old* woman. I seen him . . . I seen him do it."

"Hmmm." Cole nodded. After having seen Enoch Porter in action at Double Runner's shack, after watching him display the brand of uncontrollable rage that would make a man try to rape a woman in a room full of people, it took little stretch of the imagination to see him gunning down Mary Phillips.

"And you got him dead already," Goode continued. "You done got Enoch layin' there wrapped in canvas. You could let *me* go right now 'cause you got them who did *all* the killin'."

"Doesn't work that way," Cole assured him.

"You can't charge nobody for murder that didn't do no murder," Goode asserted.

"Why'd you do it?" Cole asked.

"I *didn't* do it . . . I didn't do no murder."

"Why'd you go to the house that night?"

"Gideon said we had to kill three of 'em," Goode insisted.

"Which three?"

"Gideon didn't say. I 'spect that Enoch musta knowed, but nobody tells *me* nothin'."

"Who told you to go there?"

"Gideon."

"Who told *him* to go?" Cole asked, hoping finally to know the truth.

"I dunno," Goode shrugged as best he could in his awkward position. "Maybe nobody. Maybe it was *his* idea, thought up by hisself. Like I said . . . nobody tells me nothin'."

"What are you talkin 'bout over there?" Gideon Porter yelled from across the fire. "Goode, I told you to keep your damned mouth shut and not be talkin' to that bounty hunter."

"Shut up, both of you," Cole shouted back. "Get some shut-eye. We got an early start tomorrow."

With that, he lay his head back onto his saddle, pulled his blanket up to his chin, and stared up into the skeletons of the big cottonwoods illuminated by the fire.

His first thoughts went to his conversation with Jimmy Goode and his description of the lunatic Enoch Porter. Next, he went back to the nagging question of *why* they went to the Blaine house. Cole had found just over $200 in Gideon Porter's saddlebags. Taking into consideration that they had only received half the payment due them, and that they had probably spent a fair sum in the saloons of Diamond City and Fort Benton—not to mention whatever Doc Ashby charged—the *total* payroll for the crime, not just a sum advanced to each of the perpetrators, still only came to around $500. Now Ransdell was paying eight times that sum to have them brought in. There was more to all this than met the eye.

The snowfall, which had been coming down pretty heavily as they made camp, had finally slacked off considerably.

As the few random flakes drifting out of the sky caught the orange light of the fire, Cole thought about that night out of Diamond City when he had dozed off comparing the stars to the freckles on Hannah Ransdell's nose. It was a silly, romantic thought, but more pleasant to fall asleep to than the probable sins of Hannah's father.

Lately, of course, his thoughts of women had turned to Natoya-I-nis'kim, and now they turned to a comparison between her and Hannah Ransdell. They were both smart and intuitive. Natoya was the first woman he had met in these past years whom he had *not* compared to Sally Lovelace. Maybe this meant he was getting over Sally. He wondered too if this meant that his faith in the character and motivation of the female species in general, so severely defiled by Sally, was slowly being rebuilt.

His final thought before he dozed was that Natoya-I-nis'kim also had the distinction of being the only woman who had ever saved his life.

# CHAPTER 14

GIDEON PORTER LOOKED MORE DEAD THAN ALIVE.

Bladen Cole did not mind the inconvenience that he was suffering, but he did not want him dead. In fact, he wanted—more than anything at the moment—to keep this man alive.

After their conversation the night before, and his having learned how little was known by "good-for-nothing" Jimmy Goode, Cole understood that Porter was the *only* man who could finger the mastermind of the murder conspiracy.

"Goddamn you, bounty hunter," Gideon snarled as he woke up, greeting Cole and welcoming the new day with his characteristic lack of cheerfulness. "Damn near froze last night."

"No, you didn't," Cole said. "A chinook blew in after midnight. Besides that, I kept the fire stoked so your little stocking feet wouldn't be cold."

The face that glared at Cole really *did* look more dead than alive. The wounds from his having been whipped with a pistol the day before were healing, but they'd left jagged scabs that were nearly black with dried blood and dust.

Three or four days without a shave had made Gideon look like a beggar. At least he still had his scalp, and that was thanks to Bladen Cole.

"Goddamn it, bounty hunter," Gideon whined. "Gimme some goddamn coffee."

"No man needs coffee to stay alive," Cole said calmly as he sipped his boiled concoction. He didn't let on that, despite its inviting aroma, it was pretty bad-tasting swill.

He hand-fed the two prisoners before chaining them back to their saddles. He loaded Enoch's body on his horse, and the procession started out at first light, configured as it had been for the previous two days.

The chinook had changed the landscape, raised the temperatures, melted some of the snow, and swept the sky clear of much of yesterday's overcast. The sun was barely up, but there was a promise that the day might almost be warm.

At last, the monotonous plains dropped away, and they could see the long, narrow forest of cottonwoods that marked the Missouri River. Within half an hour, they could see it, like a blue-green snake hiding among the trees, some of which were still decked with clusters of yellow leaves.

With remembered landmarks to guide him, Bladen Cole steered his charges to turn right and head upriver. He knew they were not far from that little no-name collection of shacks where he had bought whiskey and learned of Milton Waller's impending demise. Cole knew that the shopkeeper at that place had met the Porter boys on their way north, and he really did *not* want to take the time to explain why their condition was so dramatically changed on their way south.

With the Missouri at its lowest level of the year, finding a ford almost anywhere would be easy.

Had it not been for the terrain along the way, and for the fact that the river flowed through the big centers of population between Helena and Diamond City, Cole might have followed the Missouri all the way to Gallatin City, but Cole wanted the latter to be the *only* population center he saw until the reward money was safely in his saddlebags.

As they were scrabbling up the far bank after fording, Cole saw something in the distance that gave him pause. A pair of mounted riders was coming toward them.

The thought of adopting an alternate course to avoid them was dismissed. There was little advantage that might be gained, and to do so abruptly would almost certainly invite pursuit. Cole knew that his chance of eluding these men while keeping his prisoners was a remote one.

Instead, he waved in friendly greeting.

"Howdy, stranger," one of the men shouted as soon as they were within earshot.

"Hello there," Cole shouted back.

So far, so good.

As they came closer, Cole recognized the man who had spoken. By his tall hat, Cole recalled him as the one who had been at the general store in the no-name town, the one who had berated the shopkeeper for telling Cole about the Porter boys.

This was going to be tricky.

"Whatcha got there, mister?" the man asked. "Couple Indians? They look like the mangiest coupla Indians I've seen."

"Nope, not Indians," Cole said with a shake of his head. "Couple horse-stealin' sons of bitches."

"Oh yeah, I can see now . . . white men."

The others were on top of them now, and the question that Cole feared most came quickly.

"Don't I know you from somewhere?"

"Don't think it likely," Cole lied.

"I'm sure we met . . . maybe I'm wrong . . . can't place you."

Cole still hoped for the best, though he could see that Porter and Goode recognized the man, and he figured that the man would soon notice this.

"Yeah, I remember now," the man with the big hat said. "It was down at Sumner's Landing about a week back. You were favoring a leg."

"Oh yeah, that was me," Cole admitted. "Didn't recall you. Got a bad memory for faces."

"How's your leg? You got it fixed up?"

"Yeah, it's better," Cole said, wincing so as to suggest that it was still somewhat of a bother.

After pausing for a moment, Cole resumed the conversation, hoping to conclude it. "Well it was good seein' y'all again. I guess it's time for me and my friends to get movin' on."

"What a minute," the man with the big hat said. "I recollect now that you were asking after four men who'd been through a day or so before, and now I'm seeing that you got yourself two of the four right here. Hardly recognized 'em. Look like Indians. Look like they been through hell. Guess you found 'em."

"Like I said," Cole explained calmly. "Horse thieves."

"Wait a minute," the man said suspiciously. "I'm not the sharpest bull in the herd, but I'm startin' to figure out somethin'. This feller here, who looks like some savage tried to scalp his face, handed me a twenty-dollar bill . . . You remember that doncha, mister? You paid me to tell any lawman from down in Gallatin City that I saw that you was headed *east*, not north."

Gideon Porter just looked away.

"Well, I reckon that makes you twenty dollars richer," Cole said, trying to appear calmer than he felt.

"Well . . . yes . . . it does, and you don't see that kinda money out here much, so what I got figured is that these fellers are wanted for a lot more than horse thieving . . . and you ain't no lawman . . . are you?"

"I was sent to bring back horse thieves, and that is what I'm trying to do, and if you'd excuse us, that's what's got to get done."

"Whoa . . . wait a minute," the man in the big hat said,

as his companion began to grin avariciously. "Like I said, twenty dollars handed out in the form of a single greenback is a lot for one man to be tossing around on strangers. This tells me that there's a good deal of money involved here . . . and since you ain't no lawman . . . that would make you a bounty hunter."

Cole could see where things were headed.

"Now, I'd not want to be getting in the way of what no lawman would be doing," the man with the big hat said after a long pause. "But since you *ain't* no lawman, this would be a strictly business-type deal . . . and somebody's *paying* a whole bunch of money for these fellers to be brought in. I know that you were planning on that bounty, but I think I'd like to take over from you and go down to Gallatin City . . . get that bounty for myself . . . er . . . what I mean is that my partner and me want that bounty for *ourselves.*"

"You're aiming to *steal* my prisoners?" Cole asked rhetorically as he unsuccessfully attempted to stifle an ironic laugh.

"If you'd be so kind as to step aside," the man with the big hat said, his right hand going to his holster.

Cole had seen his gun clear leather before the first shot was fired.

The partner of the man in the big hat, who had not spoken and who would speak no more, had also drawn his gun before he died.

The man with the big hat toppled to the ground as his horse reared at the sound of Cole's two gunshots, but the other man remained seated as his mount sidestepped, whinnying, for about ten feet. His previous grin had been superseded by a dumbfounded expression. He eyes dropped to the growing, reddish-brown smear on his shirt. His revolver tumbled clumsily from his hand as he reached toward the blotch, then suddenly, he jerked, like a man awaking with a start, and tumbled lifelessly to the ground.

Cole holstered his sidearm. In a space of time barely longer than it takes for the tick of a second hand, Cole had erased a potentially deadly threat with deadly action of his own.

If he'd had reason, after the near escape of Gideon Porter, to doubt his having acquired the spirit power of the grizzly, he now could wonder whether he might not have come by it after all.

Two mounds of stones surmounted with saddles marked the resting places of the two men who had chanced to express a desire to steal from Bladen Cole. The single word marked on each cross adorning those graves succinctly expressed the reason for which they were now at rest: "Thief."

The wind had picked up considerably by the time that the three men resumed their ride. About a quarter mile into this journey, they noticed an object tumbling through the brush near their route. It was an especially large hat that was quite tall in the crown.

# CHAPTER 15

—•◦✦◦•—

"SHUT UP, DAMN YOU," GIDEON PORTER SCREAMED AT THE top of his lungs.

As on the night before, Bladen Cole had chained Porter and Goode to widely separated trees so as to discourage them from communicating with each other, and as on that previous night, Jimmy Goode had taken the opportunity to engage Cole in conversation, hoping he was out of earshot of the man in whose shadow he had all his life been accustomed to cowering.

"I done told him that when this thing gets sorted, I'm gonna get let go," Goode shouted back to Porter.

"What gives you that crazy idea?" Porter shouted back.

"'Cause 'twas not me who shot them folks . . . because it 'twas that sonuvabitch Enoch and *you* who pulled the triggers," Goode said as though in triumph over the reasoning of his onetime master.

"Didn't that worthless mama of yours teach you that it ain't no good manners to speak ill of the dead? If you'd have had a father, you'd have got taught."

"Don't go bringin' my mama into this," Goode whined, omitting reference to the mention of a father he never knew, and whom his mother knew for but a short time.

"Shut up, both of you," Cole said angrily.

It was growing colder again, though the wind had died down. They had reached the foothills of the Little Belt Mountains when the shadows grew long, and they followed a deer trail until darkness overtook them. Cole planned to cross the mountains into the Smith's River drainage and stay east of Diamond City for the same reason that he had bypassed Fort Benton. Traveling with two men in chains and a dead body tended to attract the kind of attention that brought questions and unwanted intrusion.

The dark clouds that had built up in time to blot out the sunset had promised snow, but it was a fickle promise. The temperature descended from manageable to uncomfortable, and there were still patches of snow beneath the trees, but no flakes had been seen in the air as they settled in for the night.

"You see why we call him 'good-for-nothing,' doncha, bounty hunter?" Porter shouted after giving Cole's demand for silence short consideration. "This fool don't know that there's a rope waitin' for *him* in Gallatin City . . . just the same as for me."

"I reckon there *will* be a trial," Cole said.

"Like you gave those strangers this day?" Porter said. "Didn't see them get a fair trial or anything of the sort. You were pretty fast with the executioner's sword . . . I hesitate to say 'sword of justice' because there ain't no justice in what you done to them."

"I guess you didn't see that both were in the motion of drawing their 'executioner's swords' on me at the time," Cole replied in a disparaging tone. "If that was me, not them, under those rocks back there, do you reckon you'd have ended up this day ridin' upright in your saddle . . . or sideways across it like your brother?"

\* \* \*

BLADEN COLE AWOKE TO THE SOUND OF GRAVEL KICKED.

He sat up, trying to filter out the loud snoring of Gideon Porter and follow the direction of the sound. Something was obviously moving in the darkness not far from the circle of light from their fire.

Coyotes occasionally drifted near the fires of humans, especially in the desperate, hungry months when game was scarce and before the winter cold killed the weaker of the deer, antelope, and cattle, leaving them for the coyotes to scavenge. Being cowardly scroungers rather than serious predators, they were unlikely to attack an uninjured man or horse, but chasing them off was a formality necessary to prove that the humans were in charge.

Cole rolled quietly from his bedroll, grabbed his Winchester, and moved in the direction of the sound. As he did so, he glanced to the log where he had tethered Jimmy Goode. He was *gone*.

Cursing himself silently, Cole continued moving in the direction of the sound. He had expected Porter to repeat his escape attempt, and had taken special care to anchor him to a tree. He had meanwhile chained Goode to a log, incorrectly assuming that he would not dare to escape. Goode had allowed Cole to believe that he really *was* good for nothing.

There was a gully which led into the canyon to the south. Goode had evidently slipped in the dark as he stumbled down the slope.

Cole peered into the gloom, though it was impenetrable to the eye, and cocked his head for further sounds.

Hearing none, he pointed his Winchester down the line of the ravine—there was no such thing as *aiming* under the circumstances—and squeezed off a shot.

He heard the *t'zing* of the bullet ricocheting off a rock, and he heard the desperate scrabbling sounds of a frightened man moving as fast as he could through the darkness and the underbrush that choked the gully.

Cole fired again, this time at the sound. Again, he heard the *t'zing* of the bullet ricocheting off a rock, and the reckless crashing of a scared man.

Cursing himself not so silently, Cole returned to the campsite, where Gideon Porter had been awakened by the shots.

"What in holy hell you shootin' at, bounty hunter?" Porter demanded.

Ignoring him for the moment, Cole went to check on the horses. He was surprised to find all four still tied where he had left them. Why had Goode not taken a horse and scattered the others? Perhaps he had decided that getting away without being heard was worth getting away on foot.

The same question occurred to Porter as Cole began saddling his horse for the day's ride.

Porter groused. "Why'd that stupid Jimmy Goode leave the horses? What a stupid fool to walk when he could ride. Course he done got one over on *you*, bounty hunter!"

"Guess he's not good for *nothing*," Cole replied, trying not to *sound* as chagrined as he *felt*.

BLADEN COLE HAD MADE A SIGNIFICANT ERROR, AND HE cursed himself for it repeatedly, but Jimmy Goode had made several. He had proved himself not to be good for *nothing*, but his failure to take a horse was a serious mistake, putting him on foot in rugged terrain—with his wrists still in chains.

By panicking and starting to run when Cole had fired at him, he had confirmed the direction that he was headed. By chance, or by design, his choice of direction took him downhill, toward the Smith's River, and in the eventual direction of Gallatin City. These errors were duly and confidently related by Cole to Porter as they rode.

The fugitive had also failed to take any food or water,

although, as Cole discovered—but did not tell Gideon Porter—Goode *had* taken the pistol that had been confiscated from the estate of the man with the large hat.

Goode also had a head start, a fact that Cole cursed, though silently in the presence of Porter. His head start, as short as it was, had been extended considerably by Cole's having not wanted to start out with the horses until there was sufficient daylight to see where they were going.

Because of the steepness, and the twists and turns required to follow the course of the dry streambed, while avoiding the periodic tangles of brush, the going was slow. Cole had planned to cross the mountains following the same deer trail that they'd been on when they had stopped for the night, but Goode had necessitated a change of plans. At least he was headed in the right direction.

Cole hoped that they would catch up with Goode, writhing in pain with an ankle twisted from a fall in the rocky gulch, but it was a wish that went unfulfilled.

Porter, who had been sullen and silent in the first days of captivity, had grown increasingly talkative. Having Goode out of the picture seemed to lift his self-imposed burden of perpetuating a facade of intransigence.

After spewing a tantrum of anger over Cole's having killed his brother over a "squaw," whom he considered somewhat less than human, he turned his attention to Jimmy Goode.

"That sonuvabitch coward could have sprung me, but he just ran off" was a statement repeated often, which summarized Porter's indictment of the man whom he considered not just a buffoon but a traitor to his leader.

"Guess he got scared when you told him he was gonna hang," Cole replied.

"I don't plan to hang," Porter said defiantly.

"Why is that?"

"No way they're gonna *let* me hang."

"Who's *they*?"

"You'll see."

"Wasn't it *they* who put you up to this?" Cole asked, getting to the question that had been on his mind for days.

"Put me up to *what*?"

"Shooting those two men . . . and that *woman*," Cole said, putting emphasis on the fact that Mrs. Phillips had been among those murdered.

"I seen you shoot more people in the last four days than I shot in my whole life."

"I doubt it."

"Go ahead and doubt it," Porter said defiantly. "And you done murdered my *brother*."

"Murder's a strong word," Cole replied.

"What do you call shooting a man in the back?"

"Saving somebody."

"All's he was doing was tryin' to have a little fun with a squaw," Porter explained.

"Your brother seems to have had him a weakness for hurting women," Cole observed.

"Wasn't a woman," Porter insisted. "It was a *squaw*."

Cole bit his tongue.

As the ravine widened into more of a valley, Cole found it necessary to take the lead in order to look for evidence of Goode's having come this way. The clumsy man made himself easy to track. He had kept to the path of least resistance, running downhill and following the streambed, while not making any effort to hide his tracks. Every fifteen feet or so, Cole could see the fresh footprint in the gravel of a man who was running hard.

If it had been flat, open country as in previous days, men on horseback would have caught up with Goode by now, but the present terrain favored a runner. Goode had remained ahead of them by running in a straight line, while they had to pick their trail carefully with the horses—*and* a frightened man running downhill can move very quickly.

As the ground grew more level, where Goode no longer

had the momentum of a steep slope, Cole's own progress was now slowed by the necessity of looking for his tracks. Where the streambed meandered into an oxbow, Goode had cut cross country, and it took time for his pursuer to find his tracks.

Each time Cole seemed to lose the trail, Gideon Porter was eager to point out the fact with a taunting phrase reminding him of his failings.

"Good-for-nothing Goode done got you there," he would laugh.

For Cole, it was no laughing matter. The narrower that they cut the distance, the more likely that Goode would hear the ranting Porter, and know they were closing in. If that happened, Goode would either quicken his pace or abandon the streambed. Cole hoped for the former, because a day of running would exhaust him, and he feared the latter, because tracking Goode on the hillsides, now covered with more and more ponderosa, would be much slower.

A third possibility troubled Cole even more.

What if Goode got tired of running and decided to ambush them with the purloined pistol? Cole guessed that Goode was not a good shot, but he did not *know* this. He did not want to ask Porter.

Gradually, the air grew colder, and the clouds became darker and more ominous. If it started to snow, the footprints in the gravel would be lost, but these would be replaced by footprints in the snow, which would be easier to follow. Even if he was a few hands short of a full deck, Goode would certainly be able to figure this out.

Coming to a place where it looked like Goode had stopped for a while and moved in circles, Cole dismounted. He let the roan graze, took Porter's reins away from him and led his horse.

About thirty feet farther on, they came to a place marked by the exposed roots of a large cottonwood that had been toppled a couple of years ago by a spring flood.

In among the tangle of roots, bleached white, and as thick and stiff as limbs, two roots had been broken to form some sort of tool. Cole could see that they were spattered with blood.

Goode had, with a frenzy born of desperation, tried and failed to use the roots to remove the manacles from his wrists. There was no way that steel would yield to cottonwood, but it looked as though the man had torn at least one of his wrists trying.

Cole reached out and touched the blood. It was fresh.

# CHAPTER 16

JEREMIAH EATON TURNED HIS EYES FROM THE MORNING sky to the dark ridgeline in the west. The contrast of the flakes against the heavily timbered hillside gave him a better take on how hard the snow was falling than to look upward into the uniformly gray sky.

"She's a-comin' down," he said to his wife, who stood a short distance away, in the doorway of their log home.

"Be comin' down *hard* before long, I reckon," Rebecca said as she glanced down to see whether six-year-old Thomas had bothered to put on a coat before he ran out to see the flakes. He hadn't. Early snowfalls were always a point of curiosity for youngsters, she thought to herself, before admonishing him to "Gitcher self inside and gitcher coat."

"Reckon I better ride on down the river and scare the cattle back up this way," Jeremiah said with resignation.

"Reckon," his wife nodded in agreement.

Early snowfalls were always a reminder of that moment in the cycle of months when it was time to button up their affairs, time for Rebecca to be glad that she had finished canning the vegetables and crabapples, and for Jeremiah to hope that he'd put up enough hay to get the milk cows through till spring.

Four years now separated this cold autumn day from a moment of blissful, romantic dreaming on an Ohio front porch.

Rebecca had first heard the glittering tales in her mother's dining room. She had sat there, an infant on her knee, as a gentleman who was a cousin to her mother's best friend, related tales of the open spaces of Montana Territory. He had been there, having gone west to the gold fields around Diamond City, and he had experienced the land for himself. He had seen its sights with his own eyes. There were opportunities to be had—if one was of a mind for homesteading.

Four years ago, Jeremiah Eaton had come home to his wife and toddler, dejected and complaining. It had taken him nearly a year to get on at the mill, and now there was talk that those hands who were newly hired might soon be let go. Two years on, and the nation was still digging out after the Panic of 1873.

Somehow, it seemed to the young married Eatons that a place like Montana Territory was across the line that delineated the limit of the part of the world that could be affected by panics such as that of 1873.

Thanks to vague directions given by the cousin, and a great deal more luck than they'd realized they had, the Eatons found the end of their rainbow in a mountain valley in Meagher County, Montana Territory.

Canvas from the wagon that brought them had become the tent that was their home until the house was built. The team which had drawn their wagon maneuvered the ponderosa logs felled by Jeremiah, and the house was ready by Christmas.

The first year was hard, but the fact that it was the *hardest* separated the Eatons from the majority of homesteaders who came west in the decades following the Civil War. For most, each successive year was worse than the one previous, and by the third or fourth, dreams faded like dust devils in a field gone dry.

Jeremiah Eaton rode down along the stream that differentiated his 160 acres from those of the majority of homesteaders. At a time when most western homesteads required the sinking of a deep well at great expense and great labor, the Eatons' land was blessed with a running stream. Unlike those in some of the adjacent valleys, it ran all year. The fact that it had run all year for many, many years meant that the soil was good—once you got at it. Like the soil in every corner of the territory, it had never been tilled, and that was back-breaking work. Though Rebecca had vigorously opposed his taking up most of their emigrant wagon with it, she finally admitted that the single best possession they brought west with them was the old, one-runner plow.

Little Thomas—his mother called him Tommy—had grown up not knowing the Ohio reality of streets and streetlights, but the pains and pleasures of a lonely mountain valley. Sometimes this pained his mother, but mostly it made her glad. What mostly pained her was the fact that Tommy's younger sister would never know these things, and that the complications from her birth meant that, for certain, Tommy would grow up an only child.

For this reason, Rebecca had developed a protective attachment to the child which Jeremiah dared not describe as "spoilin'." There was one time that he had, but his wife's tears and his wife's words had told him it would be the last.

Jeremiah could, and often did, count their blessings. They had each other, and they had a "place" which had stood the tests of the seasons.

When she counted her blessings, and like her husband she often did, Rebecca arrayed few things in the opposite column. The one thing that most often headed this list,

though, was the loneliness. The needs of the place kept her
here. Except for a rare trip down to the small town at Camp
Baker, or their annual ride all the way to Diamond City, she
rarely saw another soul.

It was for this reason that the rapping at her door caused
her an alarm that nearly found her jumping out of her own
skin.

It seemed only natural that she should open the door. It
was not locked, as doors in Ohio homes would often be, and
Rebecca had long since forgotten her Ohio instincts.

Nothing among her faded memory of Ohio instincts, or
her recently acquired Montana instincts, however, had quite
prepared her for the sight she faced on her doorstep.

"Mornin', ma'am," said the stranger.

The sight of him pronounced the definition of "stranger"
on many levels. He was the very embodiment of dishevel-
ment, with his scraggly beard, his dirty clothing, and his
hair askew. However, that which struck Rebecca as most
peculiar were his scabby wrists and those gray chains that
bound them together.

"I'm starvin,'" he insisted in a hoarse voice. "Could I
trouble ya for a bite to eat?"

While it was not exactly a neighborly thing to be impolite
to a stranger, the extreme strangeness of *this* stranger invited
pause.

"Well . . . I never," was the first phrase to fall from
Rebecca Eaton's lips.

"You look a fright, sir" was the second.

"If I'm forgetting any niceties might be due a lady," the
man said, "I am powerful sorry . . . but I'm powerful
hungry."

"I reckon . . ." Rebecca said, regarding the flakes of snow
nestling in his unkempt hair, and nodding for him to enter
her home.

She shot Tommy a "stay away from this man" glance,
then ladled a bowl of the same cornmeal and elk fat porridge

that she had served her family for breakfast and set it on the table for the newcomer.

"My husband'll be back soon," she said, staking out the fact that she was not alone in this remote location and that the stranger would soon be dealing with the man of the house.

"That would be good," the man said between bites. "I reckon he's got tools what might get these irons from my wrists."

"Looks like you been tryin' at that yourself," she observed as she watched him eat. "Looks like you cut yourself bad doin' it too."

"Guess so, ma'am."

"Who put those things on you?" Rebecca asked. "Are you runnin' from the law?"

"No, ma'am. It is God's honest truth that these were not placed here by no lawman."

"Then . . ."

"I was *kidnapped*," he explained nervously. "Me and my partner was. We was kidnapped by an angry stranger done have designs on sellin' us to the Indians up north."

"Well . . . I never," she began. She had been planning to add the phrase "heard of such a fool notion" to the usual expression, but she caught her tongue. "For what purpose?" Rebecca asked.

"Servitude . . . slavery . . . who knows what a savage would do to a God-fearing man."

"Who knows?" Rebecca nodded in mock agreement. "Where'd you get yourself caught?"

"Up north, up around Fort Benton."

"Guess you got away?"

"Yes, ma'am . . . been runnin' for days. He's after me."

"Who's that?"

"The slaver, ma'am. He's a mean one, he is. I fear he'll kill me."

"You must be an awful important slave to get yourself chased all the way from Fort Benton," she said sarcastically.

She had heard of Indians *taking* slaves, but never of them *buying* slaves.

"Reckon I am," he said modestly, not catching the sarcasm in her tone.

Rebecca glanced out the cabin's one small glass window, anxious to see Jeremiah coming up the trail, but the trail that wound its way downstream to where the milk cows usually went to graze was empty.

"Reckon I could have some more?"

"Where are you from, sir?" Rebecca asked as she ladled another helping into the bowl.

"I'm from down toward Gallatin City. Headed home, I am."

"That's real nice," she nodded. "What did you say your name was?"

"Oh . . . I'm truly sorry . . . I reckon I failed to give my name. My name's Goode, James J. Goode."

"Good to meet you, Mr. Goode." She smiled. "You lived long down there?"

"My whole life," he said, as though a life spent in Gallatin City was an accomplishment in which a man could take great pride.

"Your people been there long?" Rebecca asked. She was growing more and more anxious at the fact of having a strange man in her house and was hoping to prolong the conversation as a distraction until the image of Jeremiah appeared in the small window.

"Yes, ma'am. They been there since before the war. Don't recall exactly when . . . 'Twas before my time."

"I reckon," she nodded. "What do you do down yonder?"

"Mostly what comes up that needs doin'. Nothing regular."

The small talk continued thusly for a time, but at last the limits of Jimmy Goode's attention span were reached.

"You said your husband's comin' back soon?"

"Yes, I expect he'll be showin' up at any moment," she replied with a nervous lump in her throat.

"You reckon you could show me to your husband's tools so's I could take care of this iron on my wrists?" Goode said. "The itchin' is something fierce, and I'm longing to be loose of these."

"As much as I'd like to help you, Mr. Goode," she said. "My husband's tools are not something I handle . . . any more than I would have him thrashing around in my kitchen."

"If you'd just point me at 'em, I'd be much obliged," he said with a suggestion of irritation in his voice. "You would not need to touch nothin'."

Looking into his eyes, she could see that the sustenance provided to this disheveled man had revived him from trembling hunger to an almost cockiness.

As he traced his tongue across his lips, her imagination did not like the way those eyes now regarded her, not as a good samaritan sating the pain of his empty stomach, but as a female body that might satisfy other hungers.


HAVING ROUNDED UP HIS CATTLE, JEREMIAH EATON HAD paused at the southern extremity of his 160 acres to restore some lodgepoles to the top rungs of several sections of his fence. It was a chore that would be exponentially more difficult in deep winter snow, and hence it was better to address it when the snowfall was still measured as less than an inch or two.

The snow had stopped for a while but was picking up again as he made his way home. There were few chores awaiting him other than getting the cattle situated in the pasture nearer the house, so his ride home was not done with particular urgency.

As he neared the house, the column of smoke promised a fire before which he might warm himself, but as he rounded the bend and came within sight of his homestead, he was startled to see his wife walking toward the barn with a man.

He had to blink a couple of times to assure himself that his eyes were truly seeing this. Visitors were a rarity out here, and unexpected visitors unheard of.

Leaving the cattle to graze lazily in the yellow, foot-tall grass that rose above the thin dusting of snow, he galloped toward the barn.

His wife and the man turned to watch him approach.

"This would be Mr. Goode, Jeremiah," Rebecca explained as her husband dismounted. "He has a problem that he's anxious to have your help in getting out of."

"Would that be those irons that you got on your wrists, Mr. Goode?" Jeremiah asked.

"That would be right, sir," he answered, his tone reverting to its earlier politeness.

"You're a long way from anywhere, Mr. Goode. How'd you get way out here?"

"He's on the run from kidnappers," Rebecca said with a note of sarcasm that was not lost on her husband.

"Done escaped . . . but they're after me. Trailing me right now too," Goode explained.

"You sure it wasn't the law that put these on?" Jeremiah asked skeptically.

"Like I told your missus, I would swear on a stack of Bibles that it wasn't no lawman what chained me up."

"Kidnappers?"

"Yes, sir."

"But why . . . ?"

"They planned to sell me and my partner into slavery among the Indians," Goode insisted.

"Never heard of no Indians *buying* slaves from white men," Jeremiah said. "Heard of people . . . fair sum of people . . . gettin' theirselves taken by Indians, but I never heard of Indians *buying* slaves . . . but then there's lots of things I've never heard of. Lemme take a look."

Jeremiah's credulity concerning Goode's story held no more conviction than his wife's had, but he figured he would give him the benefit of the doubt—at least until he figured out what was really going on with this man.

"These are built to last," Jeremiah observed. "Lot heavier steel than handcuffs. I see by the markings that they are U.S. Army issue."

"I reckon he musta stole 'em," Goode said. "I seem to reckon the slaver told how he stole 'em from somebody over at Fort Ellis."

"I have no saw that will cut steel," Jeremiah told the man. "Breaking the locks with a hammer could not be done without breaking your wrists . . . somethin' it looks like you damned near done already."

As he spoke, Jeremiah's eyes began flicking toward the ridge opposite the cabin. Instinctively, Rebecca looked in that direction, and Goode noticed this.

"Whatcha lookin' at?" Goode demanded.

"Nothin,' " Jeremiah told him. "Just the snowflakes in the air."

"You was looking and she was looking," Goode said nervously, following their gazes. "You'd be lookin' at something."

After a moment of silence, Goode gasped.

"Christ almighty," he hissed. "That consarned slaver done caught up to me!"

As the three of them watched, a lone rider made his way down a hillside three-quarters of a mile away.

Suddenly, Goode reached beneath his long coat and pulled out the Colt .45 that had once been carried by the man with the big hat. With his other hand, he grabbed Rebecca's wrist and pulled her close to himself.

"No way in hell I'm gonna let that man take me," Goode

said, shoving the muzzle of the pistol painfully into the small of Rebecca's back and pulling her backward toward the cabin. "When he comes by here, tell him . . . I don't know what to tell you to tell him . . . Just get rid of him or this lady gets a hole blowed in her . . . *please.*"

Jeremiah saw fear on his face and tears in his eyes.

# CHAPTER 17

⬦━━━⬦━━━⬦

BLADEN COLE HAD NOT LET ON TO GIDEON PORTER THAT he had lost the trail of Jimmy Goode in the fading light of yesterday. He had rousted the outlaw so as to be on the trail at dawn, hoping to see the smoke from Goode's campfire somewhere ahead—but he hadn't. Either Goode had known that a campfire would reveal his location, or he had not been able to get one started. Cole was hoping for the latter.

Cole had allowed Porter to believe that he was still following a trail, when the only thing he was following was a hunch. He figured that a man who was in desperation to the verge of recklessness—which he believed to be the case—and who was increasingly tired, cold, and hungry—which was sure to be the case—would follow the path of least resistance. Therefore, they continued south, down the southern slope of the Little Belts.

"How the hell can you see where he went?" Porter demanded.

"Practice," Cole lied.

"Reckon it's easy to trail somebody who ain't good for

nothing except givin' the slip to a bounty hunter," Porter said to taunt him.

"Hmmm," Cole replied, thoughtfully staring at the ground, at an imaginary track that, obviously, Porter could not see.

About a half hour out, they came across a gently flowing stream, and Cole paused to water the horses. In a silent, thoughtful way designed to convey to Gideon Porter the illusion that he knew what he was doing, Cole figured that Jimmy Goode would probably have followed this stream.

By now, it had started to snow. Cole held out hope that he would soon be seeing the footprints of a cold and desperate man who had spent a night nearby in this wilderness without a fire.

After another hour or so on the trail, they could see a column of smoke rising into the windless skies in the distance.

When this turned out to be coming from a homesteader's cabin, Cole chained Gideon Porter to a ponderosa, tethered the horses, and circled around to approach the cabin from high ground so as to make himself visible—and coming from a direction away from the place where Porter was chained.

A man was standing alone near the barn as Cole rode toward him through the scattering of randomly floating snowflakes.

"Mornin,'" Cole said as he rode up.

"Mornin,'" the man said, returning the greeting. "You're a fair distance from anywhere."

"Yep," Cole agreed.

"Where ya headed?"

"South . . . Gallatin City."

"You got some ridin' to do."

"Yep," Cole agreed. "By the way, I'm looking for a man who'd be passing through this country yesterday or today."

"Haven't seen nobody," the man replied quickly.

"You sure? Skinny fellow with a long gray coat and no hat?"

"Can't say as I have. We don't see too many people out here."

"We?" Cole asked.

"Me and the missus."

"How long you been living out here?" Cole asked, making conversation and trying to get a read on the man. He wondered where the wife was. If they did not have many visitors, as the man said and as Cole believed to be the case, why had she not appeared at the cabin door, out of curiosity if nothing else?

"Four years last summer," the man replied. "Goin' on five."

"That's pretty good. Most homesteaders don't make it that long. By the way, my name's Bladen Cole."

"Jeremiah Eaton," the man said, reaching up to shake Cole's hand. The slight tremble in Jeremiah's hand told Cole that Jimmy Goode and the stolen pistol were not far away.

"Well . . . nice makin' your acquaintance," Cole said, reining his horse to ride away. "Reckon I'll get going."

"So long," Jeremiah said, watching him go. As the stranger rode away, he wondered whether he was a lawman or a slaver. He had showed no badge, but Jeremiah still doubted the latter. What other possibilities could there be? At the moment, it really did not matter.

"DON'T MAKE A GODDAMN SOUND," JIMMY GOODE whispered nervously as he trained the pistol on Rebecca Eaton with a shaking hand.

"What would your mother say?" she asked in a low voice. "Cursing at a woman in that foul tone?"

Jimmy was in deep. He was in over his head. He cursed the day that he had met Gideon Porter. Had that never happened, the road of Goode's life would never have reached this place.

Everything about the way that his mother had raised him, everything in his being, told him that he was wrong to drag a woman into her home at gunpoint—but circumstances had forced this as the only course of events he could imagine. He was doing, in short, what one of the Porter boys would have done.

Tommy sat in the corner, trying not to be seen, and looking with great trepidation at the man's pistol and the way he pointed it recklessly at his mother.

Rebecca watched as Jeremiah waved halfheartedly, and the horseman rode away.

"Your mother would have a fit if she knew what you was doin'."

"Leave my poor, widowed mother out of this."

"Sorry to hear your papa died, but I reckon he spared the strap one too many times when you were growing up."

"Never knew him. He was with mama but a short time."

"How'd he die?"

"Nobody ever said."

"You ever ask?"

"Nope."

They both turned their heads as Jeremiah entered the room.

"Well, I done got rid of your slaver," Jeremiah said. "Told him I never saw you."

"Did he believe you?" Goode asked, his voice quavering.

"Didn't seem to disbelieve me."

"Now it's high time for you to be gettin' along, mister," Rebecca demanded angrily.

"I don't know . . ." Goode said, gritting his teeth. "I don't know what to do."

"Gettin' along would be a darned good start," Rebecca repeated.

"Shut the hell up," Goode shouted, raising his voice

louder than either of them had heard him speak previously. "I'm tryin' to *think*!"

There was a long pause. Thinking was clearly something that came to him with considerable difficulty. His earlier tale of kidnapping and slavery *had* displayed ample imagination, though it had been short on believability.

The silence was broken by the crash of breaking glass.

Goode turned, pointing the muzzle of the Colt in the direction of the sound.

Had it not been for the saucer-shaped eyes of a terrified six-year-old boy, he would have pulled the trigger.

A faint trace of what Goode's mother *had* taught him grabbed his wrist and whispered in his ear that it was a very big mistake to shoot a little child for breaking a jar of crab-apple preserves.

"Tommy," Rebecca said, standing up and moving quickly toward her child.

"I'm sorry," Tommy said, apologizing for breaking the jar.

"Oh . . . my baby," his mother said, embracing him. "It's all right, it's just preserves."

Both mother and son were crying, and this made Goode both nervous and agitated.

"All of you *sit down* where I can see you," he demanded in an almost pleading tone. "And shut your mouths while I'm trying to *think*!"

He could feel himself starting to sweat as he gritted his teeth and tried to decide what to do. Gideon Porter would know. He would have figured things out by now.

Or would he?

If Gideon Porter was so smart, why was *he* still a prisoner of the bounty hunter while Goode walked free? This thought gave him hope. He took a deep breath and tried to relax.

"Like the missus said, it's time for you to be movin' on and leave us be," Jeremiah said. "I done told the man that you were not here, and there's no way that we could tell anybody else that you'd *been* here. It's more than a day's ride to any town. Why would we even want to? You were the victim of a man who wanted to enslave you."

"Let me *think*," Goode said, trying to be stern.

The man was right. He couldn't stay here. He really *did* have to get moving—and sooner, rather than later.

"I'll even saddle a horse for you," Jeremiah said. "It would be a neighborly thing to help a man who has been through what you been through . . . with the slaver and all. With a horse you could get down to a town where a blacksmith would have the tools to get the irons from your hands."

His wife gave him a glance that said "How dare you offer one of *our horses* to this evil man?"

Goode gritted his teeth. This sounded pretty good. He was being handed a free horse. It seemed too good to be true. Was it?

"That sounds mighty fine, mister, but how do I know you ain't got a trick up your sleeve?"

"We got no bone to pick with you," Jeremiah said. "We didn't even *know* you until an hour ago. All's we want is to have you get on with your travels and leave us alone."

Goode anguished over the decision he had to make. He was not used to making decisions. What would Gideon Porter do?

At last he seized upon the course he would follow. He would take a *hostage*.

"As you say, it is mighty neighborly of you to offer a horse," Goode said with renewed confidence. "But I want you to saddle up *two* horses . . . and gimme all your guns."

"Don't got but that one," Jeremiah said, nodding at an early model Winchester repeater that hung above the doorway.

Jeremiah Eaton swallowed hard. The man obviously planned to take a hostage with him when he departed. He did not mind being a hostage to the crazy man if it meant leading him away from his home and family. The man had not yet pulled the trigger, and Jeremiah figured that he was not anxious to do so. Somewhere down the road, when the crazy man felt less boxed in, he would be able to trade both horses for his freedom and walk home.

The expression on Rebecca's face, however, was a mix of fear and anger.

The Eatons had just four horses, two riding mares and the aging draft horses who had pulled their wagon from Ohio and who now pulled the plow and did general work around the place. Jeremiah offered to scatter them so that Goode would not fear a double cross, and he did so.

With both horses saddled, Goode ordered a rope to be strung between them as he had seen Bladen Cole do with him and Porter.

Goode then lurched aboard one of the horses as gracefully as he could with his hands still in irons.

Jeremiah hugged his wife and started to mount the other mare.

"Not you," Goode said.

"What?"

"Not *you*," Goode repeated. "Put the *boy* on the horse."

Jeremiah was dumbfounded, his wife apoplectic.

"You are *not* taking my boy hostage," she spat in a venomous rage. She impulsively grabbed Tommy by the hand and pushed him behind her.

"I have the guns," Goode asserted. "I have the guns and I'm in charge . . . you gotta *do what I say*!"

"Not my boy," Rebecca pleaded, tears running down her cheeks.

"If I was to take his daddy, he might get tricky on me," Goode said. "This boy's gonna do what he's told . . . aren't ya, boy?"

"You can't do this!" Jeremiah insisted.

"Boy's a helluva lot better hostage than a man," Goode said with a smirk. "No way a lawman is gonna question a man ridin' with a boy."

"*Lawman?*" Rebecca screamed. "You said you was the

victim of slavers and not an outlaw! Why are you worried about a *lawman* if you're a poor victim?"

"That's what I meant to say," Goode said, becoming jittery. "And you're tryin' to confuse me with your talk . . . Now, get that boy on the horse or I'm gonna start shootin' and I'm gonna start with *you*."

REBECCA EATON SAT SOBBING IN THE YARD OF THEIR HOME, oblivious to the growing number of snowflakes floating down around her and oblivious to the cold.

The only thing of which she was aware was that her boy had been taken by a violent man with a gun.

She had been oblivious to what her husband had said about the mistakes that the kidnapper had made—such as not tying them up or searching the house for more guns, and thereby not finding Jeremiah's shotgun. She was oblivious to the fact that it might have taken hours for them to get themselves untied, meaning that the kidnapper might have had half a day's head start—instead of half an hour's—by the time that her husband had rounded up a draft horse and set out, riding bareback, in pursuit.

The only thing of which she was aware was that her boy—her *only* living child—had been taken by a violent man with a gun.

JEREMIAH EATON HAD BEEN SEETHING WITH ANGER AND sick with guilt at not being able to protect his family, but unlike his wife, who sat powerless, unable to do anything, he had at least the small satisfaction that he was taking action.

Jeremiah took some solace in the fact that the boy had value to the man only if he was alive, and distress in the fact that he was an erratic and impulsive man who could not be relied on to make entirely rational choices.

The draft horse was slow, and the shotgun afforded but two shots between reloading, but at least he was doing *something*—though he had yet to decide exactly *what* he would do if he actually caught up with them.

The lightly falling snow allowed Jeremiah to follow their tracks, and to guess the timing of their progress by how much snow had collected *in* the tracks. He could see that the two-year-old mares were moving faster than the old draft horse and extending their lead. He hoped that they would stop at some point and that it would not start snowing hard enough to smother the tracks.

YOUNG THOMAS EATON WAS AFRAID FOR HIMSELF AND afraid for his family. In all his life, he had never been alone with a stranger, or indeed with anyone other than his parents.

He didn't know what he was supposed to think, but he *did* know he did not like this. He had stopped crying, but he was still afraid that the man would hurt him and nobody would be there to see it.

He was so preoccupied with his situation that he had forgotten for the longest time to worry about being cold. Except for the tips of his ears and his fingers, he wasn't, but he expected that later, he would be. He was glad that his mother had earlier demanded that he put on his coat, and he wished that he had picked up his gloves.

He had said nothing to the stranger, and the man had said nothing to him. He seemed to Thomas to be the kind of man who did not like to talk unless he had to.

As the miles went past, the snowfall slowed, stopped for a while, and then started up again, heavier than before. Thomas looked at the flakes settling on the horse's mane and remembered how his mother had told him that every snowflake had a design all to itself, and that no two snowflakes in all the world were exactly the same. He had enjoyed this special time with his mother—last winter, when he was five—and it made him cry to think of how much he was missing his parents.

The woods were thicker and darker now, and Thomas grew more frightened. He choked back his fear, wanting to be the kind of man of whom his father could be proud. He knew that his father was liable to say something about a man not being afraid in a dark forest.

He wondered whether his father would come for him, and whether he would see his mother again.

This made him cry.

The angry man growled when he saw the tears, and Thomas wiped his cheeks.

Soon, Thomas had another worry.

"Mister . . ." he said tentatively. "I gotta pee."

"Okay," Jimmy Goode said, after a moment's thought. "Make it quick."

The boy slid off the mare and began walking up a slight incline toward some trees.

"Where the hell you goin'?" Goode demanded.

"Ma says I should always go into the bushes," the boy replied.

"Okay," Goode said impatiently.

Deciding that he too could use a pit stop, Goode climbed off his horse, but he did not venture near the "bushes."

He paused to congratulate himself on his good fortune. He had made the transition from desperate fugitive to the man in control. He had gotten the bounty hunter off his trail, he had a horse, and he had a *hostage*. He was the man in control.

Nobody would call him "good-for-nothing Goode" today!

With his hostage, he could walk up to a blacksmith and say that he had rescued the kid from slavers. Nobody would question a man with a kid. They'd get to the next town, whatever it was likely to be, and go straight to the blacksmith, and then they'd get something to eat. Goode had no money—he wished now that he had taken some from the homesteading family—but who would deny a *kid*?

The kid. Where was the damned kid?

"*Kid!*" Goode shouted. "*Kid!* Get yourself back here and let's get goin'."

There was no hint of a reply from the "bushes" to which the boy had gone. Goode cursed himself for not keeping an eye on him.

Where was the damned kid?

He walked up the slope in the direction Thomas had been headed when Goode last laid eyes on him.

"*Kid?*" Goode shouted. "Get yourself out wherever you're hidin'. *Kid!* If you don't show yourself, I'm gonna have to get tough and tan your hide."

There was no reply.

Goode cursed himself again for not having kept an eye on him, but he dared not allow his mind to drift into thoughts that "good-for-nothing Jimmy Goode" may have been outsmarted by a six-year-old.

*Where was the damned kid?*

Goode decided to appeal to the boy's emotions.

"Whatcha gonna do when it gets dark out here . . . ? *Oooeee*," he shouted, attempting to make a ghostly sound. "Whatcha gonna do when it gets *cold* out here? Whatcha gonna do when you get *hungry*?"

No reply.

"Whatcha gonna do when the *coyotes* get hungry? They're gonna *eat* you . . . *eat you alive!*"

Still no reply.

"Okay, kid, that does it," Goode shouted. "I'm mad. I'm goin' hunting."

Lifting the muzzle of the Colt, he squeezed the trigger.

The sound of the gunshot in the deep pillowy quiet of the snow-blanketed woods was startling even to Jimmy Goode.

"*No.*"

Jeremiah Eaton nearly jumped out of his saddle when he heard the gunshot.

"*No*," Jeremiah said to himself when he heard the thunderclap reverberate through the trees.

He prodded the big draft horse to run as fast as he could. In his prime, the big horse had had some pretty respectable speed in him, but age had tempered him. He moved as fast as he could, aware that his rider desperately needed him to do so.

"*No!*" Jeremiah repeated as he broke into a clearing and saw a man, *that* man, with a pistol.

He did not see his son. Was the boy lying injured on the ground somewhere? Was he lying . . . ? The anguished father could not finish the thought.

Jeremiah gripped the shotgun with his right hand as the horse closed the distance between them and *that* man. He ached to use the shotgun *now*, but he knew that the range was too great.

Goode turned his attention from the bushes to the oncoming rider and took careful aim. He cursed himself for not tying up the homesteader and chasing the draft horses farther, but fate had given him a second chance. It is not hard to hit an object that is coming directly at you.

Suddenly, a withering pain tore through Goode's elbow.

He felt himself rendered helpless, knocked off balance, and thrown to the ground like a block of salt being kicked off the tailgate of a wagon.

Jeremiah watched this as he came on, clutching his unfired shotgun and wondering who had shot the man.

He arrived near Goode a moment later, slid off the horse, and looked around. The woods were silent but for the heavy, heaving breath of his horse and strange, animal-like sounds being uttered by Jimmy Goode.

As for most of the day he had imagined himself doing, he leveled the shotgun at the man who'd kidnapped his son.

"Where's my *boy*?" Jeremiah demanded angrily. "What did you do with my *boy*?"

"Don't shoot him."

Jeremiah looked up to see a man emerge from the trees carrying a lever-action Winchester and leading a group of horses. He recognized the man as the same one who had ridden into his homestead that morning. He did not recognize the second man seated on one of the horses, but he *did* recognize the government-issue manacles worn by this man.

"Don't shoot him," Bladen Cole repeated. "He's mine."

"Where's my *boy*?" Jeremiah demanded, pointing both barrels at Cole.

"Right there," Cole said with a nod.

Jeremiah turned to see Tommy running from the bushes at top speed.

"Papa . . . Papa . . . Papa . . ." he exclaimed as he hugged his father. Both of them had tears of joy streaming down their cheeks.

As Jeremiah turned to hug Tommy, he felt the shotgun being lifted from his grip.

"Who *are* you?" Jeremiah demanded of Cole. He made no attempt to retrieve his weapon, as both his arms were now wrapped tight around the sobbing boy. "What do you want?"

"My name's Cole, just as I said when we met back at your homestead."

He cracked open the shotgun, removed the shells, and tucked them into the breast pocket of Jeremiah's jacket.

"Like I told you, I've been trailing this fellow for a time," Cole said, handing the shotgun back to the homesteader butt-first and picking up the revolver dropped by the outlaw. This too he emptied and handed to the homesteader.

"You a lawman? He said you were a slaver."

"A *slaver*?" Cole laughed as he applied a tourniquet to the injured man's arm. "That's a pretty fanciful yarn for somebody with the imagination of Jimmy Goode . . . No, I'm not a lawman, but I *am* the man that got sent to bring back a bunch of killers."

"Bounty hunter?"

"Yes," Cole replied. "Can you read?"

"Of course," Jeremiah said, slightly offended.

Cole took a scrap of paper from his pocket and pointed out the names and charges on the warrant.

"I knew from your manner that you were in trouble when I talked to you at your place this morning," Cole explained. "When I didn't see your wife, I figured that she was inside your house with a gun to her head, so I just backed off and trailed this man when he left with your boy. I knew that he wouldn't hurt him unless he was provoked, so I wanted not to provoke him . . . It was your boy who provoked him."

"What?" Jeremiah gasped.

"Gotta give you credit." Cole smiled at Tommy. "What's your name, son?"

"Thomas J. Eaton, sir."

"Yes . . . Thomas J. Eaton," Cole laughed. "Well, I watched where you were hiding. He was not even close to finding you. You were awful brave not to let out a sound even when he started yelling about coyotes eating you."

"I knew my papa would come to get me," Thomas said bravely, as the tears poured down his father's cheeks.

# CHAPTER 18

"FATHER, MR. PHILLIPS IS HERE," HANNAH RANSDELL SAID, putting her head in her father's office.

The banker looked up suddenly, startled by the sound of his daughter speaking those words. In his subconscious mind, "Mr. Phillips" was his violently murdered colleague, Dawson Phillips, and her use of that name was momentarily jarring. The person to whom his daughter referred was not, of course, the person to which his mind had leaped, but the son of that man.

"Send him in," Isham Ransdell said, quickly regaining his composure. "And get Duffy."

"Mr. Phillips," she smiled at the son and namesake of her father's late colleague, "my father will see you now."

She brought the younger man into the inner sanctum of the Gallatin City Bank and Trust Company. The proprietor rose to shake the visitor's hand as Duffy came in carrying his notes and ledger.

"Welcome, Mr. Phillips, it is a pleasure to meet you, though I deeply regret the circumstances that have brought us together," Isham Ransdell began. "This is Mr. Duffy, my accountant, and you've met my daughter, Hannah. She's my . . . uh . . ."

"Assistant," Hannah interrupted with a broad smile as her father grasped for words. He always did this. One of these days, she thought she might reply with a title that truly represented the work that she did for him. She could imagine his expression if she had said "general manager" or "vice president."

"First of all, let me say that I was personally acquainted with your late father. He was a fine man and a fine member of our community . . . as was your mother. I am very truly shocked and saddened by what happened to your parents."

"Thank you, sir," the younger Phillips said with an obvious lump in his throat. "Your words are much appreciated."

"The entire community of Gallatin City shares my sympathies. Your parents will be greatly missed."

Isham Ransdell then turned to the substance of his former colleague's affairs and spoke in generalities for a few moments. When the younger Dawson Phillips followed up with several specific questions, the elder Ransdell merely nodded to his daughter.

Hannah opened a folder and proceeded to explain, in minute detail, the nature and rates of all the many bank accounts and investments held by the elder Phillips. When it came to balances, she named them off the top of her head, each time asking Mr. Duffy whether the number was correct. Each time but once, he simply nodded that her numbers were accurate. The one time that she was wrong, he proudly corrected her to say that she was off by seven dollars and change, as her figure was that of the *fifteenth* of the month.

"I stand corrected," she said with a smile.

The younger Mr. Phillips began the meeting more impatient than amused that the banker was allowing his daughter to speak of financial matters, but soon he was just trying to keep up with her.

When Hannah had finished, she nodded to her father to name the total value of the elder Mr. Phillips's bank holdings, but he found it necessary to nod back to her for the balance with accrued interest at the end of the coming month.

"So there you have it," Isham Ransdell said in summary. "Are there any further questions that we might answer for you?"

"Not at the moment," the younger Mr. Phillips replied. "But there may be after I've spoken with his attorney, Mr. Stocker, about the details of the will."

"Certainly," Isham Ransdell said. "We are ready and pleased to serve you, just as we were your late father . . . and once again, you have our fullest condolences . . . Hannah, could you get Mr. Phillips a cup of coffee?"

"Yes, Father."

"WHERE DID YOU LEARN TO DO THAT, MISS RANSDELL?" Phillips asked when Hannah handed him a cup of coffee and poured one for herself.

"Do what . . . ?"

"The accounts?"

"It's basic banking practice, Mr. Phillips," she said with a shrug. "I've worked here since I was a girl."

"Where did you go to school?"

"I went to school in Gallatin City. I was very good in arithmetic. The rest I've learned working here."

"You didn't go to college . . . or a secretarial school?"

"I doubt that numbers used in secretarial school include any that had not yet been revealed to me by the time that I was in high school."

Phillips nodded. She had him there.

"If I might be so bold as to change the subject," he said, already changing the subject, "I was wondering . . . um . . . Miss Ransdell . . . if you would do me the honor of joining me for dinner at the hotel this evening?"

"I would be delighted, Mr. Phillips," Hannah said with a smile after a brief pause. It had been some time since she had been asked to dine with a gentleman, and his invitation pleased her as much as it startled her.

"Shall we say seven?" Phillips suggested, "I'll . . . I could . . ."

"I shall meet you there at that time," Hannah replied. She was delighted with the attention of a handsome young man.

"Thank you then, Miss Ransdell," he said, extending his hand. "Now, if you'll excuse me, I must go see Mr. Stocker about the will . . . Thank you for the coffee."

"My pleasure, Mr. Phillips," she said, shaking his extended hand.

HANNAH RANSDELL ASCENDED THE STEPS OF THE GALLATIN House. The restaurant in the hotel that had been owned by the late Mr. Phillips, Sr., was the fanciest and probably the finest between Bozeman and Helena. The high society of Gallatin City, to the degree that there *was* such a thing as a high society in Gallatin City, dined here. Her father occasionally took clients here, and Mr. Phillips had often entertained her father and his other associates in the bar.

She entered the front door as the hotel's big imported German clock was banging out the seven measured beats of the hour. Dawson Phillips, Jr., who was already present, rose from his chair to greet her. She smiled politely as he escorted her to the dining room.

Over appetizers, they made small talk. She asked, and he explained, about his life in Denver, and she told of life in this city, which he had visited only twice. He had spent his early years in Bozeman, when his parents lived there, but had been shipped off to boarding school in Denver when his parents moved to Gallatin City.

While she was just a tad closer to thirty than to twenty, she guessed him to be a little past thirty. This made him courting age, and had she lived in Denver, or he in Gallatin City, it might have been an opportunity worth encouraging. He was, indeed, a charming fellow, an entrepreneur like his father, *and* he did not seem to look down his nose at a woman working in a bank—at least *after* he had seen her in action.

For Hannah, more than for the man on the opposite side of the table, the subject of courtship was accompanied by the ticking of a clock no less real and tangible than the one in the lobby of the Gallatin House. In moments that alternated with her dismissive criticism of the eligible bachelors in Gallatin City she faced the reality that society had painted a narrow line between the age at which a young woman was suitable for courting and the age at which she was destined for eternal spinsterhood.

For the past few years, Hannah's life had taken its meaning from the pride of knowing she was good at her work. Young Mr. Phillips reminded her that there was more to life and gave her cause to believe that not all men were like the would-be suitors whom she had rejected thus far.

As Hannah had discovered, the typical young man in Gallatin City seemed to be quick to focus his attention on himself, before giving her an opportunity to develop a corresponding interest in him. She mentioned this to Mr. Phillips and learned that he had found much the same to be true of the young ladies whom he had courted in Denver.

"Your father has good cause to depend upon your expertise," Phillips commented when she explained her duties in the family business. "One does not often find a woman in such a role."

"'One' will likely see more, rather than fewer, of us in responsible positions in the future," she smiled. "You may be aware that earlier this year President Hayes signed a law permitting women attorneys to argue cases before the Supreme Court of the United States. One day, we shall share the voting booth with men as well."

"Speaking of Mr. Hayes, do you believe that he will run

for reelection in the new year?" Phillips asked, deciding that even politics would be safer ground for the continued conversation than women's suffrage.

"After his narrow election, or as some would say his *defeat* by Mr. Tilden in '76, I would expect that he will make good on his promise to let someone such as Mr. Garfield run for his party's nomination." Hannah smiled, impressing her companion with her knowledge of current affairs.

"This has been a very nice meal," she said, smiling again as they were beginning their desert. "Thank you again for inviting me."

"My pleasure." He smiled also. "And very nice company."

"Thank you, Mr. Phillips," she replied, still smiling. "*My* pleasure."

For both parties, it had indeed been a pleasurable evening. Both were happy to enjoy a dinner with a member of the opposite sex who was well versed in the matters of the day.

"Have you dined often here at the Gallatin House?" he asked.

"Sometimes, though not often," she replied. "I think of it as a 'special occasion' type of place. When I was growing up, my family came here for the occasional Sunday dinner. After my mother passed, I came here with my father a time or two."

"I'm sorry to hear about your mother, Miss Ransdell," he said.

"That was nearly seven years ago," she said. "And she died peacefully. I can barely conceive of the anguish you must feel about losing both of your parents so violently."

"It does cause nightmares . . . which I hope will subside with time . . . I understand that your own father was to have been present at the Blaine home that evening."

"Yes . . . and I was to have accompanied him," Hannah said. "I can only imagine the horror of having been present if a fatal shot had found him . . . but *my* nightmares of what *might* have been can only pale by comparison to *your* nightmares of what *did* happen."

"I will miss my father greatly," Phillips said, sadly.

"He was a well-respected man," Hannah said with sympathetic assurance. "He was justifiably proud of this establishment . . . it has a very excellent restaurant."

"I'm pleased to hear that," he said. "Um . . . I guess it's *my* restaurant now."

"I meant to ask how things went with the reading of the will," Hannah said, merely making conversation, under the presumption that it had been a perfunctory reading.

"Well . . . with my mother deceased," he said with a gulp, not resuming his train of thought without a sip of water. "The bulk of the estate went to me, except for the trust fund, which as you know, was set up at your father's . . . um . . . *your* . . . bank for my sister, who is married, and who lives in Cheyenne."

"That sounds reasonably straightforward." Hannah nodded.

"Well . . . it *was* . . . except for one thing," he said thoughtfully.

"What's that?"

"Are you aware of a tract of land . . . actually several parcels of land . . . that are located north and east of Gallatin City, and which were owned jointly by your father and mine, together with Mr. Blaine and Mr. Stocker?"

"Yes," Hannah nodded. "I am aware that they were buying land out there. It is not exactly prime real estate. It is in the direction of the Diamond City gold fields, but no gold has ever been found there. I know that they were buying it on the cheap."

"Were you also aware that their arrangement called for the partners to inherit the shares of their associates? With my father and Mr. Blaine gone, Mr. Stocker and your father are now the sole owners of that property."

"No . . ." Hannah said with genuine surprise. "I did not know this."

"HOW WAS YOUR DINNER WITH YOUNG MR. PHILLIPS LAST night?" Isham Ransdell asked as his daughter came into the bank.

He usually arose before she did and was frequently at his desk very early. She had arrived at the bank on time only once. When he made a comment about her keeping "banker's hours," she had made it a point thereafter to arrive at work no later than fifteen minutes before opening.

"It was very nice," she replied, hanging up her coat.

"I heard you come in," he said in an offhand manner. At one point in her life, he would have taken such a thing sternly. At this point, though, he was pleased with any attention that she might receive from any young man of courting age.

"I hope that I didn't wake you," she said as she situated herself at her own desk. She had come home well before ten and had nothing for which to apologize.

"No, not at all," he replied.

"Father, I was not aware of your arrangement with your partners about the land outside of town . . . that you and Mr. Stocker inherited the shares of the others."

"Oh yes, that's true . . . I had actually forgotten that we had drawn up the papers that way until Virgil reminded me this week. We acquired it as a partnership, and it is typical for partners to grant one another the rights of inheritance."

"I see," Hannah said, turning to her work. She had wondered why her father had made such an arrangement, but his explanation seemed reasonable. She had wondered why her father had not told her about it, but she realized she had probably been a teenager when the deal was done. Most daughters in their twenties knew nothing of their father's business dealings. The fact that Hannah knew *nearly* everything was highly unusual.

Thoughts of this deal about marginal pasture land faded as Hannah dealt with the opening rush of customers, helping them with their transactions and answering their questions. Finally, when there was a lull, she decided to pick up the mail at the post office. She called to her father to tell him where she was going. He just waved back. He was in a meeting with Edward J. Olson.

Her father's right-hand man came and went without a schedule. While she and Mr. Duffy put in more than mere "banker's hours," Olson kept no office hours whatsoever. He appeared unannounced from time to time, but he was always welcome in her father's office. To his credit, though, he seemed very competent in handling whatever task beyond the walls of the bank her father assigned.

Going to the post office reminded Hannah of that day a while back when the letter had arrived from the bounty hunter. There, she thought, was another handsome man. Unlike the clean-shaven Mr. Phillips, he had the beginnings of a beard, and she liked a young man with hair on his face. There was also a certain allure surrounding a man with danger in his life. The violence was both frightening and appealing. It gave her a thrill to think about the way he lived his life, but men like him were the ones you thought about, *not* the ones you thought about courting.

"Good morning, Miss Ransdell."

Hannah was so lost in thought that she was startled by the greeting from Dawson Phillips, Jr. He was tipping his hat as she glanced up from the mail.

"Oh . . . good day, Mr. Phillips. I was just picking up the mail."

"It's a lovely morning," he said with a smile.

"The snow seems to have stopped," she replied, also smiling. "And it looks like the sun wants to shine."

"I enjoyed our dinner last night," he said.

"And I did as well," she replied.

"I was wondering . . . um . . . if it wouldn't appear too

forward of me . . . since you made a cup of coffee for me yesterday . . . whether I might return the favor today?"

"Well . . . do you mean right now?"

"Why not?"

"Well, I have to get back to the bank," she said in a tone that conveyed to him that there was no specific urgency.

"Of course," he said, sounding a bit disappointed.

"I suppose that my father and Mr. Duffy could hold down the fort for a *little* while," she said quickly. Though she had not yet decided whether the man from Denver was courting material, she certainly did not want to close the door—at least not as impulsively as she was in the habit of doing.

They sat in the same dining room at the Gallatin House as they had the night before, sipping coffee and sharing a croissant.

When the time came for Hannah to say that now it *really was* time for her to get back to the bank, she picked up her bag of mail and extended her hand.

"Thank you again, Mr. Phillips. Perhaps we'll run into one another again before you head back to Denver."

"That would be a pleasure, Miss Ransdell . . . Oh, one thing I've discovered since last night carries good news for your father and Mr. Stocker."

"What's that?" Hannah asked.

"The railroad . . . the Northern Pacific . . . Fred Billings has got the financing together to resume construction and will be building the tracks through Gallatin City."

"That will be wonderful news for us all," Hannah smiled.

"It will *certainly* be wonderful news your father, and my father's other surviving partner, to own land through which the rails will pass."

Hannah detected a trace of bitterness in his tone, but this was quickly washed away by his changing the subject. Talk of the railroad turned to talk of railroads in general, and thence to the general topic of the "progress" that railroads were bringing to the West. Dawson Phillips, Jr., smiled when he spoke of the changes he had seen in Denver in recent years, and Hannah found herself captivated by his charm.

She almost blushed when he politely, though nervously, asked whether he might enter into personal correspondence with her.

"Of course," she said with a smile.

disliked Cole, it was just that he had an attachment to the
status quo, and having to let a bounty hunter with a warrant
use his jail cell was not part of the status quo. Cole had
negotiated a deal for the use of Morgan's single cell for two
dollars a day, plus another dollar for a place for him to sleep
in the sheriff's office.

In the long years that he had been the sheriff of Copperopolis, Morgan had seen a lot of things come and go, and
the gradual quieting down of the town suited the way that
he imagined living out his later years.

Copperopolis was not much of a town, and as tedious as
that was, Cole was pleased. For the same reason that he had
been anxious to avoid towns entirely, he liked a small place
with minimal comings and goings, which allowed him to
keep the low profile that he desired. He did not want word
of his whereabouts to get back to Gallatin City.

Copperopolis had not always been a one-horse town. In
the years immediately after the Civil War, it had been a
boomtown of sorts for the reasons suggested by its name. It
never became the metropolis that its namers had imagined,
and its fortunes began running in the opposite direction
when the fires of avarice began burning brightly at Confederate Gulch. Why work your fingers to the bone for *copper*
when you can work your fingers to the bone for *gold*?

Cole had not exactly come voluntarily to Copperopolis,
but with a prisoner lying bleeding in the snow, he had but
two choices—the obvious one, and finding medical attention
to patch him up. Cole did not want a repeat of Milton
Waller's final days, and he was determined not to abide the
"dead" part of his prisoners being wanted "dead or alive."

Jeremiah Eaton had suggested Copperopolis as the nearest place that had a doctor, and thus Cole had come. Jimmy
Goode was in a bad way when they had ridden into town
the following day, but the doctor knew his way around a
gunshot wound and lacerated wrists. That left only the wait
for Goode to be well enough to travel. It seemed a terrible

waste of energy, not to mention cash, to save a man for his own hanging, but Cole wanted to see the look on the faces in Gallatin City when he rode in with half of the Porter boys' gang still *alive*.

When he had recovered sufficiently to speak, Jimmy Goode claimed to be sorry, and he claimed to have learned his lesson. Whatever lessons he applied to whatever he had left of his misspent life, he would be applying them without the use of his right arm below his shattered elbow.

"Damn you to hell, bounty hunter," Gideon Porter barked in his usual manner of greeting, as Cole went back to check on him in Morgan's cell. "When are we gonna get out of this piss-hole?"

"You're awful anxious to get home for your own necktie party," Cole observed.

"I told you, bounty hunter," Porter said smugly, consistently insisting on calling Cole by his profession rather than by his name. "I told you my friends in high places won't let me hang."

"When are you gonna tell me the names of those friends in high places?"

"I done told you I *ain't* telling you."

"Suit yourself," Cole said, turning his back on his prisoner and slamming the outer door to the cell area.

Bladen Cole had been spending his days pacing back and forth in the snow between the jail and the doctor's office, where Goode's leg was manacled to an iron cot, and playing penny-ante poker with the middle-aged woman who owned the saloon that was conveniently located on the ground floor of the building where the doctor kept his office. To date, he had lost nearly seventeen dollars. Copperopolis was no metropolis.

"Slow this afternoon, Mary Margaret?" Cole asked as he walked into the saloon.

"Every afternoon's just peachy here in paradise," the proprietor said from behind the bar. Though her name suggested that she was a long-ago defrocked nun, it was clear that the things she had seen and done in her lifetime were beyond the imagination of most nuns. She had come with her husband in the boom years of Copperopolis and had stayed on after a mine explosion made her a widow.

"You here to lose another five dollars, Mr. Cole?" Mary Margaret asked as she turned to face him.

"Reckon," he said, pulling up a chair at the table that had become *his* table in the days he had been in Copperopolis.

Mary Margaret rolled a cigarette and sat down opposite him.

"When you gonna let me pour you a shot, Mr. Cole?"

"As I been tellin' you, Mary Margaret, I've gotta keep a clear head to keep an eye on my two rascals."

"The doc says the one upstairs there with his arm half-shot-off kidnapped a little boy off a homestead up in the Little Belts," she said, making conversation as he dealt the cards.

"That's about the size of it," Cole confirmed. He had been noticeably tight-lipped about his prisoners since he rode into town. Mary Margaret had described herself as being "not one to pry," but she was naturally curious.

"How does a feller get into a line of work like bounty huntin'?"

"Are you contemplating a career change?" Cole asked as he studied his cards and drew two.

"I figure *I'd* be the one on the lam," she said thoughtfully as she studied her cards.

"That so?"

"Yep. Figure I'm gonna have to shoot the dealer after gettin' a hand like this," she said disgustedly.

"You bluffin'?" Cole asked.

She just shook her head.

He threw a couple of extra coins on the table.

When Cole proudly displayed a full house, Mary Margaret tossed over all four jacks.

"You been at this long?" she asked.

"Not long enough to tell when a young lass like yourself is bluffin'."

"Not poker," she clarified. "Bounty huntin'."

"Few years," he said. "I had a town sheriff job down in Colorado for a while, but my feet started gettin' itchy."

"What was her name?" Mary Margaret asked as Cole shuffled and dealt.

"Whose name?"

"The woman down in Colorado that made you get itchy feet," she smiled.

"Didn't say it was a woman who made my feet itch."

"Oh, come on," she laughed. "I've been around the block enough times to know that there's only two things that'll get a man over the age of twenty-five to feel like he's gotta pull up stakes. By the fact that you've taken to deliverin' wanted men to lawmen, I can rule out the one that involves runnin' from the law."

"Sally," Cole said. He figured there to be no harm in talking about his almost wife. Mary Margaret was old enough to be his mother, and he figured her intentions to be more nosey than romantic.

"Who was the feller?"

"Cardsharp named Hubbard . . . heading out to San Francisco." He didn't ask how she knew there was a "feller."

"Were you married to her?"

"Nope . . . almost."

"Almost don't cut it for a lady," Mary Margaret said, shaking her head in a motherly way. "Did Sally marry the gambler?"

"Don't know. Reckon she has a lot more prospects out there if she didn't."

"Reckon."

"How about you, Mary Margaret?" Cole asked. "What made you decide to stay on in this town all these years?"

"In the time that I had with Mike in this place, it sort of became like home. I didn't have nothing anywhere else."

"No family?"

"We came over from County Tipperary when I was four.
My parents died in the fifties, my two brothers joined up
with the 74th Pennsylvania and got themselves shot at Chancellorsville . . . You weren't at Chancellorsville, were you,
Mr. Cole?"

"No, ma'am," he said, knowing that she knew he would
have been on the other side.

"So I stayed on here because there was no place else,"
she said with an affirmation flavored by a slight dash of
wistfulness. "How about you? Now that you know all about
me, what put you onto a life on the run?

"I can tell by your accent that you and I were not on the
same side in the war, but I consider that water to be long
past the bridge."

"No, ma'am, we were not. My family is still down around
Caroline County, Virginia. I rode with the raiders for a
couple of months in '65 . . . me and my brother, Will . . .
then we came west. We were down in Texas . . . ended up
in New Mexico."

"Where's Will now?"

"He never made it out of New Mexico," Cole said, trying
to be matter-of-fact. "Got shot in a bar fight. I got one of
them who did it. Other got away."

"You're still hunting him, aren't you?" Mary Margaret
asked sagely.

"Still looking around . . . not exactly hunting."

"Guess that's why you didn't stay settled down there in
Colorado when Sally ran off. Hope you find him. Hope you
find somebody to fill that hole that Sally left."

"I never said anything about a hole," he replied
defensively.

"Didn't have to," she laughed. "In all my years of standing behind yonder bar, I've heard it all . . . and I've heard it
so many times that I don't have to hear it . . . I can read it in
their eyes."

"Reckon I'm bothered by it to a degree," Cole admitted.

"I suspect that when you're ready for courtin,' you'll know it."

"I keep an eye open."

"I'll bet you do," Mary Margaret laughed.

"What about you, Mary Margaret?"

"Hmmm?"

"You keepin' an eye open?"

"Well . . . when Mike passed, it was not like he run off. He was taken . . . I sort of resigned myself to permanent widowhood. Once in a while there's somebody passing through."

"I suppose . . ." Cole nodded.

"I didn't mean *you*," Mary Margaret clarified. "I hope you won't take offense . . . or disappointment . . . but you're just a wee bit on the young side for me."

"My heart is broke," Cole said with a smile.

"If I was twenty years younger, it might not be," she laughed, rocking back in her chair.

"So you're keepin' an eye open yourself?" Cole asked.

"You never know what can happen," she said.

The way that her eyes flicked subconsciously in the direction of the jail, an idea came into Cole's head.

"Joshua Morgan?"

"Let's play some cards," Mary Margaret said, beginning to shuffle the deck again.

Cole had just succeeded in winning his first hand of the four they had played when the doctor came in. He looked cold and had a dusting of snow on his shoulders.

"You got something warm behind the bar, Mary Margaret?" he said.

"I'll put on a pot of coffee on," she said.

"Not that kind of warm," he said. "I just got back from delivering a set of twins out at the Edredin place. One of 'em didn't make it.

"Sorry to hear that," Mary Margaret said sympathetically

as she poured a shot of dark amber liquid from a bottle that she kept under the bar. This, Cole knew, was what she called "the good stuff."

"The missus took it real bad," the doctor confided as he sat down at the table and savored a sip of his whiskey. "So did her husband."

"How's the other one?" Mary Margaret asked in a motherly way.

"She'll be fine. Got a real set of lungs on her. Squealed herself pink in the first moments of life."

"That's a good sign," Mary Margaret said. Cole wondered if she had ever had children.

She dealt the doctor into the game without asking, and he drew a flush that topped his companions.

"Lucky day after all," he said without smiling. He raked the coins to his side of the table and took another sip.

"How's our patient?" Cole asked the doctor as they studied their next hands.

"He's on the mend," the doctor replied. "I've been keeping him pretty doped up because he's been in a lot of pain. He did almost more damage himself to his wrists than you did to his elbow. People don't seem to understand that you gotta clean a wound out real good as soon as possible or it will go to hell real fast."

"When do you suppose he'll be good enough to ride?" Cole asked.

"As I told you before when you asked that, it's been hard to say," the doctor replied. "But I reckon he could tolerate ridin' in a saddle in a day or two."

"Good," Cole said.

"You gettin' tired of us, Mr. Cole?" Mary Margaret asked teasingly.

"Not at all. I'm just anxious to get these jokers to the courthouse and get on with things."

"Hope you'll come back and see us," she said, smiling. Cole figured that she really would miss the company. With the onset of winter, there would be fewer people passing though.

"I don't know whether to think of you as a fool or a saint to pay good money to have me putting this character back together just to turn him over to the law," the doctor observed.

"In the first place, it's *his* money," Cole said, referring to the $200 that had been in Gideon Porter's saddlebags. "In the second place, there's a lot more to justice than getting these two into the dock."

The doctor just nodded.

# Chapter 20

———◆◆◆———

Hannah Ransdell had been back to the Gallatin House a time or two after young Mr. Dawson Phillips, Jr., had gone back to Denver. She had not gone there to dine, or to reminisce about a meal with a handsome city fellow, but to scrounge newspapers.

Out-of-towners of the sort who would tend to frequent Gallatin City's leading hostelry would be the type who would read newspapers. Being the out-of-towners they were, they would arrive with out-of-town newspapers, including big city newspapers, and said papers would be discarded once read. Hannah was bent on learning all she could about the railroading plans of Mr. Frederick H. Billings.

By cross-referencing the information in the news articles, she ascertained that after several years of the Northern Pacific being in bankruptcy, Billings was pouring money into it, tracks were being laid, and they were headed for Gallatin City.

Though it was not customary for a daughter to know the nuances of her father's business dealings, it bothered

Hannah that the banker's "assistant" had not known about a business deal that had so much potential.

Hannah had discerned the trace of bitterness in the voice of Dawson Phillips, Jr., when he spoke of this deal among the four partners, and in recollection, she sensed a trace of accusation when he spoke of it in light of the coming of the railroad. She knew that she was the type to overthink things, but the more she overthought this one, the more it seemed to warrant overthinking. The wheels in the back of her mind were churning like the driving wheels of a Northern Pacific locomotive.

Her father and his colleagues were certainly aware that the railroad would be coming and that they owned land across which it would come. What did it mean that her father and Mr. Stocker had inherited the interests of two men who had died violently in a crime that she considered unexplained?

Was her father somehow involved? He had not been present on that terrible night. Had this been by accident or by design? As much as she tried, she found it impossible not to think, much less *overthink*, the unthinkable.

The only way to clear her father from culpability in the unthinkable within the court of her own suspicions was to learn as much about the situation as she could.

When her father went out to lunch, she went to the old records, hoping to find out what her father had paid for the parcels of land north and east of Gallatin City. She occasionally had to look at the "old records" for one thing or another as part of her job, but when it involved going behind her father's back, it made her nervous.

She insisted to herself that she was doing nothing out of the ordinary. The old records, which were exactly that, and were *called* exactly that, were rarely consulted in day-to-day business, but *rarely* did not mean *never*.

Her heart jumped slightly when she found the first

payment issued by Isham Ransdell for property in the areas in question.

The next day, Hannah stopped by at the land office, where there were copies of recorded deeds. The clerk knew her father, but one of her school friends worked there, so Hannah waited for the man to leave before she went in.

"Hello, Phoebe," she said as she pushed open the door.

"Hannah . . . it's so good to see you . . . How have you been?"

Niceties having been concluded, Hannah explained to Phoebe that she needed to look at some old land records.

"Most of the public records are down at the county seat," her friend explained. "But we do have copies that list owners, deed numbers, tract locations, and things like that."

"That will do," Hannah said. "Thank you so much."

"Everything is filed by location," Phoebe said. "Here's a map with all the grid numbers . . . Hey . . . we should get together for lunch sometime . . . since we're both a couple of working girls."

"I'd like that," Hannah said. It really *would* be nice.

Gradually, Hannah calculated the exact locations of the property acquired by the four men. By multiplying her father's payments by four, she also knew what they had paid for the property. What Hannah could not calculate was how much it might be worth.

"GOOD MORNING, MISS RANSDELL, IT'S A PLEASANT surprise to see you here this morning," Richard Wells said as she came into his dry goods store.

In her unfolding plan, Hannah needed to talk to a businessman, and a businessman outside her father's circle of friends and associates. As a competitor of John Blaine in the retail world of Gallatin City, Wells fit the bill. The Ransdells traditionally shopped at the Blaine store because of the connection, so Hannah's coming in here was a surprise. Her smile on a cold winter day made it the *pleasant* surprise that Wells described.

"Haven't seen you here in a while, figured you to be one to shop over at Blaine's."

"I need some hat ribbon, Mr. Wells. I don't really care for what they have to offer."

"Let me see what I can do for you," Wells said, turning to a shelf. "Solid or floral?"

"Floral brightens up a winter day, doncha think?" Hannah asked rhetorically.

"Are you still working down at the bank?" Wells asked, making conversation.

"I sure am . . . Waiting for the right man to come along," she answered, telling it as she imagined he would expect to hear it.

"I'd think you'd not have trouble finding him," he smiled. "A man would be lucky."

"Thank you, Mr. Wells."

"And old Isham would be lucky too . . ." the shopkeeper continued, "lucky to have a son-in-law to take into the business."

Hannah bristled, but the retort she considered appropriate was neither polite nor in furtherance of her purpose.

She smiled, selected a nice length of ribbon, which really *would* look nice on a hat, and put a coin on the counter.

As she was putting the ribbon into her bag, she allowed a newspaper to tumble out.

"Clumsy me," she said. "Oh . . . did you see this? They're saying the railroad is coming."

"I believe it is," Wells said. "It has been long delayed, but old Fred Billings appears to be the man who will finally do the trick."

"What will that mean?"

"It'll mean that folks from right here in Gallatin City can be walking the streets of the Twin Cities in three days or so . . . or Chicago a day beyond that . . . and travel there in *style*," Wells said effusively. "It means that a merchant in Gallatin City, such as myself . . . such as Wells Mercantile . . . will be able to offer the ladies of Gallatin City the fashions of Chicago or even New York City . . . in a matter of a week or so after they have them in those places."

"My goodness," Hannah said, pretending not to have previously grasped such a concept. "What would it mean to property owners . . . landowners . . . in the area around Gallatin City?"

"Well, Miss Ransdell," he began in a schoolmasterish way, "the rails are being brought east from Tacoma, but those coming west out of Dakota Territory are likely to arrive first. That will mean that landowners out east of town will have what a speculator would call 'prime real estate,' if you understand what I'm saying."

"I certainly do, Mr. Wells," Hannah said. She did not have to pretend to be interested.

"The direction up toward Confederate Gulch and the gold fields, that would pretty much end up as prime real estate as well. There is much more advantage in those points of the compass than in the west, for instance. The rails coming from Tacoma will have to cross several ranges of mountains . . . the Cascades, the Bitterroots, the main thrust of the Rockies themselves . . . so they'll be a long time coming to Gallatin City."

"If I was buying land . . ." Hannah began with a hypothetical tone.

"Then I'd say you were a year or so *too late*," Wells chuckled with a raised eyebrow. "Those who bought before then will command a mighty pretty penny."

"My goodness," Hannah said. "I'll bet they will have doubled their money by the time the railroad gets here."

"Doubled and doubled," Wells said with a grin. "And doubled again after that . . . *at least*."

"Making the land worth eight times what it was worth just a few years ago?" Hannah summarized.

"At least." Wells nodded. "The railroad will need to lay down rails on ground, and it will have to get that ground from them who own it."


IF HANNAH RANSDELL HAD HOPED FOR HER RESEARCH TO put her mind at ease about her father, then she was disappointed. By way of the crimes perpetrated at the Blaine home, the rapidly increasing value of her father's holdings had doubled overnight. And the night of that doubling brought to her mind the most nagging of suspicions, the one which she longed not to have in her mind. He *might have* been there on that dreadful night, in harm's way, but he was *not*.

As she walked back to the bank, thinking the unthinkable, she felt tears on her cheeks.

"Are you all right?" Isham Ransdell asked as his daughter came in the front door and went straight to her desk.

"Yes . . . Why do you ask?"

"Your eyes are red and likewise the tip of your nose."

"It's cold today, Father," she said dismissively without looking up from the papers she was shuffling on her desk.

The dialogue might have taken further turns had Edward J. Olson not walked through the door at that moment.

He went straight to Hannah's father's office.

Though the door was nearly closed, she did catch fragments of their conversation. The bounty hunter was mentioned, and she heard Olson use the phrase "dead or alive."

# CHAPTER 21

JIMMY GOODE HAD BEEN MORE DEAD THAN ALIVE WHEN he had been led, slumped over in his saddle, into the tiny former mining town of Copperopolis. When he rode out, he was more alive than dead—but just barely. As he watched Bladen Cole dig the stiff and frozen body of Enoch Porter out from beneath a pile of snow behind the city's jailhouse, he knew that this might have been his fate as well.

Goode's right arm was chained to his left just as it had been on the night of his escape, but today it was chained in that manner only as an anchor, because his right arm could never again be used for anything more. His hand was still there, and likewise a healed wrist, but he had no use of either.

They had waited out a storm and left before sunup on the second day following the doctor's pronouncement of Goode's being well enough for travel.

The storm having been more wind than snow, the ground was mostly bare as they climbed down out of the Little Belts and into more level country. It was, Cole thought, to keep with Natoya-I-nis'kim's analogy of his having taken on some

spirit of the grizzly, like emerging from the hibernation of
the snowy days spent in Copperopolis.

Descending out of the mountains, Cole hoped to pick up
the headwaters of Sixteen Mile Creek and follow its canyon
downstream to the Missouri. He had not chosen the main
wagon road, which led down toward Diamond City, but a
less used trail that promised a shorter distance to his final
destination.

"You stupid pup," Porter said assertively as Goode fought
with one hand to keep his horse from snatching a bunch of
grass, exposed above the snow along the trail.

"Back atcha, Gideon Porter," Goode said defiantly.

In the days prior to Jimmy Goode's escape, the two prisoners had ridden mainly in silence—Gideon Porter brooding and angry, Goode silent and intimidated. After their
days apart during Goode's moment of freedom and days of
convalescence, the social dynamic had changed. For Goode,
who had stared down death and still rode upright, Porter
was no longer so imposing. He saw his onetime taskmaster
as an increasingly disheveled man, his long-gone fancy
boots replaced by a pair of simple moccasins that the bounty
hunter had bought for him.

Cole chuckled to himself at hearing Porter's onetime
lackey speaking his mind. All in all, though, he'd preferred
the days of sullen silence to the incessant bickering that now
filled the air.

"They're gonna hang us just for being part of this, ain't
they?" Goode asked Porter.

"Shut up your mouth, Goode. I don't want you talkin'
about that."

"I know I ain't very smart, but they wouldn't have sent a
bounty hunter after us unless they was fixin' to string us up."

"I told you to shut up about that," Porter demanded.
"You're too damned stupid to be thinkin' about that."

"Too stupid to be thinkin' about my *own neck*?"

"Ever since your mama dropped you on your head when

you was a baby, you been tryin' to think," Porter said angrily. "And you ain't very damn good at it or you'd know that they can't hang nobody for a killin' that was done by somebody else."

"I hope that those friends of yours back in Gallatin City can . . ." Goode started to say.

"I told you to *shut up!*" Porter interrupted.

Cole wondered about Porter's friends in Gallatin City, and he wondered about them a lot. Long rides are an incubator for wondering, and this was a topic to which Cole's mind kept returning.

Cole had also done a lot of self-analytical wondering about his own motivations for wanting to deliver Porter and Goode alive, when delivering them dead would have been so much easier. Had he decided on the latter course, he would have been in and out of Gallatin City by now. It would be untrue to say that the idea of shooting both Porter and Goode had not passed through his mind on several occasions. He had certainly been handed opportunities with legitimate excuses.

He could have simply delivered three bodies, collected his money, and been long gone—yet there was something that made him crave justice and truth over expedience. It caused him some degree of fright to believe this to be symptomatic of some latent nobility within himself. Bladen Cole, noble? It could not be, he insisted.

Though his mind may have been seduced into reflecting, Bladen Cole's senses were on his prisoners and on their trail. Five senses processed the routine sights and sounds and so on, but it was Cole's *sixth* sense that made him turn in his saddle and look back toward the route over which they had come.

The first reaction was the satisfaction that's always the product of surveying the miles you have put behind you on a long trip. Second came the realization that those miles behind were not unoccupied. Roughly two of those miles farther back, on a hillside in the distance, there was a lone rider.

Cole could see little at this distance except a blue coat and a brown horse, neither of which were distinctive, and neither of which he recognized. The rider was coming deliberately, but not quickly. He was visible for only a few seconds before he dropped out of sight behind some trees in the foreground.

The most likely explanation was that he was just another traveler, making his way along the same trail that Cole had chosen. It may have been a less traveled road, but it was not an *untraveled* road.

Was it simply and innocently this, or was this lone rider bent on the same intended mischief that had cost the lives of the man in the big hat and his companion?

Was the man a lone rider or was he merely one part of a whole gang who had gotten wind of Cole's passing through Copperopolis with prisoners who had a price on their heads?

Cole weighed his options. He assumed, or at least hoped, that he had the advantage of the man not knowing that Cole had seen him. The bounty hunter knew that if he had been riding alone, it would have been easy to leave the trail and double back, screening himself in the thick timber, to get behind his pursuer. With two cantankerous and sporadically bickering charges, this would be more difficult, perhaps impossible. It could also tip Cole's hand as having become aware that he was being followed.

"Let's pick up the pace," Cole demanded of Porter and Goode. "We have a lotta miles to cover."

"What does it matter if we hang on Tuesday or Wednesday?" Goode asked.

"Shut up, you good-for-nothing Jimmy Goode," Porter snarled. "I told you we ain't gonna hang."

Cole looked back, hoping to see whoever followed them. The man he'd seen was not in a hurry, and perhaps by getting Porter and Goode to speed up, he could put more distance between them and the unknown pursuer or pursuers. He hurried them across a broad, treeless area and paused when they had reached the stand of ponderosa on the far side. He was curious to see how many riders entered the meadow.

To Cole's relief, only the single rider appeared, and he was more than two miles behind.

Through the waning hours of the day, Cole managed to keep far enough ahead so that the man didn't seem to know he'd been seen.

Cole made camp quickly as the sun went down, choosing a place beside the trail in a V-shaped canyon where a man attempting to flank the campsite in the dark would find it impossible without making noise slipping across the shale that littered the hillsides.

Having made a fire, the bounty hunter positioned himself high on this hillside, telling his prisoners that he was going to take a "look around."

It did not take long afterward for the lone rider in the blue coat to emerge upon the scene of the camp. His eyes being fixed on the brightness of the fire, he would not readily notice Cole ensconced above in the shadows of late evening.

When viewed at close range in the firelight, the identity of the mystery man was revealed.

It was Sheriff Joshua Morgan.

He reined his horse to a halt and surveyed the scene briefly before he spoke.

"Looks like you got yourself in a considerably less comfortable state there than you had in my cell, Porter," he said, looking at his former lodger chained to a ponderosa trunk.

"Damn you, Sheriff," the man growled.

"Where's Cole?" Morgan asked, looking around as though he imagined the bounty hunter to be nearby.

"He ain't here," Goode offered, after a long pause in which the question went unanswered by the moody Porter.

"I can see that," the sheriff said. "That's why I was asking."

"Heard him go up yonder hillside," Goode explained. "Couldn't rightly see where on account of being chained here pointed t'other way."

"Here," Cole said from his perch.

"What are you doing way up there?" Morgan asked.

"I been watching a fellow trailing us all day, and I figured I wanted to be on high ground when he overtook us."

"That feller would be me, I reckon."

"Reckon so," Cole confirmed. "I never figured on you being one to be following us."

"Got to thinking," Morgan said. "Got to thinking as I watched you ridin' out that you might . . . could use a hand with these two scamps."

"Thank you for the thought, Sheriff, but I've come a long way on my own, and figure I can finish the job."

"I didn't mean to question your abilities, Mr. Cole," Morgan said apologetically. "I just wanted to offer my services. I hope you don't take offense."

"No offense taken."

"Good," the sheriff said with an exaggerated sigh.

"Sorry to have you come all that way for nothing," Cole said in a way that was not in the least apologetic.

"No need to apologize," the sheriff said with a smile, trying to lighten the mood.

"You're welcome to camp with us tonight before you head back to Copperopolis," Cole said, his offer framed not in the generosity of hospitality, but as a stern insistence that the sheriff clear out at first light.

COLE SLEPT FITFULLY AND AROSE BEFORE THE OTHERS when the only indication of the nearness of morning was the position of the moon in the western sky. The others still slept, Porter and Goode chained awkwardly to separate trees, and Morgan on the ground near the fire. He snored relentlessly, his head of white hair bobbing in the moonlight with each breath.

Cole entertained thoughts of kicking him to try to quiet him but did not.

The bounty hunter had no reason to doubt the sheriff's intentions, other than that sixth sense which had caused him so much consternation the day before. Was this sixth sense, this disquieting streak of exaggerated distrustfulness, part of the curse of the grizzly's medicine?

"Coffee?" Cole asked as the sheriff rolled from his sleeping bag, a sputtering sound on his lips.

"It's the middle of the night," the older man said, rubbing his eyes and scratching the several days' growth on his chin.

Cole gestured to the sliver of light on the eastern horizon.

Morgan just nodded.

"Coffee?" Cole repeated.

"Yeah . . . obliged."

"I drank a lot of your coffee in Copperopolis," Cole said, shrugging congenially.

"You're up early," Morgan said, stating the obvious, as Cole handed him a tin cup.

"Got some miles to get behind us."

"I was thinking . . ." Morgan began. "Ummm . . . I was thinking . . . about what we was talking about yesterday . . . about my offering to help you take these two in . . . and about your saying you didn't need no help."

"Don't believe I do," Cole said succinctly.

"Well, you had one of those two fellers get away from you once . . ."

"He ain't going anywhere again," Cole interrupted, referencing Jimmy Goode's crippled state. He had not mentioned to the sheriff that *both* of the prisoners had made escape attempts.

"You never know," Morgan said, shaking his head.

"Now, Sheriff, I *do* appreciate your offer . . . and I *greatly* appreciate your hospitality in letting me store one of my prisoners at your jail . . . but I paid you an agreed sum for that, and I consider our dealings to have come to a close."

"Listen, young man," Morgan said, playing the elder statesman card. "I have been in and around law enforcement and the care of desperados since long before you were saddling your own horse, and I know a situation where two gunhands are better than one when I see it."

"I will certainly grant you the years of experience, Sheriff, but I am willfully determined that I'll be carrying on alone."

Morgan sat for some time, thoughtfully staring off into the distance. At last he spoke.

"Is there any . . . ?"

"Nope."

"What if I was to *ask* you politely to include me in this?" Morgan asked.

"No. I have gone through just about everything, including coming damned near being dinner for a grizzly, to get to this point, and I am not in a mood to share the reward . . . That's what it's about, isn't it? The reward?"

"Well . . . not that I know what that reward might be . . . excepting that I can imagine it to be a goodly sum . . . but I would be a liar if I said that the thought had *not* crossed my mind."

"That's what I *thought*," Cole laughed sarcastically.

"I get barely more than room and board in Copperopolis," the sheriff complained. "I been there for years . . . ever since the town was *something* . . . and I ain't growing any younger."

"You were looking to sign on with me to bankroll a little change of scenery, then?"

"You could put it that way . . . I reckon," Morgan admitted.

"I just did," Cole said.

"I heard you talkin'. When we were sittin' around up

yonder, I heard you talkin' about not liking to be setting in one place too long."

"I've been known to use those words," Cole said with a shrug.

"Well, you aren't the only one," the sheriff insisted. "I have spent the last many years committed to exactly the opposite, to being planted firmly in one place, but a man gets to thinkin'. A man gets to wondering . . . A man gets to wondering whether it might be true that you *can* set in one place too long."

"A man *does* wonder," Cole agreed.

"So I got to thinkin' that I ought to grab hold of whatever opportunity that might come along to get on to some other landscape."

"So you rode out to give me a little sales pitch?"

"That I did."

"I see . . ."

"It ain't entirely about the money . . ."

"It ain't?"

"Well, I'd be a liar to say that ain't a *part* of it," Morgan clarified. "But I'd be a bigger liar to say that that's *all* there is to it."

"Itchy feet?"

"A man gets to setting, and he stops wondering," the older man said, looking Cole in the eye. "If you stop wondering . . . you stop thinking about anything besides what's inside of your own four walls . . . and you stop being alive."

"That's a pretty drastic view," Cole replied.

"What I'm saying is that if you get to doin' nothing but setting around . . . pretty soon you ain't good for nothing 'cept setting around."

"I suppose . . ."

"I figured that at my age, I don't have many more chances to change away from setting around. At my age, the body isn't as limber as it once was . . . even a day's ride like yesterday's makes a man feel mighty stove up. If I don't get around to goin' *now*, I *never* will."

"Isn't there *anything* left for you in Copperopolis?" Cole asked.

"Don't reckon on nothing that is worth me staying for."

"What about Mary Margaret?" Cole asked, recalling a wistful look in her eye with regard to mention of the sheriff.

"Mary Margaret?"

"Yeah, Mary Margaret?"

"What about Mary Margaret?" Morgan asked, almost indignantly.

"About her having this sort of dreamy expression when your name came up."

"Can't imagine that to be."

"Let me ask you this . . . Are you interested in her at all . . . you know . . . in her as a *woman*?"

"She's got a look about her, I'll give you that," Morgan said, barely repressing a grin. "But as far as her and me . . . I reckon she'd never give me the time of day."

"You ever ask?"

"Of course not," the sheriff exclaimed.

"Why not?"

"A man don't ask a woman nothing unless he's damned sure of a positive answer."

"Yeah . . . I understand," Cole shrugged, "but I bet you'd be more likely to get a positive answer from Mary Margaret than you seem to think you would."

"Do tell."

"It ain't my place to tell a man that he *hasn't* been too long in a place," Cole said. "That would be against my nature . . . but I *will* tell you that I think you're wrong to say you got *nothing* left for you back in Copperopolis."

# CHAPTER 22

---

THE HIERARCHY OF SOCIETY IN ANY COMMUNITY WILL have its center, its high and its mighty, and it will have its fringe. On the periphery of said fringe are the hangers-on, and the doers of odd and part-time jobs. Beyond that edge are the ne'er-do-wells, whose odd jobs are as often as not beyond the edge of what can be considered lawful.

In the hierarchy of society in Gallatin City, the latter caste certainly included the Porter boys, though they were not alone. Their names would be likely to come up in the same sentence with those of men such as Lyle Blake and Joe Clark, whom one might generously have characterized as losers.

For this reason, Hannah Ransdell did a double take when she saw Blake and Clark seated at the same table in the Big Horn Saloon with Edward J. Olson.

On her daily rounds, whether it be to the post office, or to Mr. Blaine's store for supplies, Hannah's route did not often take her on the boardwalk that passed the Big Horn Saloon. It was an institution that was not patronized by ladies—as the women who were seen inside the Big Horn were not considered to be "ladies" by the women of society's hierarchy who considered *themselves* to be ladies.

So long as she held to the pretense of her place in the hierarchy of Gallatin City society, Hannah avoided the Big Horn Saloon.

This is not to say that the place did not have a certain risqué allure, but she imagined that the allure of the laughter and the tinkling piano might not stand up to the reality of the stench of stale beer and tobacco smoke that often wafted beyond the swinging doors.

But for the company he was keeping today, Hannah would not have thought twice about seeing Edward J. Olson in the Big Horn—the rules of the hierarchy that governed ladies did not apply to gentlemen—but seeing him with Blake and Clark was surprising. What business did her father's "right-hand man" have with these lowlifes?

She wished that she could just stroll into the Big Horn, order a beer, feign surprise at seeing Olson there, and ask him point-blank—but, of course, she *could not*.

She wished too that she could just stroll into the bank and ask her father what his "right-hand man" was doing at the Big Horn in the middle of the afternoon with Blake and Clark—but, of course, she *would not*.

Hannah did not, however, refrain from asking; rather she did so indirectly.

"What errands do you have Edward J. Olson doing for you these days? I haven't seen him in the office for a day or two."

"Some things out at the ranch," Isham Ransdell replied without looking up, giving a matter-of-fact answer to a matter-of-fact question. "Getting some men to rebuild the shed so we can bring in more hogs in the spring . . . Pork prices are on the rise again . . . good time to get into hogs."

"What do you hear from your bounty hunter?" Hannah asked, not commenting on the evasiveness of his reply.

"I've heard nothing since I got that letter postmarked out of Fort Benton," he said, looking up from his desk. "Why do you ask?"

"Just wondering. I heard you and Mr. Olson talking about it the other day."

"Yes . . . we were wondering ourselves," he replied. "The man said he was headed into Blackfeet country. There's no telling what might have happened out there."

"Do you reckon that he'll bring them back alive?" Hannah asked.

"One way or another, I hope he brings them *back*," the banker said. "Could be that they'll *all* wind up under this winter's snow with Blackfeet arrows in them."

Hannah grimaced slightly at the thought of the handsome bounty hunter with the showings of a nice beard lying dead on the wild and distant plains.

"Do you prefer the Porter boys dead or alive, Father?"

"Well, wanting a man, even a *Porter*, to be dead, is not something a man likes to talk about with his daughter . . . but I will say that justice would be done either way."

HANNAH RANSDELL LEFT WORK AT HER USUAL TIME. IT was her custom to leave within an hour of the bank's closing in order to prepare supper for herself and her father, who usually remained at his desk until around seven.

As usual, the walk home took her past the Gallatin City General Mercantile and Dry Goods. Even all these weeks after the murders, people still called it "Mr. Blaine's store." If she needed something for the meal, she could always stop in and get it. Today, she had neither reason nor intention of doing so—until she saw Lyle Blake and Joe Clark walking into the place.

The embers of curiosity that remained from her having seen them in the Big Horn with Olson burst into flame. She impulsively followed them. Unlike the saloon, Gallatin

City's largest store was frequented by those from all strata
of the social hierarchy.

Hannah had no notion whatsoever of what she could or
would accomplish by following Blake and Clark, but neither
did she have any question that she should.

She inserted herself into a place where she would appear
to be examining goods on the opposite side of a large rack
from where the men were picking out beans and hardtack.

"Three days' ride, I figure," Blake said. "Gotta have
enough provisions to go up and back."

Clark disagreed. "I reckon four."

His partner admonished him "That's 'cause you're a lazy
sonuvabitch. Anyhow, I don't reckon on havin' to ride all
the way to Copperopolis."

"You reckon they left by now?"

"Yeah . . . I figure they must have," Blake affirmed.

"One of 'em's wounded, though," Clark cautioned.

Hannah wondered who they might be describing. She
remembered having heard once of a place called Copperopolis, but she could not recall where it was.

"They're not coming very fast if one of 'em's wounded,"
Clark continued.

"I figure we should get to 'em somewhere there on Sixteen Mile Creek," Blake said.

"We gotta . . . There's too much traffic comin' down from
Diamond City once you get as far as the Missouri."

"You figure we gotta kill 'em all?"

Blake's question was not the sort one should be discussing in public in the afternoon, but the whiskey provided at
the Big Horn Saloon, even with its presale watering down,
had loosened his tongue considerably.

Far from being appalled by talk of murder, Hannah was
only gripped by stronger yearnings of curiosity. Had they
had more of their wits about them, they would have seen
her craning her neck to hear them.

"Olson said that there is no way the Porter boys can show

up alive in Gallatin City," Clark asserted. "Olson said there's no way they can be allowed to point fingers at them who can't have fingers pointed at them."

"What about the bounty hunter?"

"Guess he probably knows what Olson don't want told. I guess he's gotta get himself killed too."

From this exchange Hannah recoiled.

Talk of murder was one thing when it was in the abstract, like the plot of a dime novel, but quite another when the intended victims were the bounty hunter and the Porter boys.


HANNAH RANSDELL SAT AT HER DESK, STARING AT THE notes she kept in her bottom drawer. Her head was spinning. After the conversation she had overheard the day before at the Gallatin City General Mercantile and Dry Goods, she could concentrate on nothing but her secret project.

She had found and followed the paper trail of the acquisition, and she had seen how the death of any member of the foursome would benefit his partners. She had calculated the value and confirmed that it would increase—if not eightfold as Richard Wells had estimated—at least *many* times.

Hannah had discovered that her father's net worth had at least doubled as a result of the murders. Had this been by coincidence or design?

She had dreaded the unthinkable hypothesis of her father's involvement in eliminating his partners on the eve of their jointly held land doubling and doubling in value, and then doubling again.

She had held out hope that it was all mere coincidence, despite the pronouncements of her overactive imagination. There had been no real and true reason to believe otherwise, despite the way it might *appear*.

That is, until she heard of her father's right-hand man ordering the deaths of the men who could point their fingers at Isham Ransdell himself. Lyle Blake and Joe Clark would kill the Porter boys and the bounty hunter, and with this, the fingers would never be pointed.

Her father.

Could it be?

*How* could he be involved in this?

Her *own* father.

"Hannah, what's wrong?" Isham Ransdell said as he came into the bank. "You don't look well."

She had gone to her room before dinner the night before and had left the house before him this morning. He had thought her to be ill, but in reality, she could no longer look him in the face without breaking into tears.

"I'm not," she stammered, "I'm not feeling well . . . May I go home?"

"Yes, of course," the banker said.

Once on the street, Hannah walked uncertainly in the direction of her home.

What should she do?

Conventional wisdom told her that murders and murder plots should be reported to the sheriff—but he was dead, gunned down by the same killers who had doubled the value of her father's land.

There was Deputy—Acting Sheriff—Marcus Johnson, but he was on light duty, recovering from wounds suffered in the same shootout that killed the sheriff. She could tell *him*, but what evidence did she have to offer?

None.

In the hierarchy of Gallatin City, what was the place of the daughter who accused her father of ordering brutal killings, and who did so without evidence?

What should she do?

What *could* she do?

She walked aimlessly, tossing the facts over in her mind and replaying the sequence of events.

Suddenly, it dawned on her.

She realized what she could do. She realized who she

could tell. There was *one man* she could tell—the only survivor among the Big Four of the brutal assault on the Blaine
home!


"IS MR. STOCKER IN?" HANNAH ASKED THE CLERK IN
Virgil Stocker's law office.

"Do you have an appointment?"

"No . . ."

Declining to go away and come back in an hour, she
waited in the chair offered, watching the hands on the clock
grind slowly around its face.

An hour passed, and then the better part of another.

"Mr. Stocker will see you now."

*Finally.*

The scarring on Virgil Stocker's face was still ugly, red
and not fully healed. Hannah felt pity for a man likely to be
disfigured permanently. She had seen him only a time or
two since the murders, and then only at a distance, so the
sight of the injury was jarring.

"Good morning, Miss Ransdell, how are you?" He
smiled, standing up behind his desk as she entered his office.

"How are *you*?" Hannah asked, looking at his face. "Are
your injuries healing?"

"As good as can be expected, I suppose," he shrugged.
"How is your father?"

With the mention of her father, she could not hold back
the tears. The attorney leaped up to pour her a tumbler of
water, which she accepted gratefully.

"Thank you for seeing me," she said when she had
regained her composure well enough to talk.

"Of course."

"I have come to you on a grave matter."

"What is it?" Stocker asked sympathetically.

"It's about my father . . ." she said, breaking once again
into tears.

"Is he all right?"

"I believe that he may have been involved," Hannah said between sobs. "I think that he may have been behind what the Porter boys did that night."

"That's impossible," Stocker said forcefully. "I've known Isham Ransdell for more than fifteen years . . ."

"*I've* known Isham Ransdell for twenty-five years," Hannah interrupted. "Nobody can be sadder about this than *me.*"

"What makes you think that it was he?"

"The will . . . Mr. Phillips's will . . . I learned that with this land that the partners purchased . . . the partners had right of inheritance."

"That's correct," Stocker nodded.

"I've learned that when the railroad reaches Gallatin City, the land will be worth about eight times its original value."

"It is certainly true that the value will increase as the railroad approaches," Stocker said thoughtfully. "But the fact that an investment pays off is no motive for *murder.*"

"But the right of inheritance?" Hannah replied.

"Miss Ransdell, you have a superb head for calculation . . . for putting two and two together with respect to the value of the property to the railroad . . . but by your reasoning . . . by the inheritance issue . . . *I too* would have had a motive for the killings."

"But you were hurt . . . and my father *wasn't there.*"

"Yes, but that's just circumstantial . . ."

"That's what I thought . . . until . . ."

"Until?"

"Until I saw my father's right-hand man . . . Edward J. Olson . . . with Lyle Blake and Joe Clark . . ."

"I see," Stocker said. "They're not exactly the most upstanding citizens around these parts . . . but this is still what we would call 'circumstantial' in the eyes of the law."

"Until I overheard Blake and Clark in Blaine's store," she said, dabbing at the tears on her cheeks with her handkerchief.

"What did . . . ?"

"Edward J. Olson has ordered them to go *kill* the Porter boys."

"Why would he?"

"So they can't point their fingers at *my father.*"

"I think you're just jumping to conclusions," the attorney said sympathetically. "I'm sure that it's all a big misunderstanding. Your father couldn't possibly . . ."

"I just wish I could get away," Hannah said.

"Yes," Stocker agreed. "A change of scenery can always do wonders for a person's mood. Do you have anywhere . . . ?"

"I have a friend down in Bozeman who has wanted me to see her new baby," Hannah replied. "The child must be nearly walking by now."

"That sounds like a wise course indeed," Stocker said. "While you're gone, I'll look into the matter. I'm sure that there is an explanation, and I'll find it. Everything will be back to normal by the time you return."

Hannah Ransdell thanked Virgil Stocker and took her leave.

Yes, a change of scenery *was* called for.

Visiting Rebecca and the baby would be a welcome delight. However, under the present circumstances, when a mystery so vexing had to be resolved, she questioned whether she should, indeed whether she *could*, pamper herself with an activity carried out purely in the indulgence of her own pleasure.

As she went to the stage company office to purchase a ticket on the afternoon coach for Bozeman, the wheels were turning in her mind. She knew that she needed to keep her attention on the task at hand.

Instead of returning to the bank, she went home to pack her bag.

As usual, she set the table for dinner, but she set it for one. She left a note for her father on the dining room table, explaining that she was going out of town for a week to visit Rebecca, whom she had not seen in some time. She knew that he knew that it was not like her to go off on a whim like this, but men generally thought of women as impetuous, so she was merely fulfilling a stereotype. Hannah scorned the idea of filling the pigeonhole of the inexplicably impulsive girl, but rationalized that there was no harm in using the stereotype to her advantage. Certainly, she should be allowed to use every means at her disposal in the furtherance of the task at hand—that being the resolution of the conundrum that continued to haunt her at every turn.

Yes, a change of scenery *was* called for.

# CHAPTER 23

———◆×∗×◆———

LOOKING OVER HIS SHOULDER AS HE RODE, BLADEN COLE watched the rider in the blue coat grow smaller and smaller and finally disappear in the soft haze of gently drifting snowflakes.

He hoped that he had imparted good counsel to Joshua Morgan. He was not accustomed to the practice of giving advice in matters of the heart, and he was therefore unsure that telling a man to bet his future on a woman was something he was qualified to do.

Selfishly, he was relieved to have the sheriff out of his way. Even if Morgan did an about-face the moment he returned to Copperopolis, he would still be two days behind. Cole would never see him again.

Thankfully, the bickering between Gideon Porter and Jimmy Goode had slackened. They were exhausted after a short night and their uncomfortable sleeping arrangements. Cole reckoned that Goode might even fall asleep in his saddle if given half a chance.

By early afternoon, they were within sight of Sixteen

Mile Creek, snaking between patches of ponderosa in the valley beyond. Here and there, the smoke from a prospector's cabin rose into the windless sky. Random snowflakes still fell like feathers escaping from a pillow. It was as though the sky really did not want to snow but a few flakes had slipped through the crevices in the pillowcase of low-hanging clouds.

Hoping to avoid as many of the cabins as possible, Cole left the trail. He knew that once they reached Sixteen Mile Creek it would not be hard to find it again.

Nor was he especially worried about a chance encounter with a prospector. Whereas a bounty hunter and his prisoners might raise an eyebrow elsewhere, here this fact would only convince the prospectors that they were merely passing through and not here to cast an avaricious gaze upon anyone's claim.

As he rejoined the trail on the banks of the creek, Cole was pleased to see that no one had ridden this way since the snow had begun falling early in the morning. They passed a place where a man was panning for gold. He had his gear stacked near where he was working, with his rifle at the ready.

Cole waved.

The man waved back with uncertain hesitancy and watched the three riders only long enough to be sure that they were not claim jumpers, before returning to work. Even all these years after the big strike at Confederate Gulch, everyone panning gold on Sixteen Mile Creek was certain that the next pan of gravel would be his ticket to El Dorado.

As it was growing dark, they saw another man at work on a sandbar that paralleled a stream entering Sixteen Mile Creek from the opposite side.

The man hailed them, raising his voice loud enough to carry across the sound and distance of the creek. "Howdy, strangers."

"Hello," Cole returned with a wave.

"Say there," shouted the man, "I hate to bother you . . . but could I trouble y'all for a hand?"

"What did you say?" Cole asked.

"I could sure use a bit of help from you men," he repeated. "My sluice got drug too far into the creek and I need a hand gettin' it back."

Cole surveyed the scene. At first glance, it appeared as though the man had turned one bank of the side stream into a junk yard. All manner of boxes, pipes, and other stuff was scattered along it from where the man stood to a shack that lay about a hundred feet upstream. Two large dogs wandered about, looking idly at the man. Cole could see a sluice box that was about twelve feet from shore and sitting at an angle.

"I'll see what I can do," he shouted back to the man. His mind told him to expect a trap, but his instincts told him that this was not one.

"I ain't goin' in that goddamn water barefoot," Gideon Porter snarled angrily, having overheard the conversation.

"Oh, shut up," Cole said, more annoyed than angry.

"Some sonuvabitch gave my boots to a goddamn Indian."

"Shut up, Porter. You're not barefoot."

"Moccasins ain't no damn good in a stream."

Cole sent the two prisoners to ford Sixteen Mile Creek first and followed behind them as was his custom.

"Looks like you're ridin' with a couple of captives there, mister," the man said when he saw that Porter and Goode were chained to their saddles.

"Yep," Cole said, confirming the obvious.

"You a lawman?" the man asked.

"He's a goddamn *bounty hunter*," Porter answered before Cole could say anything.

"I'll be danged to hell," the man said, looking at Cole.

"I'm just like you," Cole added. "I'm just trying to scratch out a living."

He then ordered the two men to dismount and stand next to the horses to whose saddles they were chained. The two dogs barked vigorously until the man hurled obscenities at them, whereupon they slunk away to eye the proceedings from a distance.

With Porter and Goode in a position in which an escape attempt would be awkward to the extreme, Cole directed his attention to the prospector.

"Name's Walz . . . Jake Walz," he said, extending his hand. He was an older man. He looked about sixty, though he may have been a younger man who had weathered to that appearance.

"Bladen Cole. These here are Porter and Goode. They got a date with the law down in Gallatin City."

"I won't ask why," Walz said. "Ain't in my nature to pry into somebody else's business."

"What do you need done?" Cole asked, looking at the sluice box.

"The current done moved my box out of this here channel next to the shore and out onto yonder bar."

"I see . . . and you need to have it dragged back in the channel here."

"Yes, sir . . . I been trying to get it back. Workin' at it for more than a week. I had debated callin' out for help as I done with you, but . . . I'd be mighty obliged if you could help me."

"Let's figure the best way to do this," Cole said, studying the problem as presented. "You got a horse?"

"No, sir," Walz said with a degree of sadness. "I did have, but I had to sell her off. All I got's the dogs."

By his tone, he did not hold his canine companions in high esteem.

"Sorry to hear that," Cole said sympathetically. Apparently, prospecting did not afford the steady income that would allow a man the luxury of keeping livestock. "Guess we could use mine."

Walz waded into the frigid water to attach a rope to one end of the sluice box, while Cole anchored the rope to his saddle horn. The roan then pulled the sluice a few feet through the stream.

By repeating this process several times with the rope attached to various places on the cumbersome contraption, they were finally able to reposition it to the prospector's satisfaction.

When they were at last through, the sky was dark and snowflakes were falling heavier than before.

"Since its gotten too dark to travel, and since I've helped you out here, I was wondering if we could make camp up yonder in that clearing above your house?" Cole asked.

"Well . . ." Walz said thoughtfully as he stood on the shore shivering in his wet clothes.

He obviously prided himself on living alone. Most men in his profession tended to become hermits over time, regardless of whether they had any proclivity in that direction before taking up backwoods prospecting,

"Well . . . I reckon that would be all right . . . but I don't have no grub to offer."

"That's fine," Cole said. "We got our own . . . probably even extra that we can share with you."

The man smiled at that possibility and scurried up the hill to his hovel to dry himself.

Cole was pleased at the bartering he had done. The dried meat was easily worth a campsite off the main trail along Sixteen Mile Creek, guarded by two dogs. However lazy they were, they were unafraid to bark at strangers.

Having set up camp in a place sheltered by a dense stand of tall cottonwoods, Cole took his prisoners down to Walz's house, carrying some dried buffalo meat that had been part of Cole's gift from O-mis-tai-po-kah and his people.

Walz welcomed them into his home, which was warmed by a fire in an ancient stove as potbellied as its owner. The house had the strong odor of having long been shared with the dogs, but at least it was dry.

"Nice place you got here," Cole lied. "How long you been out here?"

"Since '69 . . . I came up from Confederate Gulch in '69," he said. "Mighty nice of you to share provisions with me."

"Mighty obliged for a place to camp."

"I ain't had buffalo jerky in years. There used to be an Indian fella came through trading it, but I haven't seen him in . . . I can't remember when. I get me a couple deer every now and then . . . an elk maybe . . . put in a patch of onions and taters every year."

"You got a regular farm up here," Cole observed.

"Where'd you get this meat?" Walz asked.

"From the Blackfeet."

"Whatcha doin' up in Blackfeet country?"

"Doin' a little hunting."

"Get anything?"

"Yup."

"What's it like up there? I've heard tell those redskins up there are truly untamed creatures."

"Depends on who's writing the definition of 'tame.' "

"Well, I reckon if you can come back with your scalp intact, that's sayin' a lot."

"Reckon."

"He had him a little squaw up there," Gideon Porter interjected. "Didn't you, bounty hunter?"

"You didn't say you was a 'squaw man.' " Walz smiled lasciviously.

"Ain't a squaw man," Cole corrected, scowling at Porter. "I was takin' her back to her place after roundin' up some horses."

"How *are* their squaws?" Walz queried.

"Wouldn't know," Cole said.

"He shot my little brother for wantin' to find out," Porter said.

"Your brother got himself shot for tryin' to cut up her face."

Walz looked at Porter in disgust. Even to a recluse who had lived beyond the edge of civilization for a decade, the deliberate disfigurement of a woman's face was viewed with revulsion.

"The placers are still pretty active up this way," Cole said, changing the subject.

"People do all right." Walz nodded.

"That's good to hear."

"You thinkin' about it, Mr. Cole?"

"I don't have the patience," Cole said with a smile. "I don't like to be too long in any one place. That takes a special kind of man to put in all the years required."

"I don't reckon to be here forever, myself," said the man who had worked this obviously marginal claim for a decade. "I fancy myself as kind of a wanderer."

"I see," Cole said, wanting to laugh at the irony.

"I've got my sights set on some place warmer . . . like down in Arizona Territory."

"I've heard of some pretty good strikes down there all right. How long you reckon you got on this claim?"

"Are you sure you ain't lookin' to nose in here?" Walz asked suspiciously.

"Absolutely not," Cole assured him. "I like it warmer myself."

"Ain't in my nature to pry into somebody else's business . . . but I suspect you do move around a lot in your line of work," the prospector observed.

"Yep . . . Colorado . . . Wyoming . . . Like I said, I've developed a way of livin' that doesn't allow for staying around one place too long. I tried it down in Colorado and found out it didn't suit me."

"That's me too," the old man said thoughtfully. "I'm sure lookin' forward to gettin' a move-on myself."

"So long as you don't nose in on the bounty huntin' business."

"*What?*"

"That was a joke," Cole said. "I was just funnin' y'all . . . I would no more expect you to get into *my* line of work than I would expect me to get into *yours*."

"I see," the prospector said tentatively, before breaking into a broad smile. "Listen . . . can I let you in on something?" Walz asked in a hushed voice, dramatically leaning close so that Porter and Goode could not hear his words.

"Shoot," Cole whispered back.

"I'm gonna be outta here by fall."

"Fall's just past."

"I mean *next* fall."

"Oh."

"One more spring," Walz said confidently. "One more spring is all it's gonna take. You know how a placer works, Mr. Cole?"

"Well, I guess not exactly," he replied, sensing that a good story was about to unfold.

"A placer gets its gold from the mother lode."

"Like the one out in California?"

"Yep. It's the mother that keeps the placers populated . . . year after year after year. Every spring there's more color . . . new gold in the placer. Next spring is gonna be the *one* . . . The mother is gonna give up *so much of her color* that it will put the Gulch to shame. I can *feel it in my bones*. I know it. I can see all the signs . . ."

# CHAPTER 24

——◆◆◆◆◆——

A BITTER COLD WIND HOWLED HAUNTINGLY THROUGH THE trees. An hour after she ascended into the Belt Range, the reality of her situation dawned on Hannah Ransdell. The headstrong, single-minded woman remembered the impressionable young girl who had recoiled with horror at the terrible stories of "children lost in the woods" in these same mountains.

Hannah looked around at the thick forest, black and impenetrable, into which she had thrown herself. Her horse made slow progress, pausing to step over deadfalls and negotiate steep and slippery slopes. There were a few snowflakes in the air, but the only snow on the ground was in places where it had drifted deep in the storm a week ago and never melted.

With all the maneuvering and "going around" of obstacles that they had been doing, Hannah was sure that she and the mare would have gotten themselves completely and inexorably turned around if she hadn't had the presence of mind to pick up the old compass in the tarnished brass case which her father had given her so long ago.

Her father.

*Her father.*

Tears of anger came mixed with tears of sadness, and she wiped her cheeks on the sleeve of her riding jacket.

How could he have done this?

What would she say when she finally confronted him?

Would he say that he had done it for *her*?

Would he insist that he had done it for *her* long-term financial well-being?

Had she never known what he had done, her financial well-being would have eventually been greatly enhanced. He was far from being a poor man, but within a few years, he would be an extremely wealthy man, and she was his only heir.

Had it not been for her suspicious nature, things would be very different—and very much *easier*—at this moment.

Had she never known what she had learned in the long hours she had spent on her research, things would, indeed, be very different at this moment. She might be going home to a warm house, a warm meal, and a warm bath instead of riding though the dark forest that swallowed little children and impetuous young daughters of bankers.

What a fool she was to do this, she thought, as she listened to the moaning of the wind and the occasional whining *yip* of coyotes in the distance.

An unseen hand had snatched her and put her in this frightening place. That same hand now kept pushing her ever onward and pushing thoughts of retreat from her mind.

That hand, for better or worse, was her *own*.

Despite the leaden, overcast skies, she knew that it would soon be the hour of lengthening shadows. As it was, she knew that it would soon be the hour when darkness simply closed over these mountains like a black glove.

Part of her resolve demanded that she press on blindly.

She was single-minded about following through once she had decided to do something. Her mother had called her "bullheaded."

When she had decided that Lyle Blake and Joe Clark *must* be stopped, she had asked the question of *who* would stop them.

The answer was that she would have to do it *herself.*

*This* was definitely "bullheaded."

Now that the reality of this course of action was setting in, she wondered if she was crazy for making this impulsively imprudent decision. Before she had grown into the "bullheaded" teenager who had become the headstrong, single-minded woman, Hannah had been the impressionable young girl who recoiled with horror at those terrible stories of "children lost in the woods" in these same mountains. The dangers here were not fairy tales, though. They were real. Throughout her childhood, there *were* children who *really* never came back.

Part of her resolve demanded that she press on blindly, but another part cautioned that if she did not soon make camp, the blindness that came with night would be her undoing.

Tethering the mare to a tree in a patch of dry grass where her horse could forage, Hannah unrolled her sleeping bag on the leeward side of the root ball of a huge ponderosa, long ago toppled in a storm. She had brought a fistful of matches, wrapped in wax paper to keep them dry, but starting a fire under these circumstances took more effort—and more luck—than she had remembered, and *keeping* it going in the cold wind took even more.

The thought occurred to her that she was working up such a sweat starting the fire that she wouldn't need the extra warmth.

She thought this to be funny, and she laughed out loud.

The sound seemed so empty and so hollow when mixed with the deep baritone moan of the wind.

Her horse seemed not even to take notice.

She ate some of the bread that she had put into her saddlebags and wished she had brought more to eat. At least she
had remembered the compass and the old Winchester rifle
that was kept at the ranch.

As Hannah had boarded the stagecoach, she had made
sure that her presence was noticed by many. If her father
had inquired about her, the station agent would have confirmed her purchase of a ticket to Bozeman, and several
others would confirm that they had spoken with her about
the journey. Others had seen her waving as the stage pulled
out of Gallatin City.

When she asked to be let out at her father's ranch, she
was observed only by people who were headed to Bozeman.
None would be returning to Gallatin City anytime soon.
Even the stage driver would not be back for several days at
the earliest.

From there, she had moved quickly, driven by adrenaline
and that unseen hand. She saddled her own mare, whom she
had named Hestia after the goddess of home and hearth, and
who was kept at the ranch. She filled a canteen, tied a
bedroll to the mare's saddle, took the compass and rifle, and
headed north.

Instead of following a trail—for there was no human trail
that led straight across these mountains—she had followed
only the due north of her compass. She knew that this would
take her to the valley of Sixteen Mile Creek, where Clark
and Blake intended to intercept the bounty hunter and the
Porter boys, and she hoped that the shortcut would get her
there before either party.

Lying fully clothed in her sleeping bag with the Winchester beside her, she stared up at the sparks from her fire
soaring upward to meet the snowflakes coming downward.

HANNAH AWOKE WITH A JUMP, HER DREAM QUICKLY
disappearing into her subconscious like a prairie dog down

its hole. Hestia was snorting and sputtering and began pawing the ground nervously. Something was bothering her.

Hannah sat up and looked around. The snow had stopped
falling. Here and there she could see shafts of moonlight and
the moon itself through the trees. The fire had died down to
embers, so she jabbed it with a stick, trying to bring it to life.

The mare was growing more agitated, and Hannah wondered what was amiss.

Suddenly, out of the corner of her eye, she caught a flicker
of movement. Something was out there. She felt a nervous
chill.

Hestia reared and stomped.

Then Hannah saw it, the glint of the firelight in a pair of
eyes.

She pulled the Winchester from her sleeping bag and
stared into the dark woods.

The pair of eyes, moving in and out among the trees, was
low to the ground and about thirty feet away. It could be a
coyote, or it could be a *wolf.*

Coyotes are scavengers. Wolves are predators.

Thoughts and fears cascaded through her mind.

Coyotes are skulking opportunists. Wolves are
aggressors.

A wolf could attack her horse and leave her stranded on
foot in the wilderness—or attack *her* and leave her dead or
wounded in the wilderness. This was how people disappeared forever in these mountains.

She briefly wished that she had stayed to a more well-
traveled trail. This would have defeated her desire for a
direct route, but it would have greatly diminished the likeli-
hood of her present predicament. As aggressive as wolves
are, they generally shun places that are frequented by
people—but she was not now in such a place. She was in
the dark woods that belonged to the predator.

Hannah shouldered the Winchester. She was familiar
with this rifle. She had been firing long guns since she was

nine, and this very one since she was a teenager. The recoil
had knocked her down the first time, but she stood up and
fired again, determined not to let a piece of steel and walnut
get the best of her. Over the years, she had become quite
good with a rifle, and even her father had remarked about
her skilled marksmanship.

*Her father.*

If the wolf—if it *was* a wolf—was growling, it was not
the only one that night in the woods.

Whatever it was, its eyes were no longer visible.

Maybe it was scared off by the fire being stoked.

Maybe it sensed that Hannah had upped the ante by add-
ing a weapon to the equation. A quick kill of sleeping prey
was no longer possible.

If it was a coyote, such suppositions were within the
realm of the likely.

If it was a wolf, that would be an entirely different matter.

Hannah remained seated but eased herself back into the
protection of the tree roots. Their snarled arms, rising eigh-
teen feet into the air above her head, would protect her from
an attack from behind.

After five minutes that felt like fifty, she suddenly saw
another flicker of movement in the corner of her eye and
turned. There were the eyes again. There was that cold chill
on the back of her neck.

She aimed.

She squeezed.

The Winchester bucked in her hands as the .45-caliber
lead ripped into the darkness.

The mare reared and whinnied.

Hannah blinked her eyes instinctively to wash away the
effect of the muzzle flash on her pupils.

There had been no scream of pain or anxiety. She had
not hit whatever it was.

There was a better than fifty-fifty chance that a coyote

would have been scared off by the gunshot. With a wolf, the odds were much less.

Hannah took a deep breath and wiped her forehead on her sleeve.

Hestia continued to whinny and prance.

The monster of the dark was still out there, but she was no maiden in distress. She was armed with a Winchester. Of course, if she lost her horse, she would become a maiden in distress with a Winchester.

Time slipped by and Hannah felt herself relax. Gradually, she felt herself getting sleepy. Her eyelids grew tired.

Suddenly there was movement—*fast* movement.

Eyes—fierce orange eyes—eyes *coming*.

The rifle was more pointed than aimed.

The trigger was more pulled than squeezed.

The sharp *crack* of the cartridge being fired echoed into the night.

The scream was such as to curdle the blood.

Hannah felt the sharpness bite into her head.

A split second later, she realized that as she had instinctively jerked backward, a movement aided by the recoil, she had jabbed the back of her head on one of the gnarled roots.

She levered the Winchester to eject the cartridge, looked into the darkness, and exhaled held breath.

She saw movement and fired again.

Again, there was a yelp of anguish.

She had hit it twice.

Then she saw the eyes again, and a face contorted with both pain and rage.

Barely a dozen feet away, she saw an enormous wolf, which her eyes told her was the largest she had ever beheld.

Hannah felt her own eyes growing larger than they had ever been.

The thing was skulking away, but moving with great difficulty.

It turned, bared its teeth in an angry sneer, then crumpled to the ground.

Hannah just sat there, still holding the gun, breathing deeply as though she had just climbed a steep staircase.

At last, she stood, comforted Hestia, and thought about the home and hearth for which the mare had been named. Hannah bit into an apple that she had put in the saddlebags, and shared it with her steed. She wished that she had thought to bring coffee.

As Hannah waited for the light of dawn to penetrate the woods sufficiently for her to resume her journey, she tried not to think about the dead animal lying in her camp and cursed herself for initially forgetting that wolves hunt in packs. Fortunately for her, this one had come alone, or at least had come with easily frightened cohorts.

# CHAPTER 25

———◆✦◆———

FOR BLADEN COLE, THE THIRD DAY SINCE HE HAD LEFT
Copperopolis dawned as dark and gloomy as had the second,
though the snowfall had taken a momentary hiatus.

He bade farewell to Jake Walz and his dogs, having
poured the old man the first cup of coffee he'd had in months.
Walz explained that his fear of claim jumpers kept him from
straying far, and Cole wondered how he'd fare when he
finally did leave here—*if* he ever left the side stream off
Sixteen Mile Creek.

Cole hoped that the color really *would* run bright and
plentiful for the man come spring—but he believed that it
would not.

He could look into Walz's eyes and tell that they did not
see the same world that others saw. He had seen the same
look in the eyes of gamblers down on their luck. He had seen
that gleam of optimistic madness that expressed their firm
belief that the next hand, just *one more* hand, would make
them rich.

The gaming tables were no different than Jake Walz's

place, except that with the gambler, there was frequently a cardsharp to ease him onward with colorful promises. This thought made Cole think of Sally Lovelace and the look that had been put into *her* eyes by the guileful Hubbard down in Colorado. It was a disagreeable train of thought which Cole wished not to pursue, and he forced his mind back to the task at hand.

His father's watch told him that it was almost seven as they forded Sixteen Mile Creek to get back on the main trail, and the bounty hunter breathed a tentative sigh of relief. After today, only one more sleep separated them from Gallatin City.

There were tracks on the trail, laid down since the snow had ceased overnight, but they were headed the opposite direction. This, and the monotony and monochrome of the countryside were lulling. It was a landscape in black and white. The trees were black, and the thin covering of snow blanketed the hills and valley and merged into the clouds in a single shade of cold, bleak white.

Cole hated himself for having succumbed to this hypnotic dullness—the split second that the first shot was fired.

Porter and Goode, both riding ahead of him, jerked their heads up from their own respective daydreams at the sound, glancing around instinctively, looking for the origin of the shot.

The men each saw it almost immediately, a bluish puff of smoke hanging in the still air high on a hillside slightly ahead of them.

The sniper had chosen well, training his weapon at a place on the trail where the terrain offered no cover his targets might run for.

"*Hee-yaa . . . ride!*" Cole shouted, kicking the roan into a gallop and swatting the flanks of Gideon Porter's horse with his reins—though the two prisoners needed no urging to spur their horses into a run. Like Cole, they knew that the best reaction in a situation with no cover was to make themselves a *moving* target, and one that moved as fast as possible.

If the sniper had done well in choosing the place of his attack, his execution left much to be desired. Having failed to hit anyone with his first shot, he waited too long to fire his second. By this time, his quarry was in motion. Only luck would guide his bullet now.

Cole, of course, had problems of his own. He had lost effective control over two prisoners at full gallop on a snow-covered trail. If any horse stumbled and broke a leg in a snow-covered hole, it would greatly complicate matters. Meanwhile, there was the danger that Porter and Goode would escape. Though their being lashed together with forty feet of rope lessened the chances of this, it could not completely prevent it. Desperate men did desperate things, and both of these men had recently proven this axiom.

By the third shot, they were out of range, and soon they had put the shoulder of a hill between them and the shooter. Cole was about to order Porter and Goode to slow their pace, when another shot rang out from a different direction.

He heard the whiz of a near miss from a gunman who was a better marksman than his partner.

*"Dismount and take cover!"* Cole screamed with as much authority as he could muster. At least there now was cover to take. He might have been a better shot, but fortunately, this second bushwhacker had not done as good a job in picking a place to do his shooting.

Cole remained on the roan until both Porter and Goode had clumsily slid from their horses, then he grabbed his Winchester from his scabbard and leaped behind a nearby boulder, with his back to Sixteen Mile Creek.

As with the first sniper, the position of the second was revealed by bluish puffs of burnt powder and by the muzzle flashes of his rifle.

Having taken time to line up his own first shot, Cole squeezed the trigger.

The round impacted the rock behind which the second sniper was crouching, hitting close enough to spit up debris that the man no doubt felt on his face.

This apparently unnerved him somewhat, because he fired two shots in rapid succession which hit in the trees quite far from any of his targets.

Cole fired a second time but cursed when his bullet again hit the rock.

"Stay down," Cole growled when he saw Jimmy Goode start to move.

"He's gunnin' for *you*, not for us," Goode shouted back.

"You're wanted *dead or alive*, you idiot," Porter shouted. "You're worth as much to him dead . . . and you'd be a *helluva* lot less trouble dead!"

The impasse had the makings of a standoff.

It had taken only a few minutes to establish that neither Cole nor the sniper could easily hit the other, but *both* were pinned down.

Over the ensuing ten minutes, each side fired only as often as he thought necessary to remind the other that he was stuck where he was until the impasse was broken.

Cole realized that this would happen as soon as the first bushwhacker appeared. If the two of them could get Cole into a cross fire, things would change abruptly in their favor.

The bounty hunter's eyes were compelled to constantly scan the hillsides all around for sign of the other gunman, while the second sniper had the good fortune of knowing where his targets were.

CHANGES OF FORTUNE OFTEN COME IN UNEXPECTED FORM.

As Cole was studying the surrounding hillsides, he caught sight of a rider. What confused him was that this black horse was moving among the ponderosa on the hillside *opposite* the direction from which the other sniper was likely to come.

It was hard to get a good look in the thick trees, until the rider paused briefly in a small clearing slightly above the sniper's nest.

Cole couldn't believe what he saw.

The rider was a *woman*. By her narrow waist and the drape of her riding skirt, there was no mistaking this. She picked her way across the hillside with such ease that it made her seem to be simply taking a Sunday ride.

He was beginning to ponder the question of what a joy-riding woman was doing out here when a gunshot answered his question.

She had a rifle, and she had fired on the bushwhacker.

As Cole had been watching for himself to be outflanked, it had been his opponent who was outflanked.

The sniper turned and returned fire.

As the woman was now behind the trees, Cole could not see exactly what was happening, but the gunman's attention had definitely been diverted.

Cole squeezed off another shot, coming frustratingly close without connecting.

Suddenly, the man broke from his position and started running.

Cole fired again and missed.

He heard another shot from up on the hillside, and the woman emerged from the trees. Cole watched her put her rifle to her shoulder and fire again.

The running man abruptly slowed to a limp.

One of the woman's shots had hit him.

Seconds later, though, he was on his horse and galloping away.

Cole watched as the woman squeezed off another shot and paused to study the terrain between herself and the fleeing sniper.

Cole watched her maneuver the black horse near a deep ravine and apparently decide that it could not easily be crossed in time for a her to undertake a useful pursuit.

She turned, looked down at where Cole was, and began urging her horse down the steep slope toward him.

Cole had just caught his roan and was leading the horse back to where his prisoners were standing when she rode up.

He recognized her immediately. It was Hannah Ransdell.

She wore a snug-fitting, long-sleeved jacket over her black skirt, and a stylish, narrow-brimmed hat with a floral-patterned ribbon on it. Dressed in what ladies in Virginia would have called a "riding habit," she did, indeed, have the look of a stylish lady out for a Sunday ride. Except for the Winchester '73 which she carried in her gloved right hand.

"You're in trouble," she said soberly. "Those men are out to *kill* you."

"Wouldn't have guessed," Cole said in a sarcastic tone.

"I'm serious," she said, bristling.

"I believe you, Miss Ransdell," he assured her. "By the way . . . you *did* arrive at a fortunate time. What brings you to these parts?"

"To stop them from killing you . . . *and* Gideon Porter."

"So far that plan seems to have worked," Cole nodded, looking at Porter, who for once appeared speechless. "But they are still out there."

"I know," she said, studying the hillside. "But at least there's two sets of eyes to keep watch . . . and two Winchesters to stop them if they show themselves again."

"You're pretty good with that thing," Cole said, nodding to the rifle, which she held muzzle high, the butt resting on her hip.

"You mean good for a *girl*?"

"Did I say that?"

"You thought . . ."

"What I *think* is that *you* hit a man while he was on the run," Cole interrupted.

She said nothing more on the subject but merely looked back at the hillside.

"What have you been doing to these poor men?" Hannah

asked cynically as she observed Porter's scarred face and Goode's withered hand.

"These two fared better than Enoch," Cole said, nodding to the canvas-covered package tied to the last horse.

"I figured that was him," she said without emotion.

"We best get moving," Cole said as he mounted up. "Your hitting that one will not stop them, but at least it'll probably slow them down . . . and we'll want to get as far ahead of them as we can."

"We ought to be able to keep ahead of them if we stick to this trail," she said. "As I have learned from recent experience, riding across these mountains makes for very rough going."

"That ought to force them onto the trail, where we might have a better chance of seeing them coming," Cole suggested as he looked back down the trail. "But we need to get going and put some miles between us and them."

"Then let's make some miles," she said, touching the heels of her scuffed and muddied, though quite fashionable, riding boots to the flanks of her black mare.


THEY RODE THE FIRST OF THOSE MILES, AND MOST OF THE second, in single file because of the narrowness of the canyon, hurrying as much as possible without allowing the horses to get winded.

As the valley broadened, Cole reined the roan alongside the mare. He was curious to know what lay behind the auspicious appearance of Hannah Ransdell, especially in light of what he had concluded about her father.

"You said that you rode out here to save my hide and that of Mr. Porter there," Cole said without looking directly at Hannah. "How did you know that we *needed* saving? Who are those men?"

"Their names are Lyle Blake and Joe Clark," she said. "They're part of the same cesspool of town thugs that bred the likes of the Porter boys."

"How do you reckon that your friends were able to find us way out here?" he asked.

"They're *not* my friends," she snapped, glancing at him. "To answer your question, I happened to overhear them talking . . . talking about *you* headed for Sixteen Mile Creek from up north."

"How'd they know *that*?"

"They heard it from someone, who heard it from someone else, who saw you in a place called Copperopolis four days or so ago."

"So you followed them?"

"Not exactly," she said. "I came across the mountains. I wanted to get here first by taking a short cut. I *almost* did."

"How did you find . . . ?"

"It does not take a genius to figure how far someone would get after three or four days of riding from up at Copperopolis."

"Did your *father* send you?" Cole asked pointedly.

"My father certainly did *not* send me," she answered, her simmering irritability coming to a boil.

"When I saw you, I guessed that he might have sent you to check up on me . . . check up on how I was doing with this job he gave me."

"Well, I guess you guessed very, very *wrong*, Mr. Cole."

"Why *are* you here, then . . . making yourself the target of two men who aimed to kill us three and probably now aim to kill you as well?"

"Let's just say that I have a strong interest in seeing justice done," she said, looking at him with disdain. "Unlike *you*, Mr. Cole . . . I am not here because of a substantial sum of money."

"Well, I won't say I'm *not* doing it for the money . . ." Cole began.

"That's because you *can't* say that," she finished, biting back. "At least you can't say it with a straight face."

"If the *only* reason I have for being in this situation is the reward money, then I would have made what I'm doing a helluva . . . pardon me for my language in front of a lady . . . lot easier."

"Apology accepted, though I've heard worse," Hannah said sternly without looking at him. "How?" Hannah asked after a long pause. "How, *exactly* could you have made this any *easier*?"

"The warrant says 'dead or alive,' " he began.

"Yes, I'm well aware of that detail."

"Then you can probably imagine how much *easier* it would have been for me to bring Porter and Goode back like old Enoch. Without going through all the details, my life would have been a helluva lot easier with these cantankerous fools dead rather than alive."

"Why then, Mr. Cole?" she asked. "Why did you decide to do it the *hard* way?"

"Let's just say that I *also* have a strong interest in seeing justice done."

The canyon narrowed once again, bringing an interruption to their conversation which left many questions yet unanswered.

# CHAPTER 26

———◆✖◆———

"THANK YOU, MR. COLE," SHE SAID CRISPLY, TRYING TO maintain her facade of practical aloofness.

Late in the afternoon, the bounty hunter had offered her a slice of buffalo jerky. Hannah Ransdell was starving but tried her best *not* to appear so. She wished to deny him the satisfaction of knowing both how unprepared she had been for this venture and how much she appreciated his gesture.

She had lost her appetite after the anxiety of shooting Lyle Blake, but pent-up hunger had overtaken her and had dogged her for the past several hours. The meat tasted really good.

Hannah knew why *she* wanted Gideon Porter brought back alive, by why did *Cole*?

She had ridden to her rendezvous predisposed to his being merely a mercenary craving a reward, but his words suggested that there was more to it than she had believed.

It had surprised her greatly, and frankly confused her, that the bounty hunter had made a conscious decision to deliver at least part of the Porter boys' gang *alive* rather than *dead*. In this, his purpose coincided with her own—but she could not imagine *why*.

On the other hand, it annoyed her greatly to have heard him insinuate that she was the mere instrument of her *father* and that her motives in wishing to preserve the lives of Jimmy Goode and that detestable Gideon Porter were in the service of Isham Ransdell's interests—when exactly the *opposite* was true.

As the miles went by, the wind picked up, and with it a cold chill, although in its blowing it seemed to have parted the clouds, and there were now a few patches of blue showing.

"If it's any measure of consolation, Miss Ransdell," the bounty hunter said, "I don't think these men will try to attack us until after the sun goes down.

"Did I say that I needed consoling, Mr. Cole?" Hannah asked scornfully.

"The way that you've been biting at your lip when you look back at those yonder hills makes me think as much," he said with a slight smile.

As much as she resented the bounty hunter's verbal prods, she resented herself more for interrupting her resentment to admire the way his beard was taking shape.

"I would have to say that their presence in those hills concerns me a bit, as I suspect it does you as well," she said.

In fact, it troubled her greatly that Lyle Blake and Joe Clark were still out there somewhere stalking them. Her original plan, the plan which had taken shape back in Gallatin City when things seemed much simpler, had been to alert the bounty hunter and let him do whatever it was that gunmen did to relieve themselves of a threat. Instead, she too was now among the hunted.

"Yes, ma'am, I would be a liar to say that it is not a bother to me as well. Tonight worries me even more. Rascals like that are like the cowardly in the animal world who get their kills by attacking the unsuspecting under cover of darkness."

"I am *certainly* aware of that particular vexation," she said, referencing without describing her overnight wolf kill. She thought of mentioning it but decided such a tale would seem so improbable that he would take it as fabricated bragging, and it would therefore undermine the image of usefulness she hoped to cultivate in their mutual endeavor.

"I expect we'll have no shortage of vexations tonight, Miss Ransdell," he replied.

AFTERNOONS DON'T LAST LONG IN THE MONTHS WHEN THE cold winds begin to blow, and the clouds through which the patches of blue had appeared were starting to take on the golden hue that would precede the dreaded twilight.

Below and ahead of them now lay broad, open country stretching down toward the confluence of Sixteen Mile Creek and the Missouri. They were now less than a day's ride from their final destination, and Hannah could see the sense of relief in the bounty hunter's eyes.

Her eyes followed his, looking back into the Big Horn Mountains and the canyon of Sixteen Mile Creek, as though they were putting a monster behind them.

"I half expected that your friends wouldn't let us get this far," he said, glancing at the surrounding hillsides. "Your description of them as 'cesspool-bred thugs' suggests to me that you're just writing them off as fools. I would not have thought that of them, given that their ambush showed a certain amount of foresight in the planning."

"I did not mean to suggest that they were not wily in their conniving," Hannah clarified, "only that they were scum of the earth."

"Scum or not, I hadn't taken them for fools," Cole replied. "If the tables were turned, I would have thought it foolish to let us get this far."

"I thought you said that you didn't figure on them attacking us until after nightfall," she said.

"Didn't think it more than a fifty-fifty chance, so I didn't want to worry you."

"*You didn't want to worry me?*"

"No. Didn't much want to worry *me* either, I 'spect. We still got the most worrying time ahead of us. After nightfall will be the time when a man can slink up out of the darkness and not be seen coming on a distant ridge beyond rifle range."

"I don't appreciate your *keeping* things from me, Mr. Cole. I thought that we were in this *together*."

"We have both taken fire from these men, and we are *both* being hunted by them. I cannot abide you withholding information from me because you find me too fragile to take the worry."

"I don't much care for you keeping *me* in the dark either, Miss Ransdell," the bounty hunter replied with unexpected sharpness.

"What exactly do you mean by *that*?" Hannah replied defensively.

"I mean that Isham Ransdell's daughter shows up out of nowhere this morning with a chip on her shoulder as big as all outdoors . . . and tells me all coy-like that she's here to 'see justice done' and nothing more. If this ain't something to make a man wonder, I don't know what is."

"I am not being *coy*, Mr. Cole, and I am not lying when I say that I *am* here to see that these men get back to Gallatin City alive. That is the *only* reason I am here. If I hurt your feelings by making you think there's a chip on my shoulder, that's just *too bad*. I'm certainly not here to shelter your feelings."

She could feel her face growing red with indignation.

"It would be a lot easier on my feelings to ride with a less ornery companion," he said with a smile, reacting to her suddenly flushed complexion.

"Nor am I here to brighten your day, Mr. Cole, but to do *my part* in seeing that our common purpose is accomplished."

"Then you can tell me the *whole* truth about what's going on, Miss Ransdell?" he said, the smile gone from his face. "I suspect there is *some* truth in what you've said, but I suspect it to be *half truth*, and half truth is just the same as half *untruth*."

"I have *not* lied to you, Mr. Cole."

"Then tell me the part that's a half lie by its *not* being told."

"What do you mean by *that*?"

"I mean the part about you being Isham Ransdell's daughter . . . and him being absent from the room when those shootings took place."

Hannah felt as though the jaws of the wolf had seized her windpipe.

"What . . . makes you think . . . ?" she said, gasping and grasping for words as the tears welled up in her eyes.

*Her father!*

"Guess I touched a nerve," the bounty hunter said. "I can tell by your manner that we *both* know that the crazy notion that those people were shot over some trifle wrong that Blaine did to Gideon Porter is just a load of bull, and I will not apologize for strong language, because it serves my point."

"Which is?"

"That I figured out a long way back down the trail that Porter and his bunch got paid to do the shooting. And on his deathbed, Milton Waller *told* me so. I assume your daddy got my letter from Fort Benton?"

"Yes . . . There was nothing about . . ."

"Of course there wasn't," the bounty hunter said pointedly. "Would not have told your father what Waller said under any circumstance. But his words stuck with me since that night . . . and men don't tell lies on their deathbeds."

"What . . . ?" Hannah started to ask, fearing the worst.

"His words included something about a 'railroad,' and that there were four partners . . . three had to die . . . and only one could survive. We both know who among the four was *not* there."

*Partners. Her father. The railroad again!*

In the back of her mind, Hannah had hoped some evidence might emerge to the contrary of her worst fears, but instead, there was only this cold, hard confirmation, and also now the fact that the bounty hunter *knew*.

She turned her head, frantically wiping the tears from her cheek with a gloved hand.

"Once again, Miss Ransdell, why did your father send you out here?"

"Once *again*, Mr. Cole," she gulped between sobs as she reached for her handkerchief. "He *did not send me*."

"I guess what I've just said comes as a pretty big surprise then," he said, taunting her, watching her wipe her face.

"No, Mr. Cole," she said, blowing her nose. "It does *not* come as a surprise. I too have seen evidence of my father's hand in this tragedy."

"Oh . . ."

It was his turn to be startled.

"Are you too blind to see that *this* is why I came all the way out here to make sure that those two men riding up ahead of us . . . hopefully hearing little of our conversation . . . that those two, especially Gideon Porter, did not die before they could point their *fingers* . . ."

"Point their fingers at your *father*?"

"At the *truth*, Mr. Cole. Point them at the truth . . . whatever it is . . . whatever terrible, sordid facts surround it. I cannot live or work with my father without knowing the *truth*."

"The last time we crossed paths, you thought your father not being there was just a fortunate accident. What was . . . ?"

"What changed was the *damned* railroad . . . and I will not apologize to *you*, Mr. Cole, for strong language," Hannah said, regaining her composure. "The railroad will be coming to Gallatin City, and it will need land owned jointly by the four partners . . . whose arrangement has them inheriting the shares of partners who die. I've uncovered the same facts which you uncovered at the bedside of Milton Waller."

"I see . . ."

"What I discovered was suspicious, but open to interpretations. It is, as the lawyers call it, 'circumstantial' evidence," Hannah admitted. "However, when I saw my father's cursed 'right-hand man,' Mr. Edward J. Olson, speaking to Lyle Blake and Joe Clark, within hours of their coming to kill *you*, this was the evidence which made the other evidence *damning* evidence."

"I reckon . . ." the bounty hunter said, "I reckon we both had the same reason for wanting those two to live long enough to see Gallatin City."

"I reckon that's so, Mr. Cole," Hannah said. "Now, are you going to tell me what you have learned from speaking with Gideon Porter? As I assume you have spoken to him on this matter."

"He has been even less willing to discuss it than *you* were earlier today," Cole explained. "Though he does insist that he has friends in high places who won't let him hang."

"Who? What *friends*?"

"Didn't say," the bounty hunter replied with a shrug.

"You didn't *press him*?" Hannah asked with surprise. "Why didn't you press him to tell you? Weren't you the least bit curious?"

"You mean why did I not *beat* it out of him?"

"Well . . ."

"It's not my job. My job is to bring him in. It doesn't matter what he tells *me*. It doesn't matter what I say to anyone about what he told me. It matters what he says when he rides into Gallatin City. What matters is the look on their faces when he comes face-to-face with . . ."

"*My father*," Hannah said, completing his sentence.

"Yeah."

\* \* \*

HANNAH RANSDELL FELT A DEEP AND BROODING SENSE OF foreboding as the sun sank into the clouds on the horizon and darkness rapidly enveloped what was left of the day. To have had her worst fears confirmed by the suppositions of the bounty hunter and the deathbed words of Milton Waller caused her great anguish and despair.

A person who has lost a parent often dreads the loss of the other, but to lose him to the gallows would cast a debilitating shadow across her own life.

Still, she had to know the truth. As much as she dreaded it and wanted to prevent the pain, she *had to* see the look in her father's eyes when he looked into the eyes of Gideon Porter.

Of more immediate concern were Blake and Clark and what the bounty hunter had put into perspective about the probability that they would strike before the sun rose again.

As they crested the last rise before the Sixteen Mile Creek trail dropped into the valley of the Missouri River, she breathed a sigh of relief to see a distant stagecoach making its way from Gallatin City to the territorial capital in Helena. It seemed to symbolize their passage from wilderness to civilization.

When they reached the broad plain through which the river flowed, the bounty hunter announced that he was going to look for a campsite.

"What about near the riverbank, where there's water," she suggested. "We'd also be near the road. If there are other people on the wagon road, they would be less likely to ambush us . . . wouldn't they?"

"Being near to water is useful, but unnecessary," he said. "Our canteens will hold enough water to get us through one night."

"Then where?"

"High ground," he said, studying the hills that lay in the direction of Gallatin City. "I want to be where they got to show themselves to get close . . . *if* we have enough moon to cast light."

"It was pretty bright in the middle of the night where I was *last* night," she said. "But I don't like the looks of those clouds."

"We'll have to take what we get," he said, staring at the same gathering clouds and at the diminishing patches of deep blue twilight sky, touched by the first pin-pricks of distant stars.

AS THE BOUNTY HUNTER CHAINED HIM TO HIS TREE, Gideon Porter made a crude comment to Hannah, but Jimmy Goode just stared at her.

Noting that Cole had chained the two men to widely separated trees, Hannah decided to approach Goode with the purpose of getting the information that Cole had failed to elicit from Porter. She knew him, as many people in Gallatin City did, as the easily manipulated oaf who lived in the shadow of the Porter boys and strived for their esteem and respect.

"What have you got yourself mixed up in, Jimmy?" Hannah asked in a sympathetic voice, which she crafted so as to be inaudible to Porter.

"Nothing," he said, not looking at her.

"Don't you go talkin' to that goddamn hussy, Jimmy Goode!" Porter shouted from the opposite side of the camp. "Don't say a goddamn thing or I'll kick your fool ass from hell to kingdom come."

"Don't listen to him," Hannah said softly, trying to play a sympathetic card against Porter's threat. "He can't hurt you. He's chained to a tree."

"Not forever he ain't," Goode said in a low voice.

"What happened to your arm, Jimmy?" she asked sympathetically, sitting down on a log near where he was.

"Got shot."

"By who?"

"The bounty hunter . . . the goddamn bounty hunter."

"Why?" Hannah asked, startled. "What did you do to *him*?"

"Done got away."

"You escaped?"

"Yes, I did," Jimmy answered, looking at Hannah for the first time, and seeing her sympathetic expression.

"He shot you for *escaping*?"

"Yeah . . . sort of."

"Sort of?"

"Well there was sort of this homesteader . . . a whole family of 'em."

"Did you hurt the homesteaders?"

"No, ma'am . . . not one bit."

"What happened?"

"Well, I took the boy . . ."

"You took a boy? How old was this boy?"

"You know . . . eight or ten or something? Goode answered, his voice expressing that it had never occurred to him how old the boy might be, and that he found it difficult to guess.

"You *took* an eight-year-old boy? Whatever for?"

"I dunno . . . Guess I kind of took him . . . well, like a hostage."

"You took a hostage? Did you have a gun?"

"Yeah . . . but I swear I did not shoot the boy . . . I only wanted to flush him out when he went to hidin'."

"The bounty hunter shot you for trying to scare the boy, then?"

"No, I guess he shot me for trying to shoot the boy's pappy."

"Did you?"

"I tried, but I got hit in the elbow."

Hannah just shook her head. What had he expected for having kidnapped a child and having tried to shoot the boy's

father? *Really?* At the same time, she was pleased to hear
that the bounty hunter had not shot the man merely for trying
to escape.

"How did Gideon Porter get you mixed up in all this?"
Hannah asked, continuing to feign sympathy.

"I was part of the gang," Goode said proudly.

"I know, but this shooting of people . . . at the Blaine
home . . . ? That doesn't sound like *you.* Like you were saying, you are not one to shoot people."

"Got paid," he said. "Done it 'cause I done got paid."

"How much?"

"Thirty bucks."

"Who paid you?"

"Gideon."

"Who paid *him*?"

"I dunno."

"Do you know . . . ?"

"I don't know *nothing* . . . and I wish I didn't even know
*that*," he said sadly. "Miss Ransdell, I really wish none of
this would have happened."

"I can tell," she said with an empathetic glance at his
limp forearm.

"Did Gideon say anything about my father?"

"Just that he wasn't there that night . . . course I knew
that 'cause I *was* there."

"Anything else?"

"Not that I can remember, but I have trouble remembering sometimes . . . you know?"

"Yes, Jimmy, everybody's got trouble remembering
sometimes."

"Miss Ransdell?" Goode asked after a pause. "Can I ask
you something?"

"Sure."

"Are we gonna hang? Gideon says we ain't . . . but I figure since those folks got killed that we are."

"What makes Gideon think you *won't* be hanged?"

"Says he's got friends . . . friends who ain't gonna let it happen."

"What friends? . . . *Who?*"

"Gideon never tells me nothing."

Hannah smiled and stood up.

She walked away, regarding the man with a mixture of pity and contempt. What was it that made this man tick? Perhaps he didn't tick at all. Perhaps he was, as everyone had always said, really just "good-for-nothing Jimmy Goode."

"SOUP?" THE BOUNTY HUNTER ASKED, HANDING HER A CUP.

"Thank you . . . much obliged," she said, noticing herself smiling at the man. "Aren't you having any?"

"I just did," he replied. "This is coffee."

She nodded. "Yeah, I could smell it. But it's kind of late for coffee, isn't it, Mr. Cole?"

"I don't plan on much sleep tonight . . . or rather I don't plan on *any* sleep tonight."

"It's almost night now," she said, looking out at the landscape.

He had picked a campsite on the side of a hill that was separated from other hills by at least half a mile.

"You can see almost everything from up here," she said. "You can see everything but the far side of *this* hill."

"From up there, I *can* see everything," he said, nodding to the top of their hill, which rose another fifty feet. "And I guess it's time for me to get to work."

"You'll be cold up there," she said, regretting her forwardness in expressing concern for his welfare.

"It'll keep me awake," he said, before he disappeared around a boulder into the nearly complete darkness.

# CHAPTER 27

---

BLADEN COLE SURVEYED THE SCENE FROM HIS CROW'S NEST high above the campsite. He watched the surrounding terrain as the moonlight brightened and faded with the passing clouds. Even when the moon slipped away, though, the contrast between the sheet of snow and anyone who walked on it was still stark. Cole saw a few deer at a considerable distance and was pleased by how well they stood out against the snow, even in the cloudy diffusion of the moonlight.

After so much overcast and snow in the preceding days, he was thankful for as much moonlight as he could get and thankful for it not to be snowing tonight. A snowstorm would have been ideal cover for the two gunmen attacking the camp.

He had built the campfire down below larger than necessary, intending to have it remain burning late into the night as a beacon to lure the bushwhackers into the trap that he intended to spring.

He thought about the grizzly and the feel of dreading the animal in the darkness. If he had, as Natoya-I-nis'kim believed, inherited the medicine of the grizzly, then he hoped that he would be a force worthy of such fear when the night brought the inevitable encounter with the bushwhackers.

Suddenly, Cole was jarred into the moment by the sound of something moving on the hillside below.

There was a little bit of a scratch, the tumbling of a small stone, then silence.

What was it? A ground squirrel?

Cole was certain that he had seen no animal larger than a deer approaching the hill from any direction.

He peered into the darkness and quietly raised his Winchester. Then he saw the movement, barely fifteen feet beneath him on the slope.

*What?*

*Who?*

At first he did not recognize Hannah Ransdell. She had undone the bun into which her hair was normally wound. It framed her face and tumbled across her shoulders.

"What are you doing, sneaking up . . . ?" Cole hissed.

"Wanted to keep you awake," she whispered as she slid gracefully into a narrow hollow near where he had been lying.

"I almost shot . . ." Cole began.

"Shhh . . . I brought you some coffee," she whispered.

She had a cup in one hand and her rifle in the other. She had made the climb up from the camp with her hands full, and without making more than a trace of noise.

He took the cup with a nod. The coffee was lukewarm, but warmer than anything atop this hill, including his fingers.

Together, they crouched on the perch, scanning the approaches to their hill. He admired the skill and tenacity of this young woman. She was made of far hardier stuff than he might have imagined on that day when they strolled the streets of Gallatin City. Back on that day, he had found her

attractive, dressed in lavender gingham, trimmed in lace—
and with those three freckles on her nose which always drew
a smile when he thought about them.

Tonight, dressed in black, with a Winchester in her arms
and her long chestnut-colored hair cascading about her
shoulders, he found her even more attractive, more exciting
and untamed in her appearance—not unlike that black mare
she rode.

As they sat quietly on their perch, each studying the distance, awaiting the arrival of their foes, he occasionally
allowed his eyes the pleasure of falling upon his companion.
Once, he caught her sneaking *that kind* of glance at him.
She briefly made eye contact, smiled, and looked away.

He thought about Natoya-I-nis'kim, and how there is
something magical that is done by moonlight to the image
of a beautiful woman.

The night was passing slowly, and naturally there were
other things he would rather have been doing with a beautiful woman. He imagined feeling the softness of her smooth
skin and tasting her lips, but he forced these distractions
into the back recesses of his mind.

There were other things that must be done.

Cole consulted his father's pocket watch a time or two,
more out of boredom than anything else. The news that it
told was merely a reminder of how slow the hours were
ticking by.

The laborious ticking had moved the passage of time
closer to four than three, and Cole was stifling a yawn, when
he saw it.

There was movement in the shadow of a neighboring hill.
Was it another deer?

He strained his eyes into the darkness until they saw the
unmistakable glint of moonlight on a well-worn saddle.

He nudged Hannah, who was looking the other direction,
and pointed.

She turned and nodded.

This was it.

Two men had dismounted and were creeping toward the fire, approaching so as to screen themselves behind the shoulder of the hill. The fire had died down considerably from its original roar, but it was still the brightest thing on the ground for as far as the eye could see.

One of the men, apparently Lyle Blake, was nursing a limp. Joe Clark would walk, get ahead of Blake, and pause impatiently.

Slowly, they made their way up the slope toward the ledge where the campsite was located.

Clark prodded Blake ahead, and he stepped into the glow of the fire first. He went into action immediately, firing a pistol round into Cole's bedroll, which had been previously arranged to appear occupied.

"You missed," Cole shouted from above.

Blake turned to look up at the sound of the voice.

His eyes were narrowed by the brightness of the still flickering fire, and he fired wildly. This was his only chance at a shot, for he was promptly cut down by a bullet from Cole's rifle.

Clark, still in the shadows, fired at Cole's muzzle flash as Cole was ejecting the spent cartridge.

Hannah squeezed off a shot.

There was a loud curse, indicating a non-fatal hit, and Clark began to run.

Hannah fired again, as did Cole, but they both missed.

The moon was behind a cloud again, and Clark was moving quickly.

Impulsively, Cole set down his rifle, stood up, and ran down the hillside in pursuit.

Hannah watched as he slipped on an icy patch and fell, but managed to roll into an upright position and keep going.

She fired again and watched Clark hesitate slightly, giving Cole a chance to narrow the distance.

Clark reached the place where he and Blake had tethered

their horses, glanced back, saw Cole coming, fired two shots from his pistol, and leaped onto his horse.

Cole dropped to the ground when he heard the first shot but was running again as Clark was mounting up. He pulled his Colt and fired one shot at the fleeing man.

Without a second thought, Cole grabbed the reins of Blake's horse and jumped on. He had left his Winchester behind because he felt that he could run faster without it. Now he wished that he had not.

The clouds had passed, at least for the moment, and the pursuit continued briefly at a gallop in the stark black and blue of a moonlit night.

As the open terrain abruptly gave way to one studded with more and more trees, however, both riders slowed, knowing that to run a horse in the dark over uncertain ground and through trees was dangerous. For a horse to trip, fall, and break a leg would be the end for the animal, but this would also put its rider at a great disadvantage.

The fast pursuit had become a hunt in which stealth, not speed, would be the deciding factor.

Cole stopped, straining his ears for sounds as he had earlier strained his eyes for a glimpse of Blake and Clark.

Above the heavy breathing of Blake's horse, he heard the light wind whining in the creaking branches of the low trees.

In the near distance, the unmistakable sound of a horse walking in the brush was the proverbial music to his ears for which he had hoped. It was impossible to move silently with light snow covering broken limbs and other objects that made noise when a hoof stepped on them.

Cole moved as quickly as he could, pausing periodically to listen. He heard Clark doing the same—moments of quiet, followed by the sounds of him continuing.

He thought of taking a shot in Clark's direction. The purpose would be only to keep him on edge, because the odds of hitting him in the darkness at this range were essentially nil.

He felt around on the saddle and found Blake's rifle, an

old army-issue Henry, still in its scabbard. There was no way of knowing whether it was loaded and, if so, with how many rounds. Again, Cole cursed himself for not bringing his own rifle.

The thicker the woods became, the slower and noisier the pace became. Each man could hear the other, but neither was close enough for a decisive shot.

*Crunch.*

*Crunch.*

*Snap.*

*Clunk.*

Pause.

This could not go on all night—or could it?

*I could* walk *faster than this,* Cole thought.

Walk faster?

*Of course he could.*

At least he could walk more quietly.

Pulling the Henry from its scabbard, Cole slid off the horse, whacked him on the hindquarters, and watched him disappear into the woods.

He heard Clark, on the move again, adjusting his direction to match that of Blake's horse. The hunted was now the hunter; Clark was maneuvering to attack what he believed to be his still-mounted pursuer.

Moving carefully, and more quietly now that he was picking his own steps, Cole chose a path by which he could outflank his adversary.

Time stretched out like a reclining house cat.

*How long has it been?* Cole asked himself.

It may not have been longer than about ten minutes, but it really did seem like an hour since he had dashed down from his perch in an effort to catch Joe Clark.

Stepping as silently as possible—at least more silently than Clark's horse—Cole circled through the woods toward the place where Clark was aiming to intercept his prey.

Cole came over a small rise and peered into the woods below.

He could see Blake's horse rather clearly now, and a short distance away, a shadowy object was moving toward it.

It was Clark's horse, and it too was *riderless*.

There was a brief exchange of snorting and whinnying. Without their riders, the two horses had sought each other's company.

*Clark had the same idea as I did!*

Cole realized this with alarm.

*Which of us discovered it first?*

The bounty hunter had to credit the man from Gallatin City's cesspool of ne'er-do-wells for being smarter than his pedigree suggested he should be.

Somewhere amid the blackness, Clark was either still circling to the rendezvous of the horses, or waiting for Cole to show himself.

There was the sound of snow falling from a branch, but it was a high branch, and it was not a man-caused event. Both men would have heard this, and each would have jumped a little at the sound against the stillness and the tension of the moment.

It was Clark who first broke the silence, who first tipped his hand.

"Hey, bounty hunter," he shouted. "I ain't got no beef with you. Let's just go separate ways."

Cole was tempted to shout back that if he had no beef, why had Clark been trying since yesterday to kill him—but he resisted this temptation.

By saying nothing, he did not reveal his position, and he therefore now had the advantage.

Clark had revealed not only his position—or at least the general direction of his position—but also the fact that he was nervous about a shootout and wanted to get away.

"See here," Clark continued. "There's nothin' personal . . .

I'm just gunnin' for you for pay. You done shot Lyle . . . that should be enough for you to be satisfied with your night's work and be ready to let bygones be bygones . . . *I'm* willing to just let bygones be bygones."

Again, Cole chose not to reply.

Again, time seemed to slow to a crawl.

There was no sound but that of the light wind in the trees and the two horses scraping in the snow for easily uncovered bunches of grass.

At last, Cole could hear Clark walking through the snow toward the horses. He waited for sight of the shadow moving through the trees and took aim with the same Henry rifle with which Blake had taken aim at him the day before.

He would not let Clark reach his horse.

*Krrr-ack!*

The sound of the shot shattered the peaceful stillness and impacted a tree very close to where Clark was walking.

Clark paused to fire a shot in the direction of Cole's muzzle flash.

Clark was nervous, and he was anxious to escape. To save himself, he ran.

As at the beginning of this misadventure, Cole again found himself running down a hill to pursue the man on foot.

They crashed and thrashed through the brush for a few hurried moments, then the woods fell silent. Somewhere up ahead, Clark had decided to make a stand.

Cole moved as quietly as he could, trying to close the distance.

*K'pow!*

Cole ducked.

The shot came from very close, and it was a pistol shot. Had he, like Cole at the beginning of the chase, left his long gun behind?

Cole squinted into the darkness and got lucky.

He took aim with the Henry on the silhouette of Joe Clark's bobbing head.

*Click!*

The hammer fell on an empty chamber. Blake had left his Henry with just one round in it.

"I heard that," Clark shouted. "You're out of bullets!"

"I've been counting, and I think you're nearly down to none yourself," Cole shouted back confidently. "I know you got yourself nicked back at the fire. Why don't y'all just give up and we'll go back and sit by that nice warm fire."

In fact, he had *not* been counting and wasn't sure how many shots the man had left. It might be one, and he was sure it was no more than two. Meanwhile, Cole now had the advantage of Clark believing Cole had an empty gun, when he still had five rounds left in his Colt.

Cole braced himself.

The intuitive next step for a man facing another who was out of ammunition is to attack and finish him off.

Instead, however, Clark turned and resumed running. Maybe it was Cole's overconfidence, expressed in his invitation to the warmth of the fire, that made Clark believe that he was doomed unless he got away.

Cole jumped a downed tree that crossed his path, and gave chase. Maybe Clark really was almost out of bullets.

They came to an open area, and for a brief moment, Clark was exposed.

*K'pow!*

Cole fired once and missed.

He eyed a boulder in the middle of the clearing and ran toward it, knowing that Clark would turn and return fire as soon as he reached the dark woods at the far side.

*K'pow!*

Clark's shot hit the rock inches from Cole's hand. The shards of granite kicked up by the lead stung his flesh.

*K'pow!*

Cole fired again as Clark resumed running through the woods.

The pursued man grunted. Cole was unsure whether this meant that he had been hit.

The stillness of the forest was bisected by two men running as fast as the underbrush permitted.

Not far ahead, Cole heard the sound of feet slipping on loose gravel and the scrabbling noise of a man trying to keep his balance.

"*Aargh . . . ahhh . . . eeyoooooh!*"

Gasps turned to a single scream, which trailed off into the distance.

Suddenly, Cole found his own boots scruffling in the uncertain footing of gravel mixed with snow.

His feet went out from beneath him, and he fell on his back.

Briefly winded, he caught his breath, sat up, and looked around.

Barely two feet away, the ground dropped into a dark void. The patch of gravel on which he found himself seated was, literally, a slippery slope into nothingness.

The moon drifted out from behind a cloud, and Cole stared at the broad canyon that lay before him. He was at the top of a vertical cliff. Had he not slipped and fallen where he did, he would have gone over.

Grabbing a nearby tree root to steady himself, he stepped out to a rock outcropping where he could look into the chasm.

Far below, he saw Joe Clark, lying faceup and motionless on a slab of light-colored rock. The inky darkness spilling from his broken skull told the bounty hunter that he was never going to arise from this place.

# CHAPTER 28

———◆◆◆———

"WHERE'S CLARK?" HANNAH RANSDELL ASKED AS SHE entered the campsite. She had remained in the crow's nest high above until she had seen Bladen Cole ride out of the woods.

"He didn't make it," Cole answered.

She didn't ask how or why. She did not really care. The day ahead demanded her attention more than did the last loose end from yesterday.

She had breathed a sigh of relief when she laid her peeled eyes on the bounty hunter and had come down from her perch to greet him. She was tempted to do so with a hug, but forced herself to remain focused on the business at hand.

For Cole, the first order of business was a perfunctory examination of the other bushwacker, who had not moved since Cole had drilled the man the night before.

"That's Lyle Blake!"

Gideon Porter recognized the body as soon as Cole rolled the corpse to face the gathering light of day. "What the hell?"

"Meet the man who's been trying to kill *you* since

yesterday," Hannah said, holding her rifle in a posture that Porter found a trifle threatening. "Him and Joe Clark."

"They won't now," Cole said tersely.

"Why would they do this?" Jimmy Goode whined.

"Because somebody wants you *dead*," Cole answered. "It looks like Gideon's 'friends in high places' don't want to see you hang after all . . . they want to see you killed off *before* you get anywhere *near* a gallows."

"Gideon, is that right?" Goode shouted. Apparently, even after all the shooting on the previous day, it took the vacant stare of Lyle Blake to finally bring it home to Goode that someone was actually gunning for *him*.

"Shut up, damn you . . ." Porter roared back.

"If I'm not mistaken, these boys were paid by the same person who paid *you*," Hannah said.

"That would make you a loose end," Cole continued. "How does it feel to have your high-placed man turn on you and want you erased . . . squashed like a bug so that you can never talk?"

"But . . . he still owes me money."

"*Who* is it?" Hannah demanded. "Is it . . . ?"

"I ain't talkin'!" Porter shouted. "I ain't sayin' a word till I get to Gallatin City."


THERE BEING ADEQUATE ROCKS NEAR THE CAMPSITE, COLE put Porter to work in the construction of a rock pile mausoleum as the resting place of Lyle Blake. The flood of profanities that accompanied this task offended Hannah's sensibilities less than his stubbornness.

"That man is insufferable," she said, glancing at Cole as she saddled her mare and Cole stacked the saddles and tack belonging to Blake and Clark on top of the cairn.

"By this time tomorrow, he'll be somebody else's problem," he reminded her as he turned loose the horses that had been ridden by the late bushwhackers.

"I fear this will be a very long day," she said, revealing a trace of melancholy.

"Sometimes the last day of anything is the longest," Cole said. "But same as any day, they're all eventually over."

"Mr. Cole," she said, looking back at him.

"Yeah . . ."

"I'm really worried about today."

"After what we been through, what I've seen you able to take in stride, I can't picture you being too much of the worrying type."

"I've never had to face my father like this."

"I can't even imagine it," he said, betraying a shade of sympathy despite the overarching outrage he felt toward her father.

"Is your father still alive, Mr. Cole?"

"No, ma'am. He died in the war."

"I'm sorry . . ."

"It's been a while," Cole shrugged. "Lot of good men died in the war."

"I used to think of my father as a good man," Hannah said sadly.

"I'm sorry about that," he replied, trying not to appear cynical.

"Thank you . . ." she said, her voice trailing off.

She smiled, but he could see the tears in her eyes. He felt her hand close tightly on his wrist.


THEY WERE A CURIOUS CONTINGENT, THIS RAGTAG PARTY making its way south along the Helena–Gallatin City wagon road on that cold, early winter morning.

The bounty hunter brought up the rear behind an assortment that included two well-worn men chained to their saddles and a ripening corpse that was beginning its foul decay even in the sub-freezing temperatures. Leading the way was a young woman. Despite a generous spattering of mud and dirt and her two mostly sleepless nights of camping in the wilderness, she still managed to present the manner and appearance of a lady out for a Sunday ride.

She cheerfully greeted a freighter whose wagon they passed on his way north toward Helena. He smiled and tipped his hat when she waved, but his jaw dropped a little when he saw the others. He was still looking back at them and scratching his head a quarter mile after they had passed.

Though he was tempted to breathe a sigh of relief at having gotten through the last night on the trail alive, Bladen Cole knew better. There was no guarantee that Blake and Clark were the only ones with a mandate to prevent Cole and his prisoners from setting foot again in Gallatin City alive.

Snowflakes drifted in the air more like paint flaking randomly from the white sky than harbingers of a serious storm.

About two hours from the campsite and the final resting place of the late Lyle Blake, Hannah Ransdell reined her mare into an about-face and trotted back to where Cole was.

"Did you see?" Hannah asked urgently.

"Yeah . . . three riders about a mile and a half out."

The three had dropped out of sight behind a low rise, but he too had been watching them for about ten minutes.

"I think I recognize one of them," she said.

"Oh yeah . . . Who?" Cole said cautiously.

"I think the one in the black coat is Edward J. Olson, my father's . . ."

"Yeah, I know," Cole nodded, instinctively tucking his long coat behind the holster that held his Colt.

"What should we do?"

"If we've seen *them* . . . they've certainly seen *us*," Cole said. "If we leave the trail now, they'll know that we have misgivings about crossing their path."

"Then we shan't leave the trail," Hannah said confidently. "We'll face them. I'll continue to ride point."

"Are you sure you want to do that?" Cole asked. "You're

a good shot, but there's three of them, two of us, and we have a pair of caged pigeons to keep from getting killed."

"I don't mean for us to face them with *guns*," she said. "I mean to face Edward J. Olson with *words*. He *knows* me, and I think I can figure out what to say. He doesn't know that I know that *he* sent Blake and Clark out here, and there is no indication that we met up with those two. The best thing we have on our side is that he's in very big trouble if he lets anything happen to Isham Ransdell's daughter."

"He could say that you got hit in a cross fire," Cole said.

"Thanks for suggesting that comforting possibility," she said with an almost smile. "I'm betting there will not be a cross fire."

"I don't know . . ." Cole said hesitatingly.

"Do *you* have a better idea, Mr. Cole?"


THE TWO GROUPS OF RIDERS APPROACHED EACH OTHER cautiously but deliberately, without overt demonstration of caution.

When they were within shouting distance, it was Hannah who spoke first.

"Good morning, Mr. Olson." she exclaimed with a merry smile, as though she were greeting Olson on the street in Gallatin City. "What a pleasure to see you."

His companions, whom she dismissed with a nod, were a pair of men she recognized as being among those who did occasional odd jobs around town.

"Good morning, Miss Ransdell," he replied, touching the brim of his hat. "I'm surprised to see you out here this morning."

"It *is* such a nice morning, isn't it? A bit on the cold side, but it doesn't look like we're in for a lot of snow."

"No, ma'am. It doesn't look like much of a storm."

"Good morning, Mr. Olson," Cole said with a wave, riding up to a place near Hannah. Following her lead, Cole smiled broadly, though he kept his right hand close to his Colt.

"Mr. Cole," Olson said, nodding an acknowledgment of the bounty hunter. "I can see with great satisfaction that you have succeeded in your mission of rounding up the Porter boys . . . or at least *one* of the Porter boys."

"Enoch's right there," Cole said, nodding to the canvas-wrapped parcel tied across the saddle on Enoch Porter's horse.

"I can smell him from here," Olson nodded.

Olson was trying to appear cordial, but the two men with him had nervous, edgy expressions. Perhaps it was merely Cole's endemic distrust of Olson's employer, but it seemed to him that these two were keeping their gun hands at the ready.

Cole was sizing up how fast he could take them if they *did* draw on him, and which one to take first. Unlike the more seasoned and calculating bushwhackers of the day before, these two appeared very young and very inexperienced, the sort who were prone to being easily spooked into drawing weapons without adequate thought. That sort was, Cole knew, the worst kind.

Cole watched Gideon Porter exchange knowing glances with Olson. This man, as Olson's knowing nod and the expression on Porter's face revealed, was one of Porter's friends in high places.

"What are you boys doing out for a ride today?" Hannah said cheerfully. "Heading up to Helena?"

"No. Actually, we were riding out to meet Mr. Cole," Olson said warily. Whatever he was doing or saying that he was doing, he obviously had not in his wildest dreams expected to run into Isham Ransdell's daughter.

"Mighty good timing, I'd say," Cole smiled. "How'd you pick *this* morning?"

"There were some travelers who passed through Gallatin City a couple of days ago who had word of a bounty hunter with two prisoners who had been in Copperopolis about a week ago," Olson explained. "Figured it had to be you."

"Guess you figured right," Cole smiled calmly.

"Hadn't expected to see you out here, Miss Ransdell,"

Olson said, repeating his earlier words to her. "Does your father know you're out here?"

"Of course he does," Hannah lied with an innocent smile.

"He didn't say anything to *me* about you being out here on the road with this bunch."

"Well, you know Daddy," she laughed. "He doesn't necessarily tell everyone about *everything*. He often doesn't tell me about the errands he sends *you* on."

"He *sent* you?"

"Certainly," she said with a nod. "You don't think I'd come out here and associate myself with such riff-raff on my own, do you?"

"Well . . . I reckon not," Olson said. He had to admit that having his boss send her was the only possible explanation that he could imagine.

"Why do you suppose . . . um . . . Why did he do that?"

"Well, Mr. Olson, as Mr. Cole put it, he wanted me to 'check up on his bounty hunter.' Why do you suppose he didn't tell *you* that I was coming?"

Hannah wished immediately that she had not made the latter barb, but she could not resist the temptation to insinuate that the right-hand man was not briefed on everything.

"I reckon he was busy with various affairs at the bank," Olson said weakly, trying to save face.

"Folks, if you'll excuse me, I've got some outlaws to move along," Cole interjected at this break in the conversation.

"Of course." Olson nodded. "But I must say that I'm certainly concerned to see Miss Ransdell being in harm's way like this, with these ruffians. Since things seem to be in order here, I'd like to escort her on ahead and get her back to Gallatin City as soon as possible, while you bring in your villains, Mr. Cole. I'll leave the boys here to give you a hand."

"Thank you *so* much for your offer," Hannah said. "There is really *nothing* I'd rather do right now than get away from this mess . . . especially now that Enoch Porter has started to reek with such an atrocious odor."

"I'm happy to oblige . . ." Olson smiled.

"*But* . . . and it pains me to say it, Mr. Olson, I would not be true to my father's instructions to accompany this motley crew if I were to do such a thing." Hannah smiled.

"I'm sure that if he were here, Miss Ransdell, he would . . ."

"He might or he might not." Hannah shrugged innocently. "But of course if he *were* here, he wouldn't have asked *me* to be here . . ."

"Okay, Miss Ransdell," Olson said, holding up a hand. "If that be your wish. Let us all hasten back to Gallatin City . . . together."


"YOU FELLAS WORK FOR MR. RANSDELL?" COLE ASKED innocently of Edward J. Olson's hands as they continued south toward Gallatin City.

While Olson joined Hannah in the lead of the procession, the other two had joined Cole in bringing up the rear.

"Ummm . . . yep," answered one. "Sometimes. Mainly do jobs for Mr. Olson."

"He sure seems to be surprised that Mr. Ransdell sent his daughter out to check up on me," Cole said in a casual, "making conversation" way.

"Does seem curious, I guess," the kid said. "But I guess he figured she was up to the job."

"She's a willful one," the other interjected. "Too damned smart for her own damned good from what I've heard. Like some kind of filly bronc."

"Like to ride that filly bronc, though," the first kid said.

"Not me," said his partner. "I'm not rightly fond of uppity women. That one looks to be nothing but trouble."

"Still, she's a looker," the first insisted. "What do you think, Cole?"

"She's a looker, for sure," Cole said, nodding, in a casual, "making conversation" way.

# CHAPTER 29

❦

As Isham Ransdell unlocked the front door to the Gallatin City Bank and Trust Company and stepped inside, the big clock on the far wall chimed once. Half an hour until opening time.

Mr. Duffy was at his desk, hard at work under his green eyeshade. Hannah's desk was empty, of course.

"I wonder why Hannah decided so impulsively to take off for Bozeman," Duffy said as he noticed his boss staring at the empty desk.

"She has a friend down there who had a child recently," the banker replied. "But I do not know why she decided on this visit so abruptly. I have long ago discovered that the females of our species are given to flights of spontaneity. In any event, I looked forward to her return. I'm tiring of making my own breakfast."

"Maybe you'll hear from her by mail today," Duffy said hopefully.

"When she travels, she usually drops a line to tell that

she arrived safely, but young people often forget such things when they get busy. I hope she is having a pleasant visit."

Pouring himself a cup of the coffee which Duffy had made—more poorly, admittedly, than Hannah—he sat down to review a stack of papers that Duffy had placed on his desk for his signature.

After signing off on a couple of very routine documents, he leaned back in his heavy oak desk chair to take a sip of coffee. On the wall there hung a map of Gallatin City and adjacent parcels, with various properties marked with color-coded snippets of ribbon carefully attached with banker's pins. Red stood for mortgages, green for commercial loans, and so on. To the east of town, his eyes fell upon the tract of land that he and his partners had acquired some years back for practically nothing, and on which he and his lone surviving partner stood to make a fortune. Upon this reflection, he could not stifle a contented smile.

As the clock struck the hour, Isham Ransdell was raising the curtains and unlocking the front door. This was normally Hannah's job, but in her absence it fell to him. It was, he thought, only for the week. In any case, he was delighted, as always, to see a line of customers at his door.

Standing at the teller's window, performing the routine tasks of the bank teller—cashing checks, making change for the boy sent over by the mercantile, and so on—reminded him of his own early days in banking. He was glad, though, to have that part of his career behind him.

ISHAM RANSDELL STEPPED INTO THE COLD MORNING. A few snowflakes were in the air, but there seemed no threat of a storm.

Not only had he been compelled to fill in at the teller's window this morning, but he now had to make the daily trek to the post office *himself*. He could have sent Duffy, but the man was more useful to the bank beneath his eyeshade working with his pen.

Standing in line, waiting for his mail, was another task Ransdell was glad to have behind him.

At last, he got his bundle, and he had stepped aside to thumb through it, when the door opened and in walked Virgil Stocker.

"What brings *you* to the post office, Virgil?" Ransdell asked with a smile..

"Same as you, I suppose," Stocker answered with a shrug. "My secretary is off today . . . Caught something . . . It's the weather, I suppose. These girls these days . . . they get the sniffles and suddenly they cannot work."

"Not like when we were starting out," Ransdell observed nostalgically.

"In those days, we'd have come to work with a broken leg."

"Indeed," the banker agreed, noting the injuries and scars that were still prominent on the attorney's face.

"Isham, I was thinking that if you are available, you and I should perhaps dine together at the Gallatin House, as we have *not* done in some time."

"That is a capital idea," Ransdell said, his eyes brightening. "What about this evening? With my chief cook and bottle washer off to Bozeman to call on her friend, dinner at my home is a lonely affair. Your company would be much appreciated."

"Excellent. We could make it an early dinner. We'd dine in my private booth, of course . . . perhaps around five?"

By now, Stocker had reached the head of the line and was rewarded with his own stack of mail.

Isham Ransdell was about to say "good day" and leave his partner to look though his mail alone, when Stocker turned to him with a letter, addressed to "Mr. Virgil Stocker, Attorney," which he showed to his friend. It had been postmarked in St. Paul, Minnesota, and the return address was that of the Northern Pacific Railway Company.

Stocker looked at Ransdell and back at the letter.

"This may be what we have been waiting for," Stocker said, licking his lips.

"Are you going to open it?" Ransdell asked.

"I suggest that we open it *together*," Stocker said with a smile. "We *could* wait for dinner, but why don't we retire to my offices *now* and open it over a glass of something to warm us."

Neither man spoke as they made their way through the lazily drifting snowflakes to Stocker's law offices. The two men sat down, and Stocker ceremonially uncorked a half-filled whiskey bottle.

"Special occasions." He smiled, pouring generous portions for himself and his colleague. "I save this bottle for special occasions. I think you were here the last time . . . When was that?"

"Nearly a year ago, as I recall," Ransdell said, picking up his glass. "There were *four* of us on that day."

"Indeed, there were," Stocker agreed with sadness in his voice.

"Shall we drink to a satisfactory conclusion of a sad affair?" Ransdell said. "To the bounty hunter's having resolved the situation once and for all."

"To the end of the whole sordid mess," Stocker suggested, touching his partner's glass. "And to brighter days ahead."

"Hear, hear," Ransdell agreed with a smile. "Now, are you going to open the damned letter?"

"Indeed . . . after much adieu," he said, crisply slitting the envelope with a letter opener.

Isham Ransdell leaned forward as Stocker unfolded the missive.

Beneath the formal letterhead of the railway company, and above a signature that carried the legend, "on behalf of

Mr. Frederick H. Billings," was a typescript containing more zeros than either man could have imagined.

"Jackpot," Isham Ransdell said. It was the only word that came to mind.

Stocker smiled after a long pause. "This is but their *opening* offer."

# CHAPTER 30

———◆◆◆———

EDWARD J. OLSON FOUND HIMSELF IN THE KIND OF
situation his mother had always referred to as a "pickle." He
never understood why, to her, a conundrum was like a
canned vegetable, but the analogy had permanently stained
his vocabulary.

When he had ridden north out of Gallatin City at the
crack of dawn, he had expected to meet Blake and Clark on
the trail with a line of horses bearing the bodies of the
bounty hunter and the Porter boys. Just in case Blake and
Clark had not accomplished their task, he had brought a
further pair of hired guns to help him finish the job.

One way or another, he had expected to reach Gallatin
City with a line of horses that represented a line of loose
ends, each of them neatly tied off.

Then *she* appeared, unexpectedly, and as though out of
*nowhere*!

When he had ridden north out of Gallatin City at the
crack of dawn, the *last* thing Olson would have imagined

himself doing was riding back to Gallatin City beside Isham Ransdell's daughter—and with Gideon Porter still *alive.*

Where were Blake and Clark?

They must be out here *somewhere.* If *she* had found the bounty hunter, certainly they could have as well. Were they complete fools or had they been spooked into inaction by the presence of Isham Ransdell's daughter?

If they had done their job *before* she had showed up, then Edward J. Olson would not be in this pickle, but he *was,* and he knew he must either eat it or choke on it.

One way or another, Gideon Porter *could not* reach Gallatin City alive. If Gideon Porter pointed his filthy finger of accusation in front of everyone in Gallatin City, Olson himself would be in danger of the gallows. He cursed everyone involved in that fatal calamity at John Blaine's house and himself for agreeing to be part of it.

*Her* presence complicated everything. He *must* get rid of Gideon Porter, but he could not have her as a witness. He had to get her away so that his boys could take care of business.

"Miss Ransdell," Olson said at last, steering his horse close to Hestia. "May I have a word?"

"Yes, Mr. Olson," she said, smiling innocently.

"I'd like to beg you to reconsider my offer to ride on ahead with me. I would very much hate to see you get hurt if there were to be trouble. These men are dangerous criminals."

"They don't appear very threatening at the moment," she said, mocking him with a naive giggle. "They're both chained up. I don't see *how* they could hurt anyone in such a state."

"Miss Ransdell, I'm afraid that this is not something that is open to discussion."

"*What?*"

"As your father's right-hand man, I am afraid that I must *insist* that we get away from these men and that you allow me to escort you back to Gallatin City in safety. The men have the situation well in hand."

"As you should know better than anyone, sir, *his* wishes must be respected," she said, displaying a temper not previously in evidence. "I'm afraid that I cannot do as you've requested."

"This is not a request, Miss Ransdell," he said, displaying a temper of his own. "I must *insist*."

"Then I *decline* your insistence, as I declined your request, Mr. Olson."

"You *will* do what you are *told*!" he said angrily. "I was your father's right-hand man when you were in pigtails, Miss Ransdell. If you will not obey me, I'll turn you over my knee as your father should have done long ago."

"I should like to see you *try* to do such a thing," she said antagonistically.

"You are a disrespectful girl demonstrating the behavior of a wench, young lady," he cautioned.

With that, he desperately grabbed for her reins.

She deftly sidestepped the black mare, and his grasp fell short.

"*Aha*," Hannah exclaimed, taunting him.

"Damn you," Olson said, turning his horse to get near to her.

The mare reared suddenly, but Hannah leaned into Hestia's neck and did not fall.

"What's going on up there?" Bladen Cole yelled from the back of the procession, having seen Olson make a grab at Hannah's mare.

Olson grasped again for Hannah's reins, and again he missed.

"What the hell are you tying to do?" Bladen Cole shouted angrily, as Olson glanced back toward him.

"Boys!" Olson shouted. "Take him *now*!"

The young man closest to Cole, the one who had described Hannah as a "filly bronc," went for his pistol.

Alerted by Olson's shout, the bounty hunter ducked as the first shot rang out, and fired the second himself.

As the man toppled from his horse, the one behind him reached for his gun.

The .45-caliber lead from the bounty hunter's Colt impacted just below the man's clavicle, ripping into his chest before he had a chance raise his gun.

Cole glanced once at his dying face and at hands thrashing clumsily in the warm, rapidly flowing blood, and turned the roan in the direction of Edward J. Olson.

As Olson was watching these events unfold, his gaze turned to Gideon Porter, the man who could, under no circumstance, ever set foot in Gallatin City.

He pulled his own pistol from the holster within his coat and took careful aim. Porter was so near, and so paralyzed with fear, that he could not be missed.

As he aimed his pistol at Porter, Olson felt what seemed to be a freighter's wagon crashing down on his head.

The sight of the near and vulnerable Gideon Porter melted into a dizzying grayness.

Turned awkwardly in his saddle, and spinning in dizziness, Olson felt his balance lost.

He had the sensation of the pistol tumbling from his hand as he reached out to break his fall.

The collision with the ground was nearly as painful as the blow to his head.

*I must finish the job . . . Gideon Porter cannot live*, Olson thought.

Through the dizzying grayness and the seeing of "stars," his eyes fell upon his pistol. He crawled and reached out to it as it lay on the ground in the light dusting of newly fallen snow.

"Don't do it!"

Someone was shouting.

*K'pow . . . T'zing*

A shot had been fired.

The bullet had ricocheted of the metal of the cylinder.

Something had hit him in the eye.

He rolled over and looked up.

With his other eye, he saw Hannah Ransdell, still on her mare, pointing a rifle at *him*.

"Put that gun down this instant," he demanded in a creaking, sputtering voice.

"Or what?" Isham Ransdell's daughter asked. "Will you turn me over your knee?"

*K'pow . . . T'zing*

The second shot missed him by inches.

"That's for calling me a *wench*," she explained. "Next time, I won't miss."


"DAMN YOU, BOUNTY HUNTER. HE'S THE *ONE*," GIDEON Porter asserted as Bladen Cole rode up to find Edward J. Olson lying on the ground with Hannah Ransdell pointing her Winchester at him.

"One *what*?" Cole asked

"One what hired me to shoot those people."

"*Now* you tell us," Cole said. "After all these days of keeping your mouth shut about your 'friends in high places.'"

"Looks like he was not your friend after all," Hannah suggested.

"And not in such a high place at the moment," Cole added wryly.

"He told me he'd take care of it . . . said that he'd take care of everything," Porter insisted angrily.

"Looks to be that his plan was to take care of *it* by taking care of *you*," Cole mused.

"You fool, you *stupid* fool," Olson said to Porter as he stood up and brushed off his hat.

"Is the fool *right*?" Cole asked. "*Did* you hire him to do those murders?"

"You are *all* fools," Olson said emphatically, walking toward his horse. "This is not over yet!"

"Whoa, there, Mr. Olson," Cole said. "You're not dressed to ride just yet."

For Isham Ransdell's right-hand man, being "dressed to ride" meant the proper jewelry, specifically the manacles that then held Jimmy Goode to his saddle. Because Goode was without the use of his right hand, Cole decided to secure him to his saddle with rope and to use that set of irons for anchoring Edward J. Olson instead.

# CHAPTER 31

AS THE BANKER ENTERED THE LOBBY OF THE GALLATIN House, the hotel's big imported German clock was banging out the five measured beats of the hour.

He felt a tug at his sleeve and looked down to see John Blaine's widow.

"Mr. Ransdell, might I have a word?"

"Mrs. Blaine . . . I didn't see you. Good evening, ma'am."

"Mr. Ransdell, I must speak with you. Is there somewhere that we could talk . . . privately?"

"Certainly," Ransdell said. "Come by the bank in the morning . . . say around nine, before opening hours . . . you shall have my undivided attention."

"I'm afraid you don't exactly understand, sir," Leticia Blaine said in a hushed tone. "I must speak with you *now*."

"I'm sorry, ma'am. I'm meeting Virgil Stocker for an early dinner at the moment."

"He should hear this as well . . . I have no secrets from my husband's associates . . . May I join you?"

"Well, I . . . uhhh . . ."

"Then it's settled," Leticia Blaine announced. "I don't see him in the dining room. When will he be coming?"

"*I* was to meet him at his private booth," Ransdell clarified.

"Lead the way then, sir."

Isham Ransdell was in no small way unnerved by the way that Mrs. Blaine had inserted herself into his evening plans, but politeness demanded that the widow of his former partner could not simply be dismissed and told to go away to mind her own business.

"Virgil, ummm . . . Mrs. Blaine has asked to join us," Ransdell said as he slid back the curtain and they entered Stocker's booth. "She has a matter of pressing urgency which she would like to discuss with *both* of us."

"Good evening, Mrs. Blaine, what a pleasant surprise," Stocker said, standing politely.

"Thank you and good evening to you, Mr. Stocker," she said, taking a seat at the table and seizing a napkin.

"Isham, I took the liberty of ordering a plate of oysters," Stocker said. "I know that you like oysters . . . Can't stand them myself, but I know that you . . ."

"I *love* oysters," Mrs. Blaine said, helping herself. "Thank you very much, sir."

Stocker poured a glass of claret for Ransdell and offered to pour one for his late partner's widow. She nodded.

"A fine evening." He smiled as he filled her glass and topped off his own. "No sign of snow yet, I believe."

"None that I could see," Leticia said, eating another oyster. Given the complexities of shipping to a location not yet reached by a railroad, oysters were rarely served here, and a prized delicacy.

Stocker offered the plate of oysters to Ransdell, who took it but did not put an oyster on his own plate.

"Now, what is the matter you wish to discuss with us?" Ransdell asked, getting to the point at hand.

"It is the matter of my husband's murderers," she explained.

"Yes . . ."

"It has been some weeks since you engaged that bounty hunter to track them down."

"Yes, that is correct." Ransdell nodded.

"I may be a foolish old woman, but it seems to *me* that a great deal of time has elapsed without his return. He was, as I recall, in pursuit of these scoundrels less than two days after they ran away."

"As I recall, that *is* correct, Mrs. Blaine," he said.

"In that case, may I be so impertinent as to ask what is *taking so long*?"

"These things do take time," Ransdell said in a reassuring voice. "As you recall, I *did* bring you up to date on that letter I received from Fort Benton."

"I do recall that letter, but as I *also* recall, that communication had been postmarked less than a week after your bounty hunter departed from Gallatin City. I *further* recall that your bounty hunter was headed into Blackfeet country, and you speculated that he and the Porter boys might come to their demise in that hive of merciless savages."

"Yes, I did," he said cautiously.

"Have you heard anything with regard to this?"

"I *have* had reports since then."

"And when were you planning to share these 'reports' with *me*?" She bristled indignantly. "I *am* the widow of your own partner, sir, not just another old woman off the street."

"The simple answer is that these are unconfirmed reports . . . which one might call hearsay."

"And what exactly did this *hearsay* have to *say*?"

"Some travelers who were passing through from up north claimed to have seen them in Copperopolis," Ransdell said in a confiding sort of way.

"Where on God's green earth is *Copper . . . opolis*?"

Leticia Blaine replied, raising a eyebrow. "I don't believe I have heard of such a place."

"It's located across the mountains, this side of the Little Belts, up in Meagher County," Stocker interjected. "As you might surmise, it was once a mining town, but like so many mining towns, it withered practically to nothing after the easy ore played out. This would explain why you've never heard of it."

"A ghost town, then?"

"Practically . . ." Stocker said.

"And what in God's name was your bounty hunter doing in this place?"

"Apparently one of the Porter boys had been injured, and medical attention was being sought," Ransdell explained.

"*Medical attention being sought?* My husband was *murdered* by those thugs and *medical attention* is being sought?"

"That's what the reports tell us," Ransdell said. Her rage was making both of the men more than a little nervous.

"Mr. Ransdell, I was under the impression that the Porter boys were wanted dead or alive," she said angrily. "Is that not correct?"

Ransdell nodded.

"Why is it that your bounty hunter is wasting time to seek *medical attention* for a murderer who by all rights should be brought back to this city *dead*?"

"I do not know the answer to that," he said. "I don't even know whether it is true that it *really was* Mr. Cole and the Porter boys who were in Copperopolis."

"If it *is* the case, I hope that whichever of the Porter boys was sick has by now gone to follow Milton Waller to *Hades* . . . and that your bounty hunter sees the light and brings the others back *dead* . . . not alive."

"Believe you me, Mrs. Blaine," Stocker said. "My associate and I could not agree with you more that the lives of those nefarious criminals aren't worth saving for the luxury of a trial."

"Can you . . . Is there a way to determine whether this hearsay is true?"

"In fact, Mrs. Blaine, I hope to do exactly that," Ransdell told her with a smile. "This very morning, my right-hand man, Mr. Edward J. Olson, started north on the most likely route between Gallatin City and Copperopolis to investigate. I'm not certain what he will find, nor indeed, whether Mr. Cole and the Porter boys will be found at all, but at least we may know *something* within the next few days."

"I certainly, hope so, Mr. Ransdell," she said, not returning his smile.

THE PALPABLE TENSION IN THE PRIVATE BOOTH GRADUALLY dissipated as the steaks and boiled potatoes were served and conversation turned to other topics.

Mrs. Blaine seemed visibly relieved at having unburdened herself, and the claret seemed to have somewhat lightened the mood at the table.

"Would you care for some more horseradish, Mrs. Blaine?" Ransdell said, offering her the condiment.

"Yes . . . I mean no . . . I'm afraid . . . that I am not feeling well," she said, dropping her fork clumsily on the table.

She had suddenly gone pale and her eyes had glazed over.

"Here, take some water, madam," Stocker suggested.

"I don't feel well . . . I feel that I am about to be . . ."

She coughed as though about to vomit, then gagged.

"Is something caught in her throat?" Ransdell asked.

As both men stood to come to her aid, Leticia Blaine began convulsing, then collapsed into a heap on the floor.

"I can't . . . breathe . . ." she gasped.

Pushing back the curtain enclosing the private booth, Virgil Stocker shouted to the head waiter. "Get a doctor! Quickly . . . *get a doctor!*"

# CHAPTER 32

❖◈❖

AS THE AFTERNOON HAD SLOWLY FADED, THE SNOW HAD come and gone. The closer they got to Gallatin City, the more traffic they met on the road. There were more wagons, and even the stagecoach headed up toward Diamond City or Helena. As they passed, people regarded this group of chained men escorted by a young woman and a bearded man with great curiosity, but no one said anything beyond exchanging simple greetings.

It was growing dark when they reached the crest of what both Bladen Cole and Hannah Ransdell knew would be the last ridge before Gallatin City. When he saw her pause and look down at the city, he ordered the others to stop and rode up to join her.

He looked at his father's pocket watch. It was close to six o'clock. The lights of the city were coming on.

"Are you ready for this?" Cole asked.

"No . . . of course not," she said bitterly. "Could I *ever* be ready for this?"

"Guess you'll just have to take it as it comes."

"Oh, oh," she said suddenly.

"What?" Cole asked.

"I just saw the light in the bank come on."

"Is that bad?"

"Actually not . . . I'd much rather this confrontation take place *there* than at home . . . with the memories of mother . . . and . . ."

Cole could see tears in her eyes.

"I understand," Cole said, nodding toward the city below. "We'll deliver this bunch to Deputy Johnson's jail, then we'll go over to the bank and . . ."

"No," Hannah interrupted. "I need to go to see him *alone*. I know that you will have to get your money . . . but I'll go to see him first, and I'll go alone. You won't need me with you when you deliver these people to the sheriff's office."

"But . . ."

"Don't argue with me." She smiled, glancing at Edward J. Olson. "You saw what happened to the last man who tried."

"Be careful," he said.

"I will."

"You don't know what may happen," he said.

"No . . . I do not," she admitted. "I'll be covering new ground."

"He may have more hired guns," Cole suggested.

"I don't know." She shrugged. "Probably, I guess . . . What a cheery thought."

"Let me give you something," he said.

"What?"

"It's a little something I picked up down in Green River," he said, reaching deep into his vest pocket.

"What is that?" Hannah asked. In the gathering darkness, she could not identify the small object wrapped in dark cloth that he had in his hand.

"It's an over-and-under Remington derringer," he said. "I got it from a man who has no further use for it. It's more discreet to carry than your rifle."

"I'm not planning to *shoot* my own father," she said, taking the little gun.

"Like we were saying, that which you *are* planning may involve people other than your father."

"Okay . . . I suppose it wouldn't hurt. Is it loaded?"

"Two shots, .41-caliber."

BLADEN COLE'S LONG-AWAITED RETURN TO GALLATIN CITY came just past dark, so few people noticed that the procession riding into town included three horses with men fastened to their saddles and three carrying men *across* their saddles.

They paused when they reached the intersection of Main Street and Cottonwood. Down one block on the latter, there was still a light on at the sheriff's office. Two blocks away on the former, they could see the light burning inside the Gallatin City Bank and Trust.

"Wish me luck," Hannah Ransdell said as she bade the bounty hunter good-bye. She reached for his hand, and he took it.

"Good luck . . . Stay safe," he said.

"You too . . . Bladen," she replied, calling him by his first name for the first time.

IT WAS ALMOST SEVEN O'CLOCK WHEN DEPUTY—ACTING Sheriff—Marcus Johnson heard someone knocking at the door of his office.

He was already in the back room, which functioned as his sleeping quarters, putting a pot on for his supper, and was ready to call it a day.

It had been a slow and quiet day, the kind that he preferred— that is, it had been until about an hour ago, when he had been summoned to the restaurant at the Gallatin House.

Poor Mrs. Blaine.

The recently widowed Mrs. Blaine had died a dramatic

death on the floor of a private booth, and naturally the law must be summoned under circumstances where a clamorous demise occurs in a public place. However, the doctor, who was also summoned, ruled it a death from natural causes, so there was nothing for the lawman to do but tell the gawking onlookers that nothing could be done. You can't arrest an oyster for being tainted.

Now, back in his office, about ready to turn in for the night, Johnson was startled by the knock on the door.

"Who's there?"

"Bladen Cole . . . the bounty hunter . . . I got some wanted men for that jail of yours."

Johnson quickly opened his door, looked at Cole and up into the face of the infamous Gideon Porter.

Weeks had passed since the murders at the Blaine house, but the crime was still on the minds of the people of Gallatin City. So too, especially for Johnson, who was there when it happened, was the murder of Sheriff John Hollin.

"You done brought back the Porter boys," Johnson observed with satisfied wonderment. "Least one of 'em, or two, I guess, with Jimmy Goode here."

"Enoch's tied across that horse yonder," Cole said. "You better call the undertaker. He's started to rot. You've also got two others out there, but they're not nearly so ripe."

"Good evening, Mr. Olson," Johnson said, spotting Edward J. Olson sitting on his hitched horse. In the dark, he did not notice that the banker's right-hand man was chained to his saddle.

"Okay, you scum, lets dismount," Cole said, walking first to Porter's horse. Having detached him from his saddle, he handed him off to Johnson, who happily, though roughly, escorted the defiant outlaw to a waiting cell.

"What happened to you, Jimmy Goode?" Johnson exclaimed, looking at the man's debilitating injuries.

"It's what you get for kidnapping a six-year-old," Cole answered.

"Do tell," the sheriff said.

Goode glanced at him mournfully and looked away as he was led to a waiting cell.

"Here's the last of 'em," Cole said.

Having locked up both Porter and Jimmy Goode, Johnson turned back to the door, where Cole stood with Olson.

"That's Mr. Olson," Johnson said with alarm. "You got him in *irons*!"

"Yes, I do," Cole explained. "Meet the man who paid for the Porter boys' rampage over at the Blaine house."

"Damn right!" Porter shouted from his cell. "He's the one, all right."

"Mr. Olson?" Johnson asked. "But you are . . ."

"Nobody . . . none of you. Nobody understands the whole picture," Olson said angrily.

"And he tried to shoot poor old Gideon to keep him from talking," Cole added.

Johnson looked at Olson in disbelief and had an almost apologetic expression on his face as he closed a cell door on this erstwhile pillar of the community.

"I'll be damned if this bastard didn't try to shoot me," Porter shouted to Johnson. "Ain't that right, Jimmy Goode?"

"Damned right for sure," Jimmy Goode said. "Would have too, but for that Ransdell girl done whacked him . . . whacked him *hard*. I done saw it."

"The Ransdell girl?" Johnson asked, addressing his question to Cole.

"She came out to help me round 'em up," Cole said.

"*What?*" Johnson gasped incredulously. "Where is she now?"

"Over at the bank having words with Mr. Olson's employer," Cole explained. "I think that she is—"

His words were interrupted by someone rapping at the door.

"Who's there?" Johnson asked.

"It's Virgil Stocker, Sheriff."

# CHAPTER 33

HANNAH SWALLOWED HARD AND TOOK A DEEP BREATH, gently nudging Hestia down the street. She passed the post office, which she had visited routinely every business day for as long as she had worked for her father. She passed Blaine's store, where she had shopped since she was a little girl.

It was a street that she had traveled so often throughout her entire life, but tonight things were so very different, and they would never be the same again.

She peered into the bank. It was closed, of course, and the shades were drawn, but through a slit, she could see her father at his desk.

Having steered Hestia to a hitch rail in front of the closed store adjacent to the bank, she dismounted and made an effort to smooth her badly wrinkled skirt. She wished she had a mirror so that she could fix her hair, but she decided this was the least of her concerns.

The bank's front door would be locked, but Hannah had a key in her jacket pocket.

Isham Ransdell looked up in alarm when he heard the

front door open, wondering who it could be and whether he had forgotten to lock it.

"Hannah," he said in surprise.

To him, having no idea that she had been camping in the wilderness for two nights and on the trail for three days, his daughter looked terrible. Her clothes were wrinkled and dusty, her riding boots muddy. As he watched, she threw her hat on the counter and let her unkempt hair fall down across her shoulders.

"I'm so glad to see you," he said, standing up from his desk chair.

"Hello, Father," she said icily.

Her cold demeanor surprised and greatly disturbed him.

"You look like you've seen a ghost," Hannah said without emotion.

"Yes . . . I have," he said. "I just watched Leticia Blaine fall dead . . . less than an hour ago."

"*What?*"

This was a twist that Hannah had not seen coming.

"It was tainted oysters . . . over at the Gallatin House."

"She's *dead*?"

"Yes . . . she's dead."

"There have been a lot of deaths in Gallatin City of late," Hannah said, her insinuation clear, assuming he chose to hear it.

"A lot has happened since you've been in Bozeman," her father said.

"I didn't go to Bozeman," she replied, still disallowing herself from expressing emotion, aside from a perfunctory bitterness in her words.

"But you said . . . you were on the stage . . ."

"It was a ruse," Hannah said, folding her arms.

"Why? Where?"

"I went up into the Sixteen Mile Creek country," she explained. "I took Hestia and went up to Sixteen Mile Creek to find the bounty hunter."

"Did you . . . ?"

"Yes, Father," she said. "I *found* the bounty hunter."

"Why?"

"Why did I go? . . . Or why did I go looking for a *bounty hunter*?" Hannah asked before proceeding to answer. "I went looking because I overheard *your* right-hand man—Mr. Edward J. Olson—sending Lyle Blake and Joe Clark to *kill* the bounty hunter, and to *kill* the Porter boys. I went looking for the bounty hunter because I wanted to *stop* that from happening."

"But why would they . . . ?"

"Because, *as you know*, Father, dead men cannot point fingers," Hannah said angrily. "Can they?"

"Point fingers at what?"

"*Really?* Don't insult my intelligence, Father. I'm not your little girl anymore."

"I don't understand . . ." Isham Ransdell gasped. His daughter had never spoken to him like this.

"I know it *all*, Father," she asserted. "I know the whole, sickening story."

"What story?"

"*What story?*" Hannah repeated. "Let's start with 'Once upon a time there was a railroad that was coming to Gallatin City.' Then there were four businessmen who owned some land that was not worth too much until the railroad was coming. Do you know this part of the story, Father?"

"Yes, that's true, of course, but . . . ?"

"But it's not anything out of the ordinary, is it?" Hannah fumed.

"No . . . not at all," her father answered, becoming perturbed.

"Until you add on rights of inheritance," she said, counting one by one on her fingers. "And you add to *that* a series of *murders* . . . and *next*, the shares go not to families, but to surviving *partners*."

"You can't believe . . ."

"I did not *want* to believe," she said, fighting back tears. "You asked whether I found the bounty hunter . . . and I said I did . . . and I learned what he *did not* write in that letter from Fort Benton."

"Which was?" Isham Ransdell demanded, his own ire growing.

"Which was Milton Waller's deathbed words. His *death-bed* words about him and the Porter boys being *paid* to go to the Blaine home that night. And *why* did they go there? Because there were *four* partners. 'Three must die,' Waller said, 'and only *one* can survive.' Who was the *only* man of the four who was *not* there that night?"

"I wasn't there, but . . ."

"*Exactly!*" Hannah shouted.

"What are you saying?"

"Gideon Porter knows, and Gideon Porter is *alive*. You sent the bounty hunter to bring him back, insinuating that you wanted him dead. *You* sent Blake and Clark out to kill them, and this morning, *your* right-hand man, Edward J. Olson, came *this* close to killing Gideon Porter until *your* little girl slammed him across the head with the butt of a Winchester . . . but Gideon Porter is *alive!*"

"I did *not* hire Gideon Porter to kill *anyone*," Isham Ransdell shouted back angrily, though he could tell that this woman who said she was no longer his little girl did not believe a word he was saying.

# CHAPTER 34

THE TALL, IMPECCABLY DRESSED MAN WITH NOTICEABLE scars on his face stepped into the sheriff's office.

"Good evening, Sheriff," he said, though his eyes were not on Marcus Johnson but scanning the other faces in the room and the cells.

"Mr. Cole, when I saw you coming down Main Street a moment ago, I could see that you had done your job," he said, not looking at Cole, but directing his angry eyes at Gideon Porter. "And here is the mangy dog who did *this* to my face."

"Gideon kept sayin' he had friends in high places who were gonna get us off," Jimmy Goode shouted in uncharacteristic anger. "Now look at him . . . at *us*."

For the first time, perhaps in his life, Jimmy Goode had spoken assertively without Gideon Porter denouncing him or telling him to shut up.

Looking at Stocker's face, Porter's expression changed from his usual countenance of bitter defiance to one of anxiety.

"And I see Mr. Olson here in a *cell*," Stocker said dramatically, as though he was performing before a jury in a packed courtroom. "Can someone explain to me how on earth a pillar of our community has gotten himself locked up?"

"These men have all said that Mr. Olson hired Gideon to do the shootings," Johnson explained.

"Edward?" Stocker asked, looking at the man himself.

Olson merely hung his head as Porter acrimoniously repeated his earlier assertion.

"The Ransdell girl stopped him from shooting Gideon . . . to keep Gideon from telling what you just heard he's already told," Johnson told the lawyer.

*"The Ransdell girl?"* Stocker said, having been caught off guard. "Where? She's in Bozeman . . ."

"Actually not," Cole said. "She rode with us down from Sixteen Mile Creek. Right now, she's over at the bank, where she's laying into the man Olson works for."

"She's *what*?"

"As you know, the man who hired Gideon Porter to do that to your face works for Isham Ransdell," Cole explained. "Milton Waller told me on his deathbed that they were paid for those killings. It also seems that the only man not present that night stood to inherit some pretty valuable real estate."

"So you've surmised . . . that Isham hired Mr. Olson here . . . to hire Porter to . . . ?" Stocker said thoughtfully, recalling that Hannah had come to exactly the same conclusion.

"Haven't heard anything to the contrary," Cole interrupted.

"You were sure lucky, Mr. Stocker," Johnson added. "They was gunnin' for you too."

"I see," said Stocker thoughtfully. "So now we know the *whole* story . . . and we have *all* the perpetrators in custody. Wait, where's Enoch Porter?"

"He's out yonder," Johnson said. "He's settin' on his horse, but not upright."

"I thought I was smelling something pungent as I walked past," Stocker said.

"Now that everything is taken care of here, maybe I

should mosey him on over to the undertaker's before it gets too late," Johnson said.

"That would be a very good idea," Stocker agreed. "We'd hate to have Gallatin City awake to his stench."


"MR. COLE, I MUST COMMEND YOU ON ROUNDING UP THE perpetrators of this crime," Stocker said after Johnson had left the office. "Including one—Mr. Olson—we had *not known* to be involved."

Cole merely nodded. His tired brain was fixed on a real bath and a good night's sleep in a real bed.

He should not have let his mind drift to such distracting thoughts.

"I commend you on figuring out all of the details . . . *except one*," Stocker said with a smirk as he suddenly drew a gun and pointed it directly at Cole's head. "Now, please carefully unstrap your gunbelt and let it drop to the floor."

Stunned by this unexpected turn of events, Cole could do nothing but comply. To attempt to draw his gun would be a fatal mistake. The man had the drop on him, and he apparently knew how to use a gun.

"Now, kick it over to the cell containing the incompetent Edward J. Olson," Stocker demanded.

As Olson reached out and took Cole's pistol from its holster, Stocker tossed him the cell keys from Johnson's desk.

"It is quite amusing, Mr. Cole," Stocker smirked, "that the *one* piece of the puzzle that you got wrong was believing that the straitlaced Isham Ransdell was the kingpin behind this affair. On one hand, I'm insulted, and on another, I find it a compliment that you *didn't* figure it out."

"If not Ransdell, then who?" Cole asked. "*You?*"

"Guilty as charged," Stocker confessed. As he laughed, the scars gave his face a macabre appearance.

"But Gideon Porter clobbered you bad with the butt of his gun," Cole said grimly.

"That was to make it look convincing, though Mr. Porter made it a bit *too* convincing," Stocker said, his leering grin fading. "While I *also* benefit from the right of inheritance, your eyes fell upon poor Isham because he was *absent* that night."

"That, and the fact that Olson is *his* man," Cole interjected.

"I also work for Mr. Stocker," Olson said, stepping from his cell and strapping on Cole's gunbelt. "Under the table of course."

"He really *did* hire the Porter boys to do the deed," Stocker added. "You had that part right."

"And I'm still owed another five hundred dollars for doing it," Gideon Porter asserted as Olson unlocked his cell.

"What do you mean?" Jimmy Goode whined. "You only paid me *thirty* bucks and you're gettin' *five hundred*?"

"That's 'cause I'm worth it, and you're good for *nothing*," Porter growled, roughly cuffing Goode alongside his head as they were released from their cell.

"Calm down, both of you," Stocker demanded. "I believe that we all need to go over to the bank and see that everyone gets what's coming to him. Mr. Cole's diligence has presented us with an opportunity."

"What sort of opportunity?" Olson asked.

"A terrible thing happened at the bank tonight," Stocker said with exaggerated mock sadness. "You see, our Mr. Cole here decided that with the banker's vault wide open to pay the bounty, the rest of the bank's assets would be easy pickings for a robbery. He took you and me hostage and went to do his dirty work."

"I follow you," Olson said smugly. "And the banker dies in the shootout?"

"Exactly." The attorney smiled broadly. "And sadly, his daughter is killed as well. Of course, *we* . . . I'll let it be *you* . . . will save the day by killing the bounty hunter. *You* will become a hero by avenging your boss's death."

"I like it," Olson said, and smiled.

# CHAPTER 35

◆━━◆◆◆◆◆━━◆

"HOW COULD YOU, FATHER?" HANNAH RANSDELL SOBBED.

"I told you, I *didn't*," her father insisted firmly. "If Mr. Olson did as you have said, he *had* to be acting alone."

"Why?" Hannah demanded. "Why did he act alone? Why did he act *at all*? What did *he* have to gain? It was *you* who benefitted from . . ."

Hannah's tirade was interrupted by the front door of the bank swinging wide.

"You should remember to lock your door at night," Virgil Stocker said as he entered the room with four other men.

Hannah stared in astonishment. Bladen Cole had been disarmed, and Edward J. Olson was pointing the bounty hunter's gun around the room.

"What's going on?" Hannah demanded, looking at Cole.

"They will want you to believe that this is going to be a bank holdup," Cole said. "But it's really a continuation of what started at the Blaine house . . ."

"Shut up!" Olson demanded angrily.

"Actually, I'm sad to say that he's right," Stocker said, looking at Ransdell.

"Virgil, can you *please* tell me what is going on here?" Isham Ransdell said. "This cannot be happening . . . This is *madness*."

"Mr. Cole here has developed a fantastic theory, which is very nearly spot-on," Stocker said, pacing the floor dramatically. The tall attorney, with years of courtroom experience, was skilled at the art of dominating a room with his presence. "He has deduced that the four of us owned land with the right of inheritance flowing to surviving partners . . . and that the purpose of the unfortunate shootings was to get that inheritance flowing to *you*."

"You can't be saying . . ." Ransdell sputtered.

"I'm afraid so," Stocker interrupted, feigning sadness. "The three of you . . . Blaine, Phillips, and *yourself* . . . were supposed to die that night. Because I was injured, and you were *not there* . . . and finally because *your* man Olson served as my intermediary with the Porter boys, Mr. Cole deduced that the guilt lay with *you*, not me, between the two of us who survived."

"I can't believe this," the banker said angrily. "Are you now intending to kill *me*?"

"Unfortunately, I must admit that tonight, your time has come," Stocker said, dramatically waving his hand. As a lawyer, he loved to pontificate with a theatrical flourish. "I had intended for your death to occur earlier this evening at the Gallatin House, in front of a room full of witnesses, but alas, poor Widow Blaine sucked down the oysters which were poisoned for *you*."

"You killed her *too*?" Ransdell said in disbelief.

"If it is any consolation, neither she nor Mrs. Phillips were *supposed* to die as part of this plan," Stocker said with a shrug. "Things just got a little out of hand."

"You weren't *supposed* to die either, missy," Olson said, smiling at Hannah.

"What are you going to do with us?" she demanded.

"As Mr. Cole has said, there is going to be a stickup tonight," Olson explained. "He has decided to take the opportunity of the bank vault being opened to pay his bounty . . . to well, empty that vault of cash, and disappear into the darkness."

"Unfortunately, Mr. Cole will murder the banker and his daughter in the process," Stocker interjected. "But, *fortunately*, the quick-thinking Mr. Olson will save the day . . . or the night, if you will . . . by killing this bounty hunter–turned–bank robber."

"What happens to us?" Jimmy Goode asked.

"Shot in the cross-fire, of course," Stocker said with a dismissive wave of his thespian hand.

"I'll be damned if I'll be a sitting duck," Goode shouted, bolting for the door.

"*Stop!*" Olson demanded, impulsively firing a shot into the darkness through the open door.

Even as he was feeling the buck of the .45 in his hand, Olson felt the body slam of Bladen Cole, jumping him from behind. The bounty hunter picked the moment of his distraction to send him crashing to the floor.

Virgil Stocker, meanwhile, took this same moment of distraction to do what he had come to do. Taking out his own gun, he aimed not at the bounty hunter, but at his former partner.

The wiry man with a narrow string tie and white sideburns looked back at the man with the scarred face, with whom he had dined as a friend that very evening.

Through Isham Ransdell's mind had run the humiliation of having lost the trust and respect of his only child, and *now* he was about to lose his *life* to an erstwhile friend who now eyed him over the top of a Smith & Wesson Model 3 with a businesslike "no hard feelings" expression on his face.

As Isham Ransdell stared into that scarred face, Virgil Stocker's head suddenly jerked sideways with a violent twist.

Isham looked then at his daughter and at the derringer in her hand.

BLADEN COLE'S GUN SLIPPED FROM OLSON'S GRIP AS HE fell to the floor. It bounced and cartwheeled across the polished surface, with both Cole and Gideon Porter scrambling after it.

Its trajectory had sent it flying toward Porter, practically as though fate wished to hand it to him.

He grabbed it, pulling it away from Cole's grasp by a mere split second.

Porter raised the gun and was working his forefinger into the trigger guard, when a sudden blast sent him toppling backward.

Bladen Cole looked up at Hannah Ransdell and at the derringer in her hand.

# EPILOGUE

NOBODY, NOT EVEN JIMMY GOODE HIMSELF, KNEW WHY he had chosen to run to find the acting sheriff at the undertaker's office instead of hightailing it to parts unknown.

Some said it was because he was the witless oaf who had *always* been called "good-for-nothing Jimmy Goode" and wouldn't have known where to *find* parts unknown.

Some said that it was because he was tired of living in the turbulent shadow of Gideon Porter and would do anything to get that terrible monster off his back.

Still others theorized that he was so exhausted, so spent, and so wasted by the experience of the previous weeks that he just could not go on.

Marcus Johnson, meanwhile, had heard the shots before Jimmy Goode found him, and had arrived at the Gallatin City Bank and Trust in time to hear the dying admissions of Virgil Stocker. The attorney had told the whole story as his onetime friend, Isham Ransdell, knelt over him, staring in disbelief. He told it in the form of an apology, and there were tears in his eyes when he took his last breath.

Those who were there interpreted his words as expressing not an apology for his terrible scheme, but only his sorrow that it had failed.

The only thing in Gideon Porter's eyes when he took *his* last breath was the reflection of an angry woman with an over-and-under Remington in her gloved hand.

Nobody shed a tear when the Porter boys were buried in a single unmarked grave. Their mother having long since died of a broken heart, there was not a soul in Gallatin City who would ever miss them.

Edward J. Olson was tried and convicted in the space of two days and was taken to the county seat to await the hangman.

Jimmy Goode got twenty years for his part in the whole affair. He might have gotten the noose, such was the mood of the jury pool in Gallatin City, but he did not.

Some say that his neck was saved by folks feeling pity for his limp and useless hand. Some say that it was because of his having gone for the sheriff that night.

Still others insist that it was because he was the witless oaf who had always been called "good-for-nothing" Jimmy Goode, and therefore, nobody ever took him seriously.


HANNAH RANSDELL WALKED DOWN MAIN STREET, BOUND for the post office.

The snow had piled up considerably over the past few weeks, and she had to maneuver through the narrow paths that had been shoveled.

During those weeks, she had also been maneuvering through the narrow path of her relationship with her father. Saving his life had gone a long way toward rebuilding the relationship they once had, but only time would heal *all* the wounds inflicted by the penetrating distrust she had expressed that terrible night, if indeed they *ever* healed.

For Isham Ransdell, the memory of having a man

considered to be a friend betray him so horrifically was a nightmare. Yet this nightmare was a mere trifle when compared to his having seen his own daughter, his little girl, say and—worse still—*believe* those things about him.

It was enough to make him yearn to have been one of those cold bodies on the floor of the parlor at the Blaine home on that *other* terrible night.

With the railroad coming, and him the sole surviving partner, he would sooner rather than later be a very, very rich man, but he would have gladly traded it all for a chance to sit down just once more with John Blaine and Dawson Phillips, or to have his relationship with his daughter back.

Stepping through the snow, Hannah passed the Gallatin House and the Gallatin City General Mercantile, the place that was still referred to as Mr. Blaine's store. She had been back to the Mercantile, long since stripped of the funereal black bunting, but she had not had an occasion to set foot in the Gallatin House since she had come back from her sojourn to Sixteen Mile Creek. She passed the building that once had held Virgil Stocker's second-story law office. Workers were carrying furniture out to load it on a wagon. She wondered who would be moving in.

She passed the intersection of Main Street and Cottonwood where she had parted company with Bladen Cole for the last time.

He had lingered in Gallatin City for a few days after collecting his reward money. They had spent some time together, and these were hours in which her heart had soared. She had finally indulged her secret desire to touch his black whiskers, and her secret passion to taste his lips. Even now, her mind returned often and happily to the memories of that time.

But they had parted. It was in his nature to be on the move, not staying long in any one place.

For a brief and fiery moment, born out of feelings kindled on that night on the hilltop near the mouth of Sixteen Mile

Creek, she had imagined that same wanderlust to be in *her nature* as well. She had made up her mind that when Bladen Cole moved on, when he rode out toward far horizons on the roan, she and Hestia would be at their side.

She had decided that she would not *ask*, but that she would simply *tell* him: "Mr. Cole, you may ride anywhere you like, but you will *not* ride alone." In her replaying of this in her daydreams, he had replied with many diverse comments, but he had *never* said no.

If this fire for the vagabond life had been in her nature, as indeed it *may* have been, it was extinguished by her father's tears, when she finally took back all that she had said to him that night, and when he had tearfully taken her in his arms.

She had never, ever before, or ever since, seen him cry.

No, her place was *not* beyond the far horizon.

As she thought about it later, she realized that the bounty hunter also recognized this, and with more sadness than he would admit to. They were each bound by their nature. Just as he knew that he must go on, he knew that she was bound to stay. She was still part of the world she had known before all of this happened.

When he said good-bye, she did not tell him that he would not ride alone. Nor did she ask where he was headed.

That night, her pillow grew soggy from her tears, a wetness she longed to be transformed into the sweat of his passion mixed with her own, but she awoke knowing that she was where she needed to be.

Hannah reached the post office, chatting briefly with a few of the regulars as she waited in the short line. As menial as it was, there was something comforting about the post office routine. It was *so* unlike the uncertainty and *wild exhilaration* of life on the trail.

When she returned to the bank, her father was in a good mood, which was gradually becoming more and more common as time went on. Time was, indeed, beginning its healing process.

As she was taking off her coat, he made an offhand comment about her being his "right-hand girl."

She froze for a moment with a lump in her throat. He had no idea of how she perceived the irony of this characterization, but that did not matter. It mattered only that he had articulated it, and this made her happier than almost anything he might have said at that moment.

Wounds would heal. She *now* knew this.

Hannah went to her desk and was sorting the mail when out dropped a letter hand-addressed to "Miss Hannah Ransdell, in care of the Gallatin City Bank and Trust Company."

It was postmarked Denver, and the return address was headed with the name, "Mr. Dawson Phillips, Jr."